PARSONS HOLLOW

DOGS OF PARSONS HOLLOW

JAMES D. MCCALLISTER

MHP
Mind Harvest Press
COLUMBIA, SC

Epigraph: *A Time for Everything*, © 2004 Karl Ove Knausgaard (English Translation © 2008 James Anderson, Archipelago Books)

Cover design by MarcCardwell.com

ISBN: 978-1-946052-04-9 (Ppbk) 978-1-946052-05-6 (ebook)

Library of Congress: 2017919159

For more information:

Mind Harvest Press
COLUMBIA, SC

Mind Harvest Press
PO Box 50552
Columbia SC 29250-0552
www.mindharvestpress.com
www.jamesdmccallister.com

1st Printing, May 2018

In memory of my mother,
Andria McCallister (1946–2015),
who instilled in me a lifelong love of animals.

Although God hadn't shown himself to any mortal since he'd appeared to Cain in the field that rainy night, and he'd therefore only lived as words among them for more than fifteen hundred years, no one seriously contested his existence. And why should they? They were there in the midst of his creation. Everything they could see bore witness to him. The sun that rose in the morning and filled the world with light, the clouds that came floating in from over the sea and emptied their water on the earth, the profusion of growth that sprang up in the fields. It was to this that they sacrificed each spring and autumn, without ever expecting that God would show himself to them. After all, what were they, except animals among animals, God's creations among God's creations?

—Karl Ove Knausgaard

1

RANDI MARGRAVE, HOPEFUL HOUSE HUNTER, BOUNCED ALONG IN THE back seat of the Escalade and stared at the chatting heads of her husband and the realtor, all three motivated by the vague but persistent notion that this latest property would be the winner. Or in the case of Cullen, only semi-motivated to that end. She supposed her hubby was a sport for going along at all—credit would be due, and duly given.

Randi sat counting every mile, especially in the minutes since they'd left the interstate to bump along forever on a county highway, and knew he'd never go for this house, not this far out. Not if the place were a crystal palace; not even if she gave him 'Cleopatra on a plate'—a line from one of the sacred movies he taught at Southeastern University back in Columbia.

Two turns later found them on Davis Macon Lane, a snaky uphill climb between walls of green. The SUV crested the ridge that bisected this deep rural part of Edgewater County, the woods fell away . . . and there, the house: As Vince and the online listing both promised, a stunner. An A-frame in cedar and stone, the home loomed imposing yet inviting, so unlike any of the suburban vinyl villages through which they'd been led. Situated on a sloping, rounded acre of cleared land like a mountain bald, the property afforded a three-sixty, blue-tinged view of the rolling country-side, with the shimmering snake of the Sugeree River visible in the distance.

Thrilled, Randi squeezed her husband's tweed shoulder. "It's gorgeous —like a ski lodge."

"Wow." Cullen checked his enthusiasm, downgrading to calling the house "interesting." Despite the loss of their son, and the daily hell that were the reminders whispering around every corner of their Victorian downtown next to campus, he didn't truly want to move. "The view feels more like the upstate than the midlands."

Vince beamed with pride, Randi thought, as though he'd built the place himself. "Ladies and gentlemen? As George Carlin once said, it's-no-bullshit."

In a flurry of enthusiasm, the three unhooked safety belts and piled out.

Standing on the circular, cement driveway, Cullen whispered, "I'm sick of him padding the square footage. No way this is thirty-six hundred."

"They always do that." Her quiet tone turned hard enough to etch glass. "Besides, it's not like we need the extra room."

"We don't for now, anyway."

Randi bugged her eyes, a sign of intense displeasure. Over the last year, discussions about having another child had been held, sure, but with acrimony, and infrequence.

"We're house hunting—I don't see how you can't-not factor that in."

"Why don't you stand by and watch how much I 'can't-not' factor that in."

Cullen, chastened, cast his eyes down to the tips of his Weejuns.

Vince stopped in his tracks and slapped the hood of his vehicle. He all but shouted, "*Damn it all.*"

The exclamation startled them both. Cullen's loafers cleared the driveway in a foppish, tiny hop.

"Vince—for god's sake."

"I swear, if y'all don't take this house?" The agent unbuttoned his blazer to reveal a substantial, ex-linebacker's gut. "I just might have to buy it myself."

Cullen, dry. "Whoa, dude. Way to create a sense of urgency."

"I'm not kidding, y'all."

"What was that getting out here?" Glaring at Randi. "An hour?"

Vince, brandishing his phone. "Not even close. Thirty-six minutes, even with that state trooper on the interstate slowing us down."

She touched her husband on the sleeve. "Honey, that was not an hour."

"So it only felt that way?"

"On a good day, it'll take you thirty and change. Not an hour." Vince held out his hands. "If I'm lying, I'm dying."

"Speaking of the phone, is there coverage up here? Out here? Whatever the hell you call it?"

"Three bars, baby—must be a tower nearby."

"Let me see that device, sir."

While the men talked signal coverage, Randi examined the surroundings: Woods, underbrush, a smattering of sunbaked, mossy boulders. The yard was rough around the edges, the grass yellowed and a little shaggy, but with decorative plantings surrounded by faded mulch—a sugar maple, a towering eucalyptus tree, a cedar hedge, azaleas that'd bloom gorgeous and pink in the spring—it was clear that someone had once put in time and effort. The hilltop lay serene and still but for the high, mournful baying, small and distant, of a dog.

Randi filled her body with the crisp air. Yes: Out here in the deep countryside, a woman could get some thinking done. Perhaps some of the purported writing.

The writing *was* helping somewhat—wasn't it?

Not really. Since quitting her job producing news at the NBC affiliate downtown, she hadn't finished so much as a single short story, nor made any headway on writing magazine articles, planning a novel, or working on a Ph.D and becoming a teacher like Cullen. Certainly not working on the Denny Memoir, which despite never being far from her thoughts nonetheless loomed as untenable rather than healing. As far as Cullen knew, she'd been putting in a couple of hours a day. A blatant lie.

On the opposite side of the crude cul-de-sac—it appeared that a mini-subdivision had once been planned, but never come to fruition—she noted a rusted chain stretched across a rutted dirt track that disappeared down the ridge into the woods.

A weathered hardware store sign dangled from the chain:

PRIVATE PROPERTY
KEEP OUT

Pointing to the sign, she called out: "So we have neighbors after all?"

"There's utility lines nearby. Probably a power company road."

"Wouldn't say 'private property' if it was the power company. Or would it?" Cullen, musing. "No—the power company's 'private property,' isn't it?"

"Does it matter? Folks, look around. Nobody but us on top of this hill."

Their footsteps crunching with sandy grit, Vince directed the couple onto a mosaic-stone walkway leading to the rustic, inviting front porch while giving a verbal rendition of the online listing she'd perused: amenities like a gourmet kitchen, fireplaces, a hot tub, a sauna, a rec room on a lower level built down the back slope, which accounted for Cullen's missing square footage.

"Sunrise from the bedroom, sunset views from these beautiful, tall windows. And Brandi, I'm wagering that with the squirrels and the deer and the antelope playing and wandering around all wild kingdom-like, you're gonna be in hog heaven."

Cullen snorted. "Sounds like a goddamn petting zoo."

Ignoring him, she instead corrected the realtor. "Randi, if you please. And—antelope?"

"Sorry, Mrs. Margrave. A little joke."

Vince removed the lockbox, opened the door, and extended a welcoming arm.

Cullen, reluctant, crept inside. His voice echoed in the expansive, sunlit family room. "Holy crap—I mean, how very interesting."

Vince grinned. "Come on, m'lady. You're gonna go ape over these interiors."

He waited for Randi, who'd glanced back at the woods. The road. She pictured being out here all alone, day-in, day-out, and frankly loved the idea.

Randi pulled her sweater tight. Since Denny's death, she'd lost so much weight. Again came the dog's distant, mournful baying and whimpering.

"You hear that?"

Vince, impatient. "Who cares—somebody's old mutt."

"Hate to think about a dog tied up outside somewhere."

"Look: you know people hunt out here."

"*Hunting?*"

Vince draped an oak-limb of an arm around bony Randi-shoulders. "No worries—just good old boys bagging themselves some venison. Hunting's good. Helps keep them pesky things out of people garden's. Besides, nobody's going to be hunting the Margraves."

"One would hope not."

"Wait till you see the master suite." He directed her inside, whispering as though concerned about being overheard. "You're gonna have kittens over it."

From somewhere along the ridge the dog continued yelping and howling, but once Vince shut the heavy door behind them, Randi could no longer hear the animal. Instead, she heard only the hollow ringing of their voices and footfalls on the hardwood floors.

By the time she inspected the lower level with its gorgeous view of the peaceful Carolina hill country, and the rushing brook, the back deck with hot tub and outdoor kitchen, and the closets, and the extra rooms downstairs, Randi began mentally packing the contents of the Victorian on University Terrace. Everything, that is, but the cruel memories of her son, and her life before the series of tragedies that had undone it.

2

On the drive back to the freeway, Randi's gaze danced across a blur of emerald as rural South Carolina rushed by outside the agent's SUV. Clapboard churches and aging ranch houses on scrubby lots didn't offer a particularly appealing sense of community, but at least the closest neighbor, at the bottom where Davis Macon Lane met the county road, seemed more middle class than poverty-stricken like so many other homes in the vicinity. Not that she was class conscious.

But if not her, Cullen would fill that role.

Randi gritted her teeth for the discussion ahead. Her hubby didn't share the urgency about moving, and it rankled her, an inexplicable, hurtful obstacle to her healing. His convenience, trumping her sanity? Check.

She had a trump card: for once the chalet, as she thought of the house, turned out to be everything a hustling real estate agent had promised. And more.

It looked like a keeper.

Vince zoomed by a group of mobile homes in a clearing, five dilapidated units in all. Laundry hanging from clotheslines. Vehicles on blocks in a cluster close to the road. Rusting barrels scored and scorched by the burning of trash. An old hound dog tied to a tree, but too far to be the one she'd heard.

Cullen cocked his thumb at the ramshackle compound. "Classy. And you had the temerity to describe this as a nice 'neighborhood'."

Randi shushed her husband, who bristled, but complied.

Signaling to turn onto the main highway to the interstate, Vince tried mitigating the tension in the vehicle with small talk, if a touch apocalyptic in tenor: "What y'all think about this Y2K hype?"

Cullen grunted. "Overblown hysteria going back to antiquity, and probably beyond. Every generation suffers some version of end-times mythology. Always just around the next corner."

"Scary, though. Our business, it depends on computers now. Look how easy Miss Randi found that awe-some effing property back there."

"Enough with the salesmanship. Christ."

"Cullen Mar-grave." Randi, again with the mommy-voice. "Cool your jets. Don't forget that all this driving and showing is a favor."

"Not necessarily." Vince, winking in the rearview. "Depending."

Randi watched her hubby rub his eyes, pat his ex-student on one meaty forearm a few times with appropriately masculine force. "Sorry about all the whining. I've got papers to grade. Too much coffee sloshing around. Yadda yadda."

"Hey, no big whoop. Y'all have been through so much."

"I'll admit it: the house was a real 'creampuff'—right, Vince?" But his voice betrayed dejection rather than interest.

"That it is."

At that, silence and torpor settled over the car.

Vince turned on the radio to a country-pop station set to a low volume. Randi cracked the window and let warm slipstream flow across her pale face. "Smell that? It's so different out here from anywhere I've ever lived. I kind of love it already."

Cullen, suspicious. "Surprising. Never known you to be much of a country girl."

"Different's what I need. Different from who I am. Different from—this."

"I hear you."

Fraught with possible meaning and subtext.

Icky.

Her husband, far from incorrect about her roots: Randi's life, before the kinda-cool seismic event at sixteen that'd been her parents' divorce, had been spent as a child of northern California: Berkeley, a college town with a vastly different vibe and temperament from bucolic, sleepy Columbia, where she'd lived since coming to college at Southeastern.

Since becoming a reluctant South Carolinian—after her mother remarried, they moved all the way across the country—Randi often missed the spectacular scenery and progressive culture of the Bay Area, as well as the few friends she'd left behind. She considered her adult home, with its diminutive skyline, decent schools, and modest cost of living, as Mayberry on the mighty, muddy Congaree River: a little dull and staid, but convenient to plenty of other interesting places not far in any direction like Atlanta, Charlotte, and steeped-in-historicity Charleston, which hadn't been decimated in the Civil War the way Columbia had. The town had risen from its ashes, however, to become a decent enough place to live.

A nice community in which to raise kids.

Have a family.

Make a life.

———

Vince dropped the Margraves off at Cullen's BMW parked on campus outside the Mass Comm College, located in a renovated, ancient campus building with wide wooden floors that creaked and moaned. The campus of then South Carolina College had been spared the wartime fires, with quite a few buildings dating back to the early nineteenth century.

"Bottom line time." The beefy realtor, leaning out of the driver's side window with a troubled countenance of concern. "If you want that house —or even think you want it—don't wait."

Cullen offered his hand. "Respect the effort, but the hard-sell? Let's table that."

Randi, smiling and warm in her gratitude. "We'll let you know."

But Vince, driving away slumped like a man who'd wasted a chunk of valuable time. Years ago he'd been one of Cullen's students, the athletic types who took the most basic of cinema survey courses as an easy elective. As Cullen would mock the Vinces of his world: "A class on, like, watchin' movies? Sign me up, Coach."

The couple sat in the BMW listening to the reassuring low-volume murmur of *All Things Considered*. Randi, waiting for him to have the first word, but getting instead only the silent-treatment, a familiar avoidance tactic she also wielded with impunity.

She broke the impasse: "I have to say—I love it. I freaking love that house."

After what seemed like the longest sigh in the history of human exhalation, Cullen asked, "Why this one, honeybunny?" His favorite pet name for her, one picked up from *Pulp Fiction*, a film the cineaste claimed, in certain circles anyway, to loathe. "I know the house is beautiful—it's the kind of place I've always dreamt of owning. But if we want, we can build. Buy some land. Closer in," he begged. "Please."

"But we won't find one like that."

"Like what?"

"High up. Able to see so far around in every direction. Like a fish-eye lens in one of your little movies."

"'Little movies.' Ouch."

She felt the sting come back on her. "I didn't mean it like that."

Cullen mulled, drumming fingers on the steering wheel. Finally he touched her on the arm. "Such a huge decision... all I ask is that we chew on this."

Randi drew breath to lobby, to argue for the house on Davis Macon Lane, then deflated. She wondered about her certitude, that perhaps she sought only to feel assured about the house on the ridge because she needed to feel sure about something. Pick a topic. Did it matter what? Since Denny, no aspect of life had felt settled or certain, but in her most raw and honest moments, she knew it'd been that way before his death, too.

Randi—when she allowed herself—knew she now clung to Cullen for reasons far afield from romantic love: despite his perfidies, he remained the life-link to Denny. The only one.

A pang in her gut, a sharp one—if she hadn't recognized it as grief, she'd have sworn a case of pancreatic cancer had sprung into ruinous being.

She shifted around in her seat and hid from Cullen her welling sorrow. "We'll chew on it, then." Randi, trying to stave off the wave. "Sleep on it."

"There we go—all perfectly reasonable, yes?"

"Quite reasonable."

Besides, Vince himself had undone any true sense of urgency: he'd slipped up earlier in the day and admitted the house had been on the market for months. So: yes yes, time enough, she thought, to decide.

Nothing but time. The last third of 1999 to grind through, and next, a new century. A new millennium, in fact.

Or else, no time left at all—Vince, with his Y2K fears, fed into her own low-level, simmering and persistent anxiety. Her resurgent, welling paranoia felt worse than the outright panic attacks that lurked, struck, and lingered, but those had gotten better over the summer, finally, after she got through the anniversary of the accident. But she had to be careful about the Xanax—an easy, pillowy solution to all this internal strife.

Too easy.

Another honest thought: since her son died—since she'd killed him by putting him on that goddamn plane—she hadn't had a purpose, hadn't had a place, hadn't had a marriage that worked. What choice had they but to start over? Split up? There was that. "Just do me the favor of taking this one seriously."

"Sure, of course." Cullen, nodding and squeezing her knee. His hand, lingering, sliding upward. Warming her thigh. "Let's go grab din. Then home. Maybe a snuggle? It's been so long."

Randi, not caring what she ate for dinner, if anything at all. "Mediterranean?"

Cullen, calling a negatory; instead, he extolled the virtues of the buffet he'd tried at a new Indian place off Rosedale Avenue. A quick agreement —Randi, hoping that the intense spices would awaken her spirit. Would make her feel sated.

Alive, again.

To avoid seeing Denny's old grammar school, Cullen took the long way around campus through the Old Market, the commercial district adjacent to the university. The streets, damp from an afternoon shower, teemed with the beer-drinking, Humpday happy hour crowd flowing down the hill from the huge campus. Randi envied them, those students and budding professionals—their youth, their innocence, their lack of obligation.

Wait—what obligations did she have? Not many. Maybe it wasn't so bad after all.

———

Now full dark, Cullen cut through the nice neighborhood up the hill from the Market, a sort of twin peak to their own hoity-toity University Terrace area visible in the rearview—Herndon Hill had been the original suburb of the downtown area, its densely packed Craftsman bungalows dating all the way back to the beginning of the century. Here began their house-hunt earlier in the summer, which in the season since had gravitated farther and farther into the outer spiral arms of exurbia, all the way into southernmost Edgewater County.

Randi's chest felt tight. The massive oaks lining the street stood expansive and mature, their shadowy, sheltering canopy only serving as claustrophobic contrast to the wondrous property on the lonely and quiet ridge.

A shape—an animal—darted across in front of the headlamps. "Cullen, *stop.*"

The BMW's tires slid on the wet road. Randi craned her neck back to see a bone-thin boxer, brown with white paws, holding one bloodied leg aloft and panting. "It's hurt."

Cullen made no move to get out. His hands remained gripped upon the leather-wrapped steering wheel. "That's somebody else's prob."

Her mouth gaping, she wrenched off the seatbelt and sprang out of the car: "Sweetheart—are you all right?"

Cullen rolled the window down. "We're not futzing around with some stray dog."

"We have to help it!"

"The hell we do." He tooted the horn.

Startled, the animal whimpered and turned tail, limping into the shadows between a pair of overvalued bungalows.

"You son of a bitch—she's injured." Randi pounded the trunk of the Beemer and darted over to the sidewalk. She cupped her hands. "*Doggie? Hello?*"

This time Cullen laid down on the horn, long and annoying. Lights came on. Silhouettes appeared in windows.

Cursing, Randi threw her skinny arms in the air and stomped back to the car.

Leaning over and facing away from her husband, she collapsed, sobbing against the window now fogged by her anguished, hot breath.

A calm Cullen smiled and nodded. He'd seen her break down so often over the last couple of years it had become part of a family routine. "Don't worry, honeybunny—just a mangy old mutt." He put the car in gear and drove on down the street. "It's Herndon Hill. One of these bleeding heart yuppies'll take responsibility. Suckers that they are," he added.

Spastic, she yanked the seatbelt across herself. "You're a coldhearted bastard."

"Randi, we cannot put a dog in this car—what about my allergies?"

Checkmate. The allergies eclipsed all.

But Randi, fuming: This, beyond the pale—cruelty to animals? A new low.

Oh, but on another level, he'd done worse. And she'd forgiven so much.

How could she make a big deal out of this latest display that her husband was an inveterate asshole?

Who would care, or be surprised? Nobody.

Newsflash.

Besides ignoring said a-hole, what she did do for the rest of the night was take her laptop into the guest room where she'd been sleeping for months and pull up the online listing of the house on the ridge. She clicked through the photo set; she closed her eyes and pictured the light and the air and the trees, the creek, the wind blowing and the high, lonesome scree of a hawk she'd heard. This hilltop in the middle of nowhere: a place to begin anew, to escape the yawning, yearning sense of unreality that pervaded her every waking moment here in Denny's house.

Satisfied and certain, with or without her husband's participation and sanction, Randi drifted to sleep believing she'd at last settled on a new place to call home.

3

OVER BREAKFAST CULLEN REFUSED TO DISCUSS THE HOUSE IN Edgewater County, or any house. "I have to teach three classes before noon. All due respect, but let me divest my mind of all this. For a few hours. If you please."

"'This?' I feel so special."

"We'll talk about the house. Just not this morning."

Since he'd left, she'd lounged bored and desperate there on University Terrace, pacing hardwood floors scuffed from the toddler years of toys and strollers and hobbyhorses.

Useless. Empty.

Anxious.

New house or not, how was she to become what Cullen was expecting, in essence a new person? A writer? Speaking of fiction, she'd dug herself deep with this phony excuse to be left alone. This would be her therapy, as she'd insisted to everyone, to colleagues from the station like Cynthia-Anne and Spencer, or to her own mother, whose advice, before or after the tragedy of Denny, had rarely been helpful, and now accused her of hiding from the world and her grief, and not getting on with things. The ice queen. Her mother had been perfect for her father—why on earth they'd gotten divorced Randi hadn't a clue.

As for her taciturn and humorless academic of a patriarch, he'd been dead to her long before his actual corporeal demise a few years ago—

Durant Montreat, brilliant and inscrutable, but a minor character, one suitable only for an occasional flashback. For backstory.

Sure—she'd gone to a community writing workshop or two at the library, and attended an on-campus series that hosted authors discoursing about craft, so even if she hadn't written a single word, around the Margrave dinner table Randi could at least fake the lingo.

At one writer's talk in the Humanities auditorium-classroom, she'd held up her hand and asked the middle-aged, Southern novelist who'd been leaning into the lectern and visibly suffering through a grinding, uninteresting Q&A, "How should one write about grief?"

"Grief?" Wary, shifting from foot to foot. "In what context?"

"When you choose a subject like grief, hasn't it all been said before?"

Cort Beauchamp, the upcountry's mid-list answer to Conroy, went *mm-hm, mm-hm* into the mic. "A problem for any writer, about virtually any subject. In the case of grief, everyone who's ever lived not only watches others pass away, but we all eventually die—a central conundrum of human existence, and ripe for artistic exploration. So with a subject like grief or loss or death, one that's so ubiquitous and endemic to the experience of being alive, it's been more than covered with sufficient grace and aplomb, both in philosophy, theology, and in modern times, fiction.

"So what to do? You must find the angle, like a newspaper reporter sniffing out a story. If the grief's inspired by your own experience with loss, figure out an oblique way to say what it felt like, without hitting them on the nose with a sledgehammer—tell it slant, as Emily Dickinson advised in her elegant metaphor."

Randi, tingling—his reference to news-gathering gave her a sense of synchronicity.

"Think of it this way," musing his way into a rhetorical groove. "It's like the Southern tradition of criticizing family members to their face around the Thanksgiving table. Talk around the truth. Treat the subject like subtext, rather than hit it head on. This approach, it's as good a template for an author as any I've read in creative writing textbooks."

Laughter, applause, and a flurry of fresh hands fluttering in the air for his attention. "So sneak up on that grief, ma'am. Find your way through the dark woods."

Green tea in hand and roiling with guilt, Randi forced herself to sit down at the dining room table with the word processor open to a new document. Her fingers poised, she dragged herself back into the past, striving to dredge up interesting scenarios and plot lines inspired by the people and places that had mattered. Times she'd enjoyed with friends back home; moments of conflict and strife, of which her mental inventory provided an unwelcome surfeit.

So, how about her college years? Coming here to Columbia. Meeting Cullen, a young associate professor ten years her senior. How they'd hit it off, explosively and passionately, and so what if she'd been his student, because by then she was all grown up and done soon enough with the J-school degree and all was well and right... until she presented as pregnant. Poof. Out of the blue. Pregnant with Denny. Pregnant with possibility, with love for the scholarly, urbane Cullen Margrave, impregnated by him with the seed of their baby boy, their spawn, their glorious progeny who'd grow into a—

Fiction. She needed to write fiction. Not think about Denny.

What about mining the marriage for drama?

Hah—now there was a source of conflict, though admittedly contrived and familiar: Before the plane crash had taken Denny, she'd done her best to move on from Cullen's ridiculous, clichéd grad student indiscretion. But at the risk of hypocrisy, Randi often rationalized his behavior by asking, what pray tell had she herself been but that: an attractive, bright pupil he'd seduced?

A huge difference: twelve years ago, when he'd begun dating her during the semester she'd taken his documentary course, Cullen Margrave had been a single man, if indeed committing an indiscretion. Randi, a smitten younger woman who fell hard for his deep brown eyes, the sharp mind, the energy and intellect and stamina, a lover like none she'd had before.

Not an indiscretion. A romance. That's the way she thought of it.

Ugh. She couldn't drag herself through all that again.

A better idea came over her, a small rush of ah-ha that made her jump in her chair: She tapped out a title, and kept on typing for over an hour before she stopped:

DAISY ON THE ROAD
by Marandi M. Margrave

The being is confused, uncomfortable, utterly alone. Its paws are scabbed over and coat damp with the rainwater that so recently fell from the slate-gray sky. It hunches its shoulders and flinches at the peals and rumbles from overhead, like great animal-gods at war with one another. It sniffs at the air, looks around, and then wanders on, careful to stay away from the hard trail over which the ugly machines roll, side by side, back and forth, belching and loud and merciless. The dog, a pet, heretofore sheltered from the unforgiving and merciless world, understands the machines only enough to stay out of their murderous way.

From what had been a life of no want, from the warmth and safety of a soft bed inside the large box of stone and wood in which it had lived with its companion, from a world of endless food and clean water and a patch of green earth protected on all sides from the unimaginable threats that lay beyond those impregnable borders, the being's existence is now an endless cycle of fatigue, fear, privation. The creature's mind understands its predicament, yes, but only on one essential and primal level:

Food, or not-food.

Or otherwise: Safe, or not-safe. And for the past few days, mostly not-safe...

Randi went on at great length describing the circumstances behind the animal's quandary: How the boxer had been frightened into bolting its fenced yard by the explosions from "the demonstrative bipeds next door, whooping and hollering as though mad"; she imagined a Fourth of July celebration, cacophonous and violent to a frightened dog. She related how it'd once worn a pink collar that said *Daisy.* What had become of the collar. The horrors of what the dog had resorted to eating on its miserable trek. The terrors and pangs and close shaves—all fabrication, of course. Randi couldn't truly know what it'd been like for the injured dog. Or why it'd become lost.

Now verifiably autobiographical elements at last came into play: the scene on the street, the blowing of the horn, the woman running after the dog, then cursing her human companion in the noisy, dangerous machine. How Daisy's heart had been broken anew. A sad sad story.

...Daisy will never know how much the woman wanted to help her, and how not being allowed to do so haunted her from that day forward.

~~A dog to replace a boy.~~

She went back and struck through this line, an inappropriate authorial intrusion of concerns lacking in context.

Hands aching, she closed the word processor window and put the laptop into hibernation mode.

At dinner, Randi announced she'd at last completed a piece.

Cullen pressed her for details. "So—is it a short story?"

"Think so."

"Ready for the blue pencil of doom?"

Pondering, she gnawed on her lower lip. "I don't think you'll appreciate it."

"Do tell."

"Let me get the training wheels off. It's not ready. But it will be."

He sipped wine, probed her with skeptical eyes. "No pressure. I've got Nouveau Vague essays to grade anyway—*tuez-moi maintenant, s'il vous plaît.*"

"I'll send up a flare when I'm ready for fresh eyes. No peeking in the oven, though. Fair enough?"

"You'll send up a flare in the oven?" He smiled. "I think that's a mixed metaphor."

"See, I don't know what I'm doing yet."

"Sure, sure—boy, you artists. *'You can't see it, till it's finished',*" sung in a reasonable David Byrne. "Take your time."

Time she had, a surplus, an endless grind of unstructured hours and days.

But how best to use these moments and hours? To her the afternoon's work demonstrated only that so long as she kept trying to force a round, new life into the square hole of what had once been their warm, reasonably happy home, she'd fail. Writing? Sure.

But not here—anywhere but the house on University Terrace.

4

THE DEBATE OVER BUYING THE PROPERTY ON DAVIS MACON LANE unfolded over several fierce episodes, but after two more trips out to view the house and surroundings—one experienced during a magic-hour sunset on the ridge, a moment Cullen, in movie-geek mode, had deemed 'Malick-esque'—Randi's husband caved. It had helped that they tried an alternative route taking only twenty-nine minutes, the half-hour mark representing an important psychological barrier for him to overcome. So what if she fudged by a minute or two?

They wandered in the yard. The light, golden. Dogs barking again, but faraway.

Lingering reluctance. "You sure about that trip time?"

Nodding. "This place—I can feel that it's right."

Standing in the light of the setting sun, he said he could get used to the solitude. Could perhaps pursue some writing of his own. Expressed that he only wanted them to be happy again, to find a way back from the abyss of their grief. "It eats away at me too. I just get buried in a fog of work and obligation to dull the pain."

"So you'll do it?"

He dabbed at the corners of his eyes. "It's a beautiful house."

Nothing else needed to be said. For the first time in months, they held one another. Kissed like lovers. Wept together yet again over Denny, and now the decision to sell his house. Despite the emotional land mines ahead, the next morning their signatures on a contract made Vince Ellen-shaw the happiest realtor in the midlands of South Carolina.

———

Time began passing like a happy daydream instead of the usual grinding nightmare that'd defined the last year: Randi, throwing herself into packing the house. Now this felt like purpose.

But in her nocturnal dreams?

The dog; Daisy, on the road. In dreams, the dog ran toward her, eyes imploring Randi for help she'd never be able to give.

Disturbing, yes, but better than the recurring nightmares of having failed Denny, the ones where he'd wept and accused her of leaving him. Hurting him. Forgetting him. An extra half a Xanax after dinner helped.

———

After nearly a month, the arrival of the moving truck.

Amidst cardboard boxes and clutter, Cynthia-Anne Goforth, Randi's friend and WKNO on-air talent, stood on the porch in a frumpy oversize Redtails sweatshirt and paint-spotted jeans, clothing she'd never deign to wear in public where her loyal viewers could see.

Cocking an elbow. "Girl, I can't believe Cullen agreed to move from downtown."

"I'm still getting used to the idea myself."

"Don't get me wrong, I dig being way out on the lake—love love *love* it —but Edgewater County? *Really?*"

Randi directed the two men struggling down the front steps burdened by half of the L-shaped living room sofa. To her friend she said, "Thanks to the settlement, we don't have to sell straight away. We'll spruce it up a bit. Maybe roll paint."

Everywhere but Denny's old room.

She could see Cyn-Anne's curiosity simmering: the size of the award the attorney had brokered. Randi's protégé had always been borderline vapid, far too impressed by money and status—a cable news anchor desk and magazine covers remained her goal, and for all Randi knew might come true.

"He argued to the last the convenience factor, but I think it's because he doesn't want to leave—" The sacred name snagged in her throat. "Leave our Denny behind."

She draped her arms around Randi's neck, pulled their foreheads together. "I know, sugar." They'd been close ever since Randi'd supervised Cyn-Anne's J-school internship, then shepherded the younger woman up the ladder at the station to evening news anchor—it went without saying that the loyalty ran deep. The women heaved and sighed together.

"It's just so far out, 3M." Randi's KNO nickname, a cutesy byproduct of the alliterative Marandi Montreat Margrave. "What a haul."

"We'll have cookouts. Walks in the woods. The trees are finally starting to turn. It'll be glorious." Randi, startled by her optimism. "I can't wait."

"So I suppose this all means you're still not coming back to work?" The on-air journalist, who could slip in and out of moods and expressions on a dime, offered a coquettish smile to the men trudging up the steps for the other half of the sofa, then hardened back into her small frown of concern. "It'd be so good for you."

Randi, hands on hips. "Did Cullen put you up to that?"

"No—but this whole writing thing?"

"Yes?"

"That's no substitute for a career. Nobody makes a living writing."

"I'm finding out that it's real work."

Cyn-Anne shrugged. "You know what they say: 'work will make you free.'"

Randi busted a gut at her friend's obliviousness of the grim origins of that particular aphorism.

The newscaster narrowed her eyes. "What's so funny?"

And another round of laughter, with the merriment threatening to tip over into mad tears. "How do you Southerners put it? You tickle me, girl. I swear but you do."

Cyn-Anne grinned. "See? There's my old 3M. God, we so need you back. Seriously, homegirl."

"Bless your heart." Randi, wiping tears—happy tears, for once. "I appreciate what you're trying to do. But the KNO chapter of my life is closed."

"Spencer misses you as well."

Her old boss would have to chill. "Too bad."

The movers buttoned up the truck. The supervisor, a middle aged

Latino thick and stubby as a fireplug, called over to the lady of the manse. "We will see you out there, ma'am?"

"I'll be along straight away. You've got good directions?"

"We have a map." He squinted at his clipboard. "Oy—it is very far."

"See? Even he thinks it's out in the boonies."

Randi felt a touch of exasperation. "Well, it's too late, baby."

Cyn again threw her arms around Randi. "I guess if I never see you again, there's always email—until Y2K hits, anyway. Think anything'll happen?"

Randi released her friend and went to close up the house. "You're the journalist. You tell me."

A quick peck on the lips and a final squeeze. Expressions of affection.

"You've always been so good to us." Randi, beaming warmth to her friend.

Cyn-Anne's cheeks colored. Stumbled over her words. "That's—what friends are. For. What they do."

Randi watched her friend drive off, a Mercedes 450 SL with a personalized plate that read KNONEWS1. Feeling a sense of release—of impending freedom—she locked the front door and leapt in her old diesel Volvo and rumbled away from the silent, empty house on Caughman Street. Odds and ends were left to do, and this wasn't goodbye, but she said the word anyway. Maybe not to Denny, but to this place that had been his? Hell, yeah she did. Time to freaking go, already.

5

"*Green Acres, it's the life for me...* farm living. Who'd-a thunk it."

Despite the clutter and lack of personal touches, the kitchen glowed with warm incandescence from recessed dimmers. While hanging copper pots one by one over the large center island, a gourmet cook's dream, Cullen, cheerful, kept humming the old TV sitcom theme song about city-folk ditching their modern life for rural farmland. He may have been crushed on every professional front—film festival planning, a paper to publish, another book proposal to pitch and write—but Randi's hubby had taken to the process of moving with vim, vigor and engagement.

"This represents quite the change of attitude." Loading perishables into the gleaming, spotless Subzero, she unpacked a large cooler in which they'd brought the contents of their old refrigerator. "Considering what it took to persuade you, aren't you more Zsa-Zsa on this than Eddie Albert?"

"That would be Eva, not Zsa-Zsa." Cullen's smile turned as cool as the fall air outside. "Honestly?"

Randi, waiting.

"It remains to be seen how I adjust to all this driving."

She felt relief—a more genuine response. "Change is what we both needed. And so that's what we have. It can come in other ways later, if this doesn't work out."

"I may have had enough change to last me. But here we are."

"It'll be beautiful. There's something out here in these woods."

"Like what?"

"Something like peace." Being out on the high ridge, alone, meant that the rest of the world, with all its tragedies, travails and concerns, seemed far away. "And hope."

"Well." He cupped her chin, stroked her stringy hair pulled back beneath a threadbare paisley bandanna. "I hope you're right."

Randi pulled a chilled New Zealand Sauvignon blanc from the cooler. "Keep an eye peeled for wine goblets—a toast to our new beginning?"

"Next box, I think. I could use a drink."

She tilted her head and offered him a pitying, insincere smile. "That bad so far?"

"No, no—look, I always planned to end up out in the sticks. To write scripts, or a novel… make my own film… or else flat-out retire and take up gardening and golf. In any case, always thought that as long as I was actively teaching, I'd stay a city boy."

Randi felt sympathy for her husband—at only 46, he'd be driving back and forth to Columbia for another decade or two before he retired. Still, this cloud of negativity threatened to spoil the mood. "At least gas is cheap."

"There's that." Cullen, pulling a stack of dinner plates separated by squares of brown kraft paper from a box on the granite counter top. "What about going back to work? Maybe not at KNO, but somewhere."

"One day, maybe," but without enthusiasm. "It's not like we need the money."

"True that. But I know it'd be good for you. We could even carpool."

A sweet sentiment, but not what she had in mind. Rather than pushing back, she merely smiled and nodded and put away plates, more plates than the two of them could possibly need.

———

Only a day or so after signing the contract on the house, news came that the airline settlement about which Cyn-Anne had been so keen to hear had been finalized. They ended up making a day of meeting with attorneys, first to close on the new property, and later with an attorney far different from the harried real estate lawyer with whom they would barely exchange a word over the signing of the small mountain of legal documents involved with the purchase of real estate:

Handling their complaint against the airline for the loss of their son was a lawyer known around town as The Mako Shark, a partner at a most prestigious of Columbia firms, a man who appeared in person as polished and elegant as the flowing cadence of his name. Hamilton Preston Sottile, sporting a cleft chin like the lost son of an old Hollywood matinee idol, explained in his sententious Charleston drawl how, yes, the airline's settlement offer, while generous, could be accepted and all could go home that night and rest as easy as they'd allow themselves to, with little loss of honor or opportunity. "If we could reduce tragedy to such base and profane terms."

Or under the right circumstances, as he said, the settlement could be made yet richer. "The death of a child? Why, the thought's traumatic even to a parent who hasn't suffered as the two of you folks have," placing tanned, manicured fingers upon aching lawyer heart, the low light in the wood-paneled office feeling to Randi like a sanctum where occult rituals were performed. "So if you'll let me, I'd be more than game to argue in front of a jury that no amount of money would be enough to make up for what you've lost."

Cullen, leaning forward. "You think it'd be worth it? Going through the trouble?"

As though burdened by the potential magnitude of his courtroom victory, Sottile, grave, rapped knuckles upon the burnished wood of an enormous, spotless desk: "Once our team is through with them, we might just own ourselves an airline."

Randi, staring at the offer on the document Sottile had handed them. "If we accept this, everything's over. Right?"

"Now hold on, honeybunny."

"What is money, anyway? Paper? Numbers in a computer? What if the computers all fail because of Y2K this year? Where'll the money be then?"

"Randi—"

Cooling her jets. Softening her glare. "I have only one question for Mr. Sottile."

"Yes, Mrs. Margrave?"

"If we sign this, we walk away, and we're done. Correct?"

He held out his hands: *well, obviously.*

"Then, may I trouble you for a fucking pen?"

Sottile blinked at the rancor in his client's voice, and Cullen had whined and begun to protest, but at the sight of his wife's tearful, pleading stare, he decided to withdraw—his acquiescence manifested as a pair of limp hands thrown briefly skyward, a slight and insubstantial gesture.

"Let us make it so, then." The attorney, calling for his assistant to produce documents of record for the Margraves. Turning to small talk. Them buying some land in the country. Sottile slapped his hands together, said he had a cabin up in Hot Springs, NC, to which he often retreated. "Healing to be had amongst nature. A wise decision."

As they left, Randi noted Sottile's tinge of resignation bordering on disappointment that they hadn't bitten, like Vince after their first visit to the house. Everyone hungry for that money-green. From the trappings of his high corner office overlooking downtown and the cut of the tailored suit, she felt certain that quite apart from taking an airline to the cleaners, Hamilton Sottile and his firm would likely survive in style.

———

After the Margraves ate frozen meals out of the microwave in their new gourmet kitchen and drank the bottle of wine, they regrouped and moved on to the bedroom: making up the king bed. Hanging clothes in the two enormous walk-in closets that, compared to their old house, Randi found heavenly. Lamps onto night tables; plugging in the digital alarm that Cullen would now be setting an hour or more earlier. Settling in.

She went to close the vertical blinds, but realized only the deserted ridge lay all around. No one to see inside.

No neighbors.

Solitude, achieved.

Cullen turned on the bedroom television. He flipped through the few channels they could receive; satellite TV, their only choice so far out in the country, would be requisitioned with all haste.

"Jesus, I'd kill for a set of rabbit ears. What next?"

"Bathroom stuff. I think that box's still in the garage."

As Cullen went back downstairs, Randi perched on the edge of the comfortable mattress and stared at a snowy, muted newscast. President Clinton, red-faced and perturbed, stood at the podium wagging a crooked finger at the White House press corps. Cynthia-Anne appeared, her lips smiling and flapping as she read off the lead-in: from the South-eastern Fighting Redtails logo that appeared chyron'd over her shoulder, sports was up next. Randi thumbed the remote and the television fell dark.

But indeed, as both the anchor and Randi's husband kept asking, what now? What would she make of herself with all this precious seclusion?

She hadn't a clue. Maybe go figure out who had that poor dog tied up. She'd heard it all afternoon, yelping and howling and barking up the ridge. Vince had been wrong about one of his selling points—somewhere close by, there did indeed seem to be neighbors.

The dog down the ridge.

Daisy, on the road.

Denny. Sweet Denny.

And now, his house—his room—sat cold and dark and empty. Pictured her boy as a confused ghost, bereft that his people had decamped for a destination unknown to him. Unable to follow them.

Like a lost dog.

Randi, her sides quivering, found herself slipping. Slipping already.

Comparing her son to a dog?

Damn, girl. Losing it.

Cullen came through the door with the bathroom box under one arm and an elegant, hand-painted Asian porcelain vase-lamp clutched under the other, a long-ago, expensive wedding gift from Randi's mother. "Well, they didn't break this one, thank god." Noticing his wife sitting in an all-too-familiar position of anxiety: "Oh, sweetie, what is it?"

Heavy tears leapt over her eyelids, an eruption, a cascade—she hadn't cried in days. Unusual for her. Mewling through a wretched apology.

He put down the lamp on the night table, sat beside her. "You don't have to be sorry. This move has just been one more layer of stress. God knows, in the middle of the semester like this, it hasn't been a cakewalk for me, either."

He pulled her close. She remained stiff.

"It's not the move."

"I know, honeybunny. It's everything." *Everything* a euphemism for Denny.

"That's not what I'm talking about."

Her throat, throttled and closed off like the time at thirteen when she'd suffered a Strep infection so virulent she ended up in the hospital. That'd been when she lost her baby fat, those days of barely eating. She'd never gained an ounce back, not even when pregnant with Denny, whose presence inside had precipitated only a gradual swelling in her lower abdomen, and then not until the sixth month. "It's—I'm having a hard time forgiving you."

Cullen drew back, a sour look on his face that spoke volumes: Was his dreadful betrayal going to come up *yet again?* "Tell me you're not still thinking about all that. Not after all this time. Not after Denny."

"All what?" Randi, observing her husband's rosy cheeks, downcast eyes. "Oh—her, you mean? No, no, it's not that. Not Rachel."

More confused than relieved: "Well what, then?"

She tried to answer, broke down sobbing anew, heaving and mewling nonsense.

"Honeybunny, I can't understand you."

"That *dog*," explosive and bitter. "I can't stop thinking about that little dog in the street that night—"

Cullen, perplexed. "What dog?"

She didn't know why the injured dog had mattered so much. But Randi couldn't shake the notion that because of her inaction—however involuntary—further ill had befallen the creature. Guilt spiral.

She struggled with explaining these feelings, but when the central heat kicked off, and the bedroom fell silent, as if on cue a faint whimpering came from out in the forest—a doleful canine wailing.

Cullen, gesturing toward the window. "That's an old hound dog, tied up in the woods."

"Tied up?"

"This is rural South Carolina. What did you expect to find out here? A nature preserve with park rangers?"

"Never mind. Forget the damn dog."

"Would that I could."

She poured another glass of wine. Cullen followed, cooing promises about how the days to come were sure to be good. Randi, thinking that whatever else lay ahead in her new life, finding out where the dog was—and how it was being treated—sat high on her list.

In other words, a project; a minor-key mystery to occupy her time.

6

One by one, cardboard boxes became empty shells consigned to the ignominy of a dusty, endless sleep in a corner of the garage.

Randi pondered the stack of boxes—were these objects aware their usefulness had passed? Did the cardboard lay sleeping, dreaming of the day the Margraves would again move? Anticipating a burgeoning intentional community of cockroaches?

Silliness. She'd truck the pile to the recycling center near Tillman Falls.

Empty Boxes.

She got a tingle. Title of a short story?

The novelist Beauchamp had said in his talk how important it was for the writer to be ready to scribble anytime and anywhere, so she'd started carrying a notebook in the back pocket of the favorite pair of threadbare jeans she wore most days. She jotted down the title idea, followed by:

A story of collapsed spaces devoid of form and meaning.

Oh-kay, then.

The new house, open and hollow in a manner different from their old home, still felt cold, sterile—in other words, a blank slate. Randi could relate; she felt a bit *tabula rasa* herself. As such, she busied herself unpacking, organizing, and considering potential changes to the interior décor, like getting some color onto the walls: the prior owners had worshipped at the altar of neutral beige. A trip to the home improvement warehouse for swatches and paint cards sat high on her meager itinerary of pressing tasks.

Every now and then? The unseen dog howled, heard best on days when the wind rushed from the river far below. She'd begun playing music all the time, not only to fill the vast empty space she occupied, but also to blot out the sounds carrying up the ridge.

One afternoon she'd lingered on the back patio, squinting and getting a fix on the direction from which she heard the dog. But as a mournful, country song-worthy train horn came a-calling from deep in the hollow, she realized with certainty the howling came from more than one animal.

———

Once she had the house squared away, a fresh crossroads: Continuing to sit in bored, desperate rumination as she'd labored on University Terrace; or, as Cullen and others expected, to become a writer. Either were endeavors she could pursue alone, at her own pace, so she had that going for her.

Writing. What words of wisdom worth offering, though?

The Daisy story had gone well—while composing the pages she'd floated in a creative trance. Healthy. Healing. More of the same couldn't hurt.

With a glorious, sun-dappled view overlooking the sloping ridge land, she slid onto a high-backed stool along the breakfast bar, opened her laptop, sipped tea and poised her fingers to revise the dog-story.

No. Forget fiction.

She tapped out the title of the only book she felt moved to write, a tome intended to both honor and lend meaning to her child's brief life:

A Song For Denny:
One Mother's Memoir of
Ephemeral Love and Eternal Grief

Repulsed by the notion, she swore at the screen and deleted the text.

Maybe one day. This made the fourth such attempt. The others had ranged from a few paragraphs to a few pages.

Again: what was there to say?

A random tragedy happened to a precocious, prepubescent member of a middle class family on Anystreet, USA. How would Randi the TV news segment-producer spin this sad story? And as a writer, what is the hook, where is the narrative through-line? Perhaps with distance, she'd be able to discern a finer thematic point in documenting Denny's life, her writing serving as more than a mere personal indulgence.

But today was not that day. That's what her intuition said. It would be wallowing, not creativity.

The house phone, newly connected, rang loud and sudden, startling Randi out of her internal debate; Cullen, returning a message she'd left for him earlier.

She lied through her teeth about what she'd been up to, pretending to have begun a fresh short story. "My fingers are positively aching."

"Hell, yeah. Can't wait to read it."

"I wouldn't be so anxious—or eager, rather." Changing the subject, and quick: "How come you didn't answer your cell earlier? Class should've been out by then." She'd tried once or twice more, too. In the time since his affair, when he didn't answer or call back right away, she suffered bouts of paranoia.

"Wasn't on purpose—in my coat pocket the mute button keeps getting pressed. I hate that phone."

"Well, get a new one."

"Question."

"Yes?"

"Was there really a need to call a dozen times?"

Uncomfortable silence. She could hear him crunching on the other end—a package of crackers, his afternoon snack. "Stop exaggerating."

"Damn near that." His tone turned smarmy and I-told-you-so. "What —you lonesome all the way out there?"

"No, smartass. I'm fine. But having said that: when are you coming home?"

He cleared his throat. "The Film Society board meeting's tonight—remember? We're screening this independent that made some noise at Sundance but didn't sell, so the producers are self-distributing, god love them. Thinking of doing these kids a solid and booking the damn thing."

Ah, yes, Cullen and his beloved Film Society meetings. Considering the huge amount of time the volunteer endeavor seemed to require, for years now Randi had wondered if the rest of his film-snob friends had families at all. Besides planning out the screening calendar, at the first of the year the group had commenced a "Relocation 2000" fundraising drive in the hopes of moving the Society's hundred-seat art house into one of the downtown, long-shuttered movie palaces that'd once dotted Columbia's Main Street. The success of the effort had been high on Cullen's list of activities, almost to the point of obsession.

"So in other words, you'll be late."

"Afraid so. If you're tired, go ahead and crash. My feelings won't be hurt."

"Want me to leave dinner in the oven?" If she were to be nothing more than a homemaker, she might as well make a game effort. "And what would you like?"

"Nah—I'm fine. Just worry about Randi."

He rang off and she stood for a long moment listening to the dial tone. Perturbed and suspicious, Randi attempted to resist the possibility that the film society screening was only a smokescreen.

However, if he didn't love her, wasn't true to her, he'd had the chance to dissolve the marriage. Before the loss of Denny they'd discussed the dissolution of their troubled union but decided against it. After Denny? He'd expressed how she was all he had left.

How wrong he'd been.

How he couldn't abide losing her, too.

The afternoon waned. She logged on and started surfing on the dialup internet connection, but found doing so excruciating—they'd need the satellite linkup for that as well as TV reception. Sitting on the patio and listening to the gurgling stream, she tried reading a novel, but found her mind wandering.

She closed the book, a South Carolina-set beach island family drama. Waited for the dog to howl. Heard only the wind and the water. A relief.

As the sun dipped down and the air turned cooler, Randi went inside and poured a glass of Pinot Grigio to enjoy as prepared herself a fresh spinach salad with walnuts, roasted red peppers, and goat cheese.

The food and wine sitting in front of her on the counter, she held herself and pondered the inky dark of the countryside. Solitude, yes, that had indeed been the plan. But as he'd warned, now she enjoyed, or perhaps suffered, a surfeit of *alone*.

She'd asked for loneliness, though. Hadn't she? *Be careful what you wish for.*

7

Unlike President Clinton, Randi managed to not only inhale but hold the rich smoke, expansive and minty-lavender fresh, deep in her lungs.

Not for too long—she had to be careful. Rare that they smoked pot anymore, but Cullen always kept a few grams around in case he wanted to get a head on before screening an Antonioni, or *Two-Lane Blacktop*, or myriad other hypnotic masterpieces filling out an extensive video collection, one befitting a cinema studies professor.

The smoke bloomed in her lungs. She coughed.

Took another puff, smaller. Managed to hold it to efficacy.

Her scalp tingled. The moment elongated.

Being a lightweight, she intended only moderate consumption. If she got too high? The blood pressure drop and the full body quivers. Stabs of paranoia and anxiety. No, no; she only wanted to get a little tweaked. She didn't even know why.

To smoke offered novelty, she supposed, in the vast and unceasing task of passing the time. Hoped the herb, if the right sort of cerebral strain, might focus and inspire her to write. Or at least distract her. She didn't want to resort to the pills. Again.

She took another small puff from the colorful glass spoon, a gift from one of Cullen's hippie students. Exhaled, languid and lovely.

She put the cannabis and pipe back into the carved wooden box that sat on a shelf downstairs near Cullen's DVD collection. In the past, he'd kept the stash well hidden in case Denny took a notion to go exploring; now, of course, no such concealment required.

Randi turned out the kitchen lights and shuffled in her sock feet through the great room, passing by the spiral stairs that led down to the lower level where Cullen had set up the home theatre as well as his office. Randi supposed if the relationship soured again, the two of them could retreat to separate floors. With each passing day she lived on Davis Macon Lane, the more she realized how much more house they'd bought than necessary.

But as Cullen had implied, they could always try again for a child, couldn't they? Randi, still in the relative prime of her reproductive life.

Her heart clenched. She thought of Denny's spirit, disappointed and forgotten, observing her with a new child. How he'd asked, once, for a brother or sister. "Someone I can look out for," he'd explained. Her conscientious little man.

They'd placed the sofa in the middle of the enormous, chilly family room, close to the as-yet unused fireplace and positioned to enjoy the lovely view of the land out the enormous windows. She turned off the globed, overhead lights hanging down from the twenty-foot pitch of the ceiling, and like the woods outside, the space plunged into cool darkness.

Her eyes adjusted. She stared up and out of the high windows—a crystalline, stunning swath of stars visible across the velvet indigo of the night sky. The starlight calmed and centered her, the immenseness of the vast impersonal cosmos offering a tonic to her earthly troubles.

The CD she'd left blaring in the kitchen, *OK Computer*, faded into silence.

The house, still. The Victorian constantly popped and settled. This one, at rest.

Her respiration measured, Randi tried to clear her mind. Back when she'd first started having panic attacks—post-Cullen's affair, pre-Denny tragedy—her boss at KNO, Spencer Mathison, had given her a short-course survey of meditation techniques by which he swore.

She chanted *AUM* for what felt like an eternity, pushing out the laughter and footfalls of her dead boy… until *AUM* became the whole of her being. Warmth spread throughout her abdomen, the space where anxiety and despair usually dwelled like twisting, venomous snakes. A pleasant floating sensation. Quiet within and without, a stillness to match the blanket of night and the vast cosmic starscape spiraling away from her.

Spencer—weary, boozy, patrician but attractive. Professional by day, but at the bar the journos frequented he could at times push the limits of sexual harassment. Worse, perhaps, he would deride their profession. Call it a game of reading government press releases, not journalism. And yet he kept coming in to work. And meditating, she presumed, but damned if she could see how the practice helped him.

Her work ethic had begun to sour. She'd begun to believe Mathison, adopt and share his jaundiced worldview. Watched as he shook his head 'NO' over pursuing a corruption tip downtown relating to a longtime, sitting city councilman. Other examples of spiking stories the local power structure would find damaging.

All that was the real problem with returning to KNO. Randi had lost what little fire she'd had in the gut for journalism, any youthful idealism squelched by the very atmosphere of insubstantial infotainment of which she'd been a purveyor. And so, a new path.

Her pulse throbbed in her temples, the only movement in the house— a moment of the genuine peace she'd sought all the way out here in the boonies. Her broken heart, if not wholly stitched back, found its raw lamentation quieted.

For now.

At first she didn't quite perceive the invasion of her placid, stony reverie, this time not the plaintive call of her phantom woods-dog—she began to hear a low rumble coming from outside. Powerful, growing in volume. An automobile engine, running rough. Light came from within the woods, a soft glow, growing in intensity.

Confused at first, Randi remembered the dirt road.

Looking out at what she thought of as 'her' cul-de-sac, she saw a boxy, old pickup truck pulling up out of the words, stopping at the chain where the dirt met asphalt.

Adrenalized, her heart thudded. So much for the chill weed buzz.

She stood at the window and watched, gnawing on the side of her thumb: a figure climbed out of the passenger side, an enormous lump of a man who moved in the light of the headlamps with a deliberateness that might have come from either from his unwieldy size, or perhaps a mental defect. As he stooped to remove the chain across the road, he kept his head bowed.

Randi picked up her birding binoculars from the coffee table, training them on the man as he fumbled around, trying to unlock the chain. His head was pink, hairless, enormous; she couldn't see his face clearly. She moved over to the driver's side, where she could make out a figure illuminated by the green glow of the instrument panel, and from the cherry of a cigarette that bloomed orange. In the truck bed she discerned a large, square object covered by what appeared to be a tarp.

She dropped the glasses and squinted with curiosity as the mountain of a man went to the back of the truck. Bouncing up and down like an excited child, he patted the top of the box and climbed back into the pickup truck, which pulled into the middle of the cul-de-sac.

The truck stopped in front of the dark driveway. The only light came from the glow of the taillights and dingy cones of yellow spilling forward from the headlamps. To better appreciate the night sky Randi had flipped off the garage floods, a decision she now regretted.

The darkness broke, abrupt and startling: a spotlight mounted on the truck's door flared into brilliance. Sweeping across the expanse of the yard, it blinded her with quicksilver streaks across her field of view.

Instinct took over: she ducked down so as not to be seen.

Randi watched with rank indignation as the illumination from the spotlight moved through the room. Shock and fury burned in her gut: Who the hell did these rednecks think they were?

The light winked out.

The engine, rumbling.

After the ancient motor roared and the truck pulled away, Randi, a ninja, rolled and sprang to her feet. She dashed through the house to get the phone, flipping every light switch her fingers could find.

8

OUTSIDE, ANOTHER SPOTLIGHT NOW SWEEPING THROUGH THE YARD, one that filled her with relief rather than dread: an Edgewater County Sheriff's Deputy in her driveway. A half-hour had passed since she'd called about the intrusion into her privacy, and in the meantime she'd become more angry than afraid.

A new worry: she realized the cop might smell the pot, her report of a neighbor's behavior delivered in a cloud of dope and wine. *Super.*

The deputy, a sturdy, bulked-up African-American man probably not quite out of his 20s, emerged from the car flashlight in hand, which he clicked off as he approached.

"Mrs. Musgrave?"

"Margrave."

"Dispatch was garbled. What's the situation, ma'am?"

Holding a hand over her mouth, she explained what happened, as well as how violated she felt at being invaded by a stranger's spotlight.

The cop grunted. "That'd probably tick me off, too."

"Took you long enough to get here, by the way."

The deputy gestured back down the hill. "It happens, ma'am, that I had a good reason to be delayed in responding: I pulled over a truck based on your description."

She noted the Deputy's clipped and flat accent. Like her, probably not native to the area. Military before cop, maybe. "And?"

"He was apologetic, ma'am," nodding to the dirt road heading down the river side of the ridge. "Said it won't happen again."

Randi felt little placated by this news. "Apologetic?"

"Mr. Macon, he lives down the ridge. Didn't know anyone had moved in."

"Macon—so the road's named after them?"

On the first visit to the house, Vince had explained that the implementation of the 9-1-1 system meant once unnamed roads like this one out in the sticks often took their new identification from nearby landowners: In driving around, Randi had noted such colorful examples as Ordell Beacham Road, Willie Nelson Lane (presumably not for the singer), Butch Alvin Footwater Drive. Randi would have no shortage of colorful character names for her fiction.

"Now that you mention it? I suppose it probably is."

Randi apologized, expressed her justifiable discomfort a final time.

He tipped his hat, proper and quaint. "From the sound of it, they didn't mean any harm. Just keeping an eye on what they thought was still vacant property."

"But the real estate sign's gone, we've been coming and going, turning lights on and playing music, and—"

"Kind of neighborly, really. But you couldn't've known that." His tone now betrayed impatience. "Anything else I can do you for tonight, ma'am?"

Randi realized she must have sounded a touch strident. "No harm done. Before tonight I just haven't even seen anyone from down there."

Before bidding her farewell, he rattled off police code into his shoulder mic. "That's what we're here for."

"Thank you. What was your name?"

"Oakley." He tipped his ranger's hat again. "Evening, now."

As he backed out of the driveway, she heard the crackling, fading voices on his scanner. She offered a wave, but couldn't see if the cop returned the gesture.

9

Randi waited up for Cullen, who came in—at last—well after midnight.

"Bitch of a drive this late." His yawn, epic and theatrical. "I almost decided to crash on the couch in the office."

She hoped he wouldn't start complaining about the commute, not after the night she'd had. "How was the screening?"

He draped his sports coat on a wooden hanger, flicked at lint with fingernails he kept manicured and perfect. "A fine line between the ridiculous and the sublime."

"Meaning?"

"We'll book the movie. Sure. But I didn't care for the piece at all. Not a bit."

"And yet the prestigious film society will run it."

"I'm only one vote anyway." He shrugged. "It played for the others."

"That's art for you."

He sat on the bed and slipped off his spit-shined loafers; they fell to the Berber carpet with two muted thumps. "These kids pulled off some great production values. And even some thematic elements of note, pretty mature stuff. Stylistically? Half-assed David Lynch. I just—it was—"

"Do tell."

"I was distracted."

"Had a few distractions around here, too."

Cullen didn't ask what. Instead, he prattled on about a vicious bout of interdepartmental politicking over a proposed high profile archival film conference to be held on campus; the idiots on the committee he chaired on the subject; the toes at the archive on which he'd stepped in securing the chairmanship; the pernicious interference from various administrators hoping to wrangle the most publicity possible out of the conference.

Halfway through his discourse, she found herself drifting off.

Coming out of the bathroom brushing his teeth, Cullen startled Randi out of her nascent doze. "Sorry to bore you with all that hooey."

"It's your life—I should be interested."

"Eh. Sometimes it barely interests me."

A loaded remark.

If it were time, finally, to truly start putting this marriage back together, Randi made the decision to set aside her concerns about the present, and especially thoughts of the past, to attempt their first intimacy in some time.

"I missed you," she said, biting her lip. "You were right—a bit lonely out here." She kicked off the sheet, pulled her knee up, ran her fingers along her thigh. "Could use some snuggling, maybe."

A slow smile. "Can do."

She reached down between her legs and ran a finger, brought it to her nose: Earthy—she hadn't showered in a day or two. Nervous and anticipatory, she yanked off her threadbare nightshirt, tossed it on the floor. Cullen, the same with his boxer briefs.

He climbed into bed and indeed snuggled up next to her. Randi noted, however, how her husband's penis remained flaccid against her thigh. In the old days the organ would by now have made for a blunt, spongy spike jutting out: Cullen, a randy boy.

When had they last made love? The night he'd agreed to take the house—a month. They'd gone much longer.

"How about in the morning, babes?" Yawning again. "I'm whipped."

She pulled away. "Sure. Whenever."

He hesitated. "You know I want to. Been dying for it."

Randi, finally in the mood, and here he was playing the tired card. "I guess we're not in sync. The morning will be fine."

He snapped off the light and rolled her back over toward him. "You sound anything but fine."

Her voice came out small and needy. "Just felt like doing it for a change."

"I don't want to disappoint my best gal." Pulling her close, he nuzzled her neck and nibbled below her ear in a special spot, one that got her going. "We don't seem to take the opportunity much any more."

At his touch, Randi's entire body flushed with forgotten warmth—like feeling alive again.

They kissed, deep, tongues dancing with passion and purpose. She tickled her fingers down his abdomen, through his pubic hair and along his penis, now coming to rigid life. She stroked, squeezed.

Cullen drew in breath, sharp, as though pinpricked.

"What's wrong?"

He grunted. "Nothing."

She sucked gently on his neck. Tugged at his half-mast erection.

"Just go easy. Easy like Sunday morning."

She pulled back, asked again what was wrong.

"I used someone else's soap at the gym today. Been itching ever since." A few years ago she'd switched brands of bar soap, and it was true he'd gotten a tenacious, painful rash. Allergies, rashes, outbreaks—poor, pasty academic Cullen's schtick, his burden. "My pieces parts feel tender."

"You poor baby. Let me kiss it."

"Yeah. Please do."

She went down. Now came a moan, but this, a sound he usually made only when close to peaking.

After only a moment or two, he sighed and touched her shoulder. "Here, baby—let me put it inside you." He rolled them both over, climbing on top. Randi, aroused more so than at any time in recent memory, beading with moisture.

Carefully, Cullen entered her. He grimaced, presumably in ecstatic pleasure.

Or something else.

"Are you sure you're okay?"

He stroked, tentative, a gentle nudging. "You're so tight… and hot."

Randi, a wave of pent-up tension releasing and overwhelming her. She began to buck against him. He increased his tempo.

The rhythm remained steady, but felt rote: Randi could sense that her husband wasn't enjoying himself. She grabbed his buttocks, hard, pulling him inside.

He yelped.

"*What is it?*"

"Nothing—it's wonderful, baby."

They continued, but Randi didn't feel her climax building. "I don't think I can get there like this."

"No worries." Without hesitation, he slipped out and commenced to kissing and nibbling his way down her slight body. Burying his face. Probing, swirling, sucking. He concentrated his attentions; her legs began shaking.

But instead of approaching liftoff, she found herself pulled from the experience by circumstantial evidence she could no longer ignore:

He's sore—the bastard is sore.

From one of his little girlfriends.

That's what's wrong.

Through teeth gritted with ire rather than pleasure: "*Stop.*"

His face, shiny and illuminated by the cool teal of the digital alarm clock. "Did I hurt you?"

"I'm done." She pushed at him with her feet. "Seriously."

"Hey, c'mon." He went to start again.

"*Get off me.*"

He fumbled his way back up beside her. "What the hell's going on with you?"

She felt degraded, closed off. "I don't know anymore."

Cullen asked if she wanted to talk instead of make love.

She started to hurl her accusation, but lost the nerve—Randi didn't want to know.

"Just one of my turns. I'm sorry," humiliated and stupefied by her apology in the face of his blatant disregard for her and their marriage. "Sorry sorry sorry."

Bitter. "I could have just gone to sleep."

Feeling filthy, she rolled away from him. "Goodnight, then," a whisper he answered only with silence. So much for lovemaking.

10

RANDI DIDN'T KNOW WHAT WOKE HER UP. NOT A SOUND—MORE LIKE A feeling. A sensation; a presence. Not in the house.

But close.

Outside.

She shuddered and threw on a housedress from a hook on the bathroom door—the bedroom, chilly. She padded across the hardwood floors back to the bed and stood still, listening.

Cullen, in restful slumber. Breathing steady. A slight nose-whistle.

She cut her eyes away from his lean torso illuminated by the light from the window. He sported an erection beneath the sheet. She scoffed and averted her eyes.

Toward the window.

The light from the pole by the toolshed, flooding in through the vertical blinds. Randi, drawn to the white glow like a moth pushed forward by instincts impossible to ignore. She parted the heavy plastic blinds and squinted down at the patio chairs and the covered hot tub, visible only in blocky shadow. She peered over to the tool shed, and the pool of light cast beside it. A light mist in the air, undulating, languid. The movement of the fog made her dizzy.

Her stomach fell to her knees—a figure, moving into the light.

An animal.

A dog.

Cautious and deliberate, the canine emerged from the darkness.

Swinging its square head around, vapor plumed from its snout. A mutt, a hound, perhaps part boxer.

Like the dog on the road.

A wild dog in the yard. A muscular, dangerous creature. She'd heard it rummaging around in the leaves. That must have been what'd awakened her.

Not like Daisy.

She stood frozen in place. What was to be done? No way was she going to confront a strange animal in the backyard at four in the morning. But she wondered if the dog might be hungry. It sniffed around, lifted its leg against the shed, stood watchful.

Did it belong to someone?

The Macons?

She cocked her head in disbelief as another dog came into view, a smaller one, a poodle. It trotted on its short legs over to the larger animal. They looked at one another. The poodle panted and glanced behind itself. A third dog, a Rottweiler, lean and powerful, trudged out of the shadows and joined them, an elegant and frightening creature.

Randi's heart, pounding.

Her throat, constricting.

Trying to call for Cullen. No sound.

She caught her breath at the sight of more dogs emerging from all directions. Dozens of them, milling around, sniffing, nosing one another, seeming at times to forage like woods-mice or other forest creatures. They came into groups, broke apart again, circled, greeted, sniffed, and finally organized themselves into a great circle into which a lone animal strode, its head held high, a true purebred and proud boxer, a boxer like the one she'd abandoned to the night, a dog, strong and healthy and alive and real, tangible as her own corporeal body, and it called, the dog called out to her in its mournful wail, called out for help—

Randi, finding her voice: "Doggie? Are you all right?"

The dogs all turned at the same time. To look up at the window of the house.

At her.

The dogs began howling a chorus of upset, one by one charging toward the patio, their numbers now in the hundreds, bodies rolling like crashing waves toward her.

She pushed away, but found herself pulled forward as though by a great magnet, her face against the cold glass, screaming and weeping and striking the triple-paned window with open palms, then fell *through* the heavy glass that melted away like water, falling, her stomach in her throat like going over the big drop on a roller coaster, a deep male voice calling out, a harsh echo—

"Randi, Randi, *Randi*." Cullen, looming over her, shaking her awake.

She blinked out of the nightmare. Her nightshirt and clean sheets, soaked; her throat, clenched. "Oh—god."

"Wake the hell up."

"A weird dream. A bad one."

"So I heard."

"How?"

"You sounded like fucking Linda Blair."

Naked, her pale body gangly and covered in gooseflesh, she stumbled out of bed to the window and flung aside the clattering vinyl blinds.

Randi, a scream catching in her throat, stared into the backyard and the gray of the woods—a gray dawn, but not misty, not ethereal, and certainly not filled with ghost-dogs.

Beating the glass open-palmed. "*Leave me alone.*"

Her husband, sitting up on one elbow. "Honey."

Breaking down. "What, *what?*"

"I think you're losing your mind."

She looked back out the window, trying to calm down, trying not to babble about dogs or Denny or the cruelties and ennui of her empty bourgeois life or whatever her freaking problem entailed.

"No," Randi finally managed. "Not my mind."

"What, then?"

"My marriage, maybe. But not my mind."

He fell back onto the bed with a groan. Cullen, taking measured breaths, gazed up at the rustic, exposed beams of the ceiling. When his wife came over and sat down, he rolled away from her without speaking.

The sun almost up, Randi floated out of her cloudy dream state and realized it was Wednesday, which meant his first class wasn't until eleven.

Faint but perceptible: A dog, quite real, howling from down in the woods.

That dog.

Back at the window, Randi pinched her arm to make sure she wasn't still asleep, caught up in a double bluff fake-out as in a cheap horror movie.

She listened.

The dog.

For real.

Randi, staring into the lightening sky. She would get to the bottom of this howling old hound dog. Cullen didn't need to know everything she did with her days.

———

Hesitant, she leaned into the BMW in the garage to kiss him goodbye. The overhead fluorescents gave them both a greenish pallor, he noted with a smirk, like a couple of extras in a George Romero picture.

"Big day ahead?"

"Nothing out of the ordinary." He rolled down the driver's side window. "Love you, honeybunny. I always have."

Randi, dry: "Is that so."

Chagrined. "Of course."

"Be careful with your friend's soap today."

"I grabbed my Ivory. It'll be fine."

"Thank goodness."

Sighing at her sarcastic tone, he thumbed the clicker and the garage door opened. The natural autumn light dancing along the ridge flooded in. Randi squinted against the sunshine and followed as he backed out down the driveway to the cul-de-sac.

"See you tonight. *Early,*" he called. "Promise."

A final, troubled look between them. And gone.

In the absence of the car's engine, she heard only silence . . . but then?

The dog.

Frantic, Randi thumbed the switch and the heavy cantilevered door motored downward, blocking out the light as well as the apparent spirit in the woods who'd been sent to haunt her into the depths of madness.

Perhaps it was Denny himself, reincarnated. Calling for her to investigate. To find him anew.

The more she thought about it? Unpacking boxes could wait.

11

With the last of the residual haze and humidity of the long Carolina summer blown out, this pristine weather almost, *almost* reminded her of her beloved Bay Area. Why she hadn't suggested they move out west—how far was far enough from a dead kid, anyway?—Randi hadn't a clue.

His family ties in the upstate, his career at Southeastern. Nothing more complicated than that.

The hell that was the reason—moving out west meant being too far away for impromptu visits to a little boy's grave. Freshen up the flowers. Keep a watchful eye over him.

His remains.

Where was 'he'?

Not here, said she.

She grabbed a pair of birding binoculars out of her trusty blue Volvo and set out for the woods. Despite the bad dream, she felt rested and relaxed. Standing on the driveway, an unfamiliar facial expression called a 'smile' made her cheeks ache. Other than her phantom dog, whose yelps and howling came and went with the direction of the wind, the hilltop felt still and lovely.

Hilltop—that's what they'd call their country estate. Get a sandblasted little wooden sign, or better, carve it into granite to last a thousand years. Cullen, from a low income family in the upstate, thrived on the notion of such elitism. The Margraves of Hilltop. She'd pitch it to him later.

But as for this dog down the ridge, that's where her focus remained: Down the dirt track that began right outside her front yard, and went for who knew how far. All the way to the river, she assumed.

Ice ran through her veins. Instead of the sunlight, the cold sweep of the rednecks' spotlight again shone in her eyes. Halfway paranoid—that was the last weed she'd be smoking for some time, thank you—she glanced around and put her hands in the pockets of a light windbreaker. Shuddered.

Listened.

Randi's entire body convulsed and her feet left the ground at a voice calling from the end of the driveway.

An elderly black man, spindly and skinny as her, straddling a bicycle. "G'morning, ma'am."

"God almighty." Breathless. "Yes? How can I help you?"

The man tipped a faded Redtails ball cap from atop gray, receding hair and apologized for startling her. "Name's Ebby Nixon—I live about a half-mile down the hill," gesturing toward the highway. "I used to keep up the yard for the last folks, so I thought I'd see if y'all needed anything done."

The idea of this elderly man raking her leaves made Randi uncomfortable. Cautious, she kept a reasonable distance. "I'd take you up on that, but, frankly—"

"Ma'am?"

She set aside her discomfort: "Yard work'd probably do me good."

His smile, sunny and knowing. "Lord knows I can appreciate that. Truth be told, retirement ain't suited me all that good. Like to keep myself busy."

"Did you really pedal up that steep hill?"

"Oh—I might've walked the last little bit back there. Keep my legs and my old ticker strong, but not that strong. Usually ride along the main road where it's flat."

"Exercise is good, isn't it?"

Nixon agreed. Said he'd made it to seventy-eight thanks to clean living and the traverse of the narrow way. "As for the yard, if you change your mind, or just want some company, I'm not a bad handyman. Can do anything but plumbing. Don't mess with that."

She accepted a business card printed on thin paper. His hand betrayed a slight tremor, either from age or possibly strong drink, but to Randi, Ebby Nixon seemed as sober as could be. "One've my grandbabies made these up for me on her computer. Can't hardly believe what all they can do these days."

His card read: *Ebby's Landscaping and Yard Service*, with clipart flowers along the bottom edge; beneath the copy, a phone number and email address. At last she shook his calloused hand, which in its brief contact felt firm and sincere.

"Now, I got my own tools and whatnot. I'm just bike riding today because I ain't got nothing else worth doing. And, I admit I might've been a bit curious about the new folks at the top of the hill."

"Understandable. I was going to stop in one day and say hello."

"Of course you were."

Randi, unsure what to make of that remark. "Busy unpacking."

Gesturing to her binoculars. "Doing some birding?"

"Trying to get a look at that hawk."

"He's up there."

"It's so beautiful here."

"You're in God's country now, my dear. Weather so nice in the fall. Some years these Indian summers just go on and on, almost like a second springtime before winter settles in—if it does at all in South Carolina." Pointing at gray on the horizon. "Well, maybe not today. Calling for rain and a cool-down, later."

"The mild seasons, they remind me of my childhood."

"Where you off from?"

"A few places. Grew up in the Bay Area."

"California's nice. I was there when I was in the service, way down yonder in San Diego. You talking about San Francisco, though."

"Berkeley and Oakland. Across the bay."

"Right on—that still what the hippies say out there?"

She chuckled and agreed they probably did.

In the pause that followed, Randi's troublesome ridge-dog yelped, yipped, and finally howled: Distant, but ever present.

Nixon followed her gaze toward the dirt road. "Y'all like it 'round here so far?"

"Like I said—it's beautiful."

"Nice little branch running through the woods, ain't it?"

"Branch?"

"The creek."

"Soothing. I love the sound."

"Wait till you hear it after we get a good rain. Where'd y'all move from?"

"Columbia—downtown. We lived a few blocks from Southeastern."

"The University? Well, I be dog. Y'all work there?"

Randi, pained by the pace of this lazy-day, country small talk. But with nothing else pressing, she told Ebby of her husband's teaching career in the Mass Communications department, her own former career producing television news, and the fact that his remained an active life while hers seemed on hold, perhaps for keeps. She resisted the urge to talk about being an aspiring writer, which felt like a bald-faced lie.

Her new neighbor, however, already impressed: "A TV producer and a college professor? All of a sudden we all big-time out here."

"Far from it."

"Speaking of that: y'all got a long drive back down to Cola-town, though."

Randi, distracted by the dog, gestured toward the woods. "So listen—"

"Yes'm?"

"That's not your dog I hear all the time. Is it?" As if on cue, more whimpering and howling. "Or, more than one dog? The wind plays tricks with the sound."

Ebby Nixon's smile evaporated. "Ain't my dog. Don't keep one no more."

"Where is it, then?"

Shaking his head. "Nope, no dogs at my house. That's most likely down at the Macons's. Best not worry too much about them, though."

"Why's that?"

He attempted a weak smile. "Folks round here, they keep to themselves, mostly. Them especially. Really just old Julius back in there now. The rest of that bunch lives up the road a piece, down in Chilton."

"Julius."

"You want to leave him alone."

Randi insisted on an explanation.

"Oh—I don't think he'd hurt nobody. But Julius Macon acts funny around people he don't recognize."

"You seem to know them well."

Nixon's face clouded. "I done lived round these folks all my life. And so that means I know what I'm talking about," a hair's breadth less cordial. "Can I be straight with you?"

"By all means."

"Them's some mean old rednecks, that family. But like I said, everybody mind they own business, nobody bother nobody, and all will stay fine in the world."

"But the dog. It sounds to me as though it's in distress."

Nixon, a dismissive, insistent gesture like an umpire calling an out. "Now look here—I'm sure there ain't nothing wrong with that dog."

"You're sure, are you?"

Looking askance at the dirt road. "Look here—missus—"

"Margrave. Randi Margrave."

"Like I said, Mrs. Brandi Margrave, I wouldn't worry about what's going on down at the end of that road. And you know why? Cause it ain't nothing worth worrying about."

"I guess I'll take your word for it."

Before pedaling away, his tone again grew warm. "If nothing else, I'll come help y'all split wood before it gets cold. I remember they got some nice fireplaces in that pretty house of your'n."

Nixon, pedal-pumping out of the cul-de-sac with more vigor than she would have suspected possible for a man of his age.

So: some country cousins lived by the river with a poor old dog tied to a tree. Not newsworthy. Not in this part of the world.

Was that a proper life for an animal, though?

She appreciated her neighbor's information, but wondered how close she'd be able to adhere to Ebby Nixon's wise counsel. Only the ringing of the phone from inside distracted her, a matter of national urgency, at least as far as Cullen had been concerned: a technician calling about her appointment to have the satellite TV installed. Her investigation of the dog would have to wait.

12

WHILE RANDI EXAMINED THE CHANNEL GUIDE—HUNDREDS OF programs now at her disposal—the technician, monosyllabic, chubby, and harried, scratched out the paperwork on a plastic clipboard. The satellite would now beam down voluminous content, including all iterations of the premium movie channels her cinema-mad husband surfed with a regularity bordering on mania. All now would be right with his world.

The installer departed. Randi thumbed the menu function on the enormous remote and scanned through until one network in particular caught her eye: *Animal Planet*, offering a show called "School for Wayward Canines."

She clicked the selection and came into the program in the midst of a speech by an outdoorsy type wearing a ball cap and a thick flannel shirt. His teeth, TV-star bleached, shimmered and reflected the outdoor sunshine.

"A dog's intelligence, while quite real and measurable," the host explained while giving a series of hand gestures and gentle commands to a handsome yellow lab at his feet, "is predicated on only four basic instincts. This dog, and all dogs, are born with these instincts, or choices, if you will, which comprise the whole of their worldview, in a sense: Fight, Flight, Submit, or Avoid," the words appearing and fading in digital chyron across the bottom of the screen.

"While a dog like this may at times seem to mimic, or even possess, intelligence and perception on the order of a human, rest assured it's one of those four choices he's considering. For the dog dealing with his trusted master, 'submit' will remain his primary emotion. For anyone else, it might just as easily be one of the other three."

Randi, feeling as though she'd been cycling through the same series of choices.

The host continued. "A fifth 'choice,' however, can be taught to a dog, and it's this one: Compliance. A dog that adds *compliance* to its selection of innate choices is a dog who'll obey; a dog you can count on as the friend and companion to mankind he was meant to be."

She clicked off the flatscreen TV. The media room fell into relative silence but for the occasional whoosh of the central heat pumping against the cool morning. She checked the time; still early yet. Thought about writing; about doing laundry; but felt enervated at the various prospects.

The HVAC kicked off. The house fell so quiet she could hear the ticking of her wristwatch. Randi pulled back the vertical blinds to the patio, gazed down the sloping land beyond.

And now came the low, mournful call from the woods.

The dog.

Enough already.

————

Randi ditched her slouchy lounging attire for a red Adidas track suit and slipped into new running shoes she'd picked up earlier in the summer. On her headshrinker's advice, she'd toyed with getting into an exercise routine. Hadn't happened, not yet anyway.

A hike in the woods?

Would that count?

She locked the house, went through the lower sliding glass doors and out onto the deck. Randi, noting fresh leaf-fall where only yesterday she'd swept, including all over the heavy pleather covering the hot tub. A chore for later.

She kicked through the leaves and down the steep steps to the yard below.

A shiver up her spine—her dream of the dogs.

But she'd already been out here to look around: that very morning, as soon as Cullen had left for campus. No sign dogs had been in the yard. Foolishness.

She made her way down the slope and into the thickening woods, already ruing the heavy bulge in her pocket: a new mobile phone purchased by her husband, a twofer deal he'd gotten when upgrading his bulky Nokia. Since leaving KNO she hadn't bothered with a cell, but Cullen said for her to think of it as a backup to the landline. A redundancy scheme; a safety net. Now that she intended to explore the woods, perhaps its weight felt like more of a comfort than an annoyance.

Having a tangible task at hand, Randi became energized: To find the dog. To see with her own eyes how the poor thing lay chained and abused. Lately she'd been hearing more than whimpering from down in the hollow —she'd also begun to notice what seemed to be sounds of aggression. As though more than one dog lived nearby, and not getting along all that well.

Knowing she would find the Macon property at the end of that mysterious, winding dirt road, she'd considered marching right down there: *Hey, just being neighborly, spotlight-boy. Now where's the dog?*

But she wasn't a fool. A newcomer to the area, dealing with these people who'd lived back in those woods for God knows how long, sounded like a recipe for stoking umbrage: Any way you cut matters, this was their turf. For now subtlety offered the safest approach, an innocent stroll through the woods and who knew where it would lead. Follow the creek, all the way to the river. Maybe coming back up a different way—an accident, stumbling upon their property. The story would check out, and depending on what she observed? It would constitute the end of her investigative journalism on this topic.

Randi crunched her way through the underbrush and made for the creek. Owing to an overnight rain, the branch, as Ebby Nixon had called the small stream, gurgled along at a fair clip. The cool air smelled of peat, and her gray New Balances sank into the leaves and straw and twigs, layers of damp matter turning by gradations into black mulch—the stuff of fecundity, of nourishment and sustenance to life yet to arrive; to life already departed.

The dog, or dogs, now seemed quiet; in the utter stillness of the woods, with only the sound of the rushing stream, Randi at last felt some of the peace she'd sought out here in the Carolina backcountry. She breathed, filling her lungs. Her spirits, if not soaring, felt at least neutral rather than downhearted.

Her pleasant reverie, interrupted: the new phone, vibrating in the zipped pocket of her jacket.

She checked the readout: her mother's number.

A rare event indeed, this. Since the tragedy of Denny a coldness had hung in the air between mother and daughter, and unless Randi initiated the call they rarely spoke anymore. Their last, acrimonious phone conversation had been a barn-burner, though one not worth remembering in any detail.

What *had* the last disagreement been about, though?

The substance of all their conversations over the last year: Randi's immaturity; her inability, whether as a parent or as a functioning adult, to make sound decisions; her lack of direction; her unwillingness to properly grieve, to move on, to find purpose in life and to seize the blah-blah fucking moment.

The subtext? That Randi and Cullen had been bad parents. Had allowed their troubled, fragile union to consume the life of their son.

Was she wrong?

Perhaps, but her mother had adored Denny, and channelled her own grief into an endless, scornful excoriation of her daughter's myriad personal failures. Randi's mother, never the warmest of parents, now showing her true colors.

What a match her folks had been. Randi had always felt Aylene and her ex-husband, the now late Durant Montreat, had been quite suited, and suitable, for one another: both with Ph.Ds, Aylene a noted sociologist at Cal Berkeley, one who'd become an administrator and later a Dean of the college where she'd resettled, at UGA, following the divorce.

Athens, where Randi had last seen her father. He'd taken a daylong layover to visit her and Aylene before he jetted off to South America as he had so many times before, as usual taking a team of grad students to do field work with the Indians there in the jungle: take the yagé from shamans. Paint himself with mud and dance around a fire. Who knew with Durant Montreat.

But this time he'd never come back, at least not alive—a fatal snakebite suffered digging around in some old ruins like a pathetic, skinny-legged real Indiana Jones had finished him. Despite all the issues and lack of warmth from the man—and the disappointment in her, rank and obvious and unapologetic—she hoped his death had been quick and none too painful.

In any case, her parents and their failed marriage had always been a mystery to the academics' only daughter, but the reasons given to her by both parties amounted only to "sometimes people grow apart," as well as other stock clichés offered without further clarification.

A series of dry pleasantries; the first of the biting comments. "With this ridiculous move of yours into some dark corner of South *Carolina*," a frightful place indeed, yet little different from the woman's own semi-rural Georgia, "I thought I'd better make sure you hadn't fallen off the face of the earth."

"We're very happy here. So far. It's like a slice of paradise back in these woods." Literally, she thought, wending her way through thickening brush, the land becoming steep, the branch running faster and tumbling down charming, miniature waterfalls.

"What will you do for fun? A church social?"

"Very amusing. You sound like my husband. Who's growing to love it."

Once the conversation took a predictable turn regarding the plans for the future, the career path awaiting the willfully unemployed daughter, Randi groaned and moaned and whined. "I was counting down the seconds until you got around to the real reason you called—to start up again."

"I'm concerned; I'm your mother. With all this house-buying, if nothing else surely you must need two incomes. Yes?"

Randi said not-really. She hadn't told her about the settlement. Figured it would be one more grief-stricken moment in an unending series, one she could put off.

"But Cullen tells me you're not selling the house on University Terrace? Is this so?"

"No rush."

"You're going to own two enormous houses? To what end?"

"If we needed the money, maybe I'd feel different about going back to work. But we don't. And when the hell did you speak with Cullen?"

"I can't speak with my son-in-law?"

"How often?"

Aylene sputtered, said she hadn't a clue. Randi asked who called who; her mother cursed and told her to grow up. That she sounded like a jealous, jilted lover. "I can speak with the father of my late grandson whenever I please."

Randi, stopped in her tracks. A long pause held, at last broken by

Aylene, who went on as though she hadn't leveled a body blow. "I suppose now you'll use the excuse that with the holidays and whatnot, you're just waiting until the first of the year, and then you plan to start *thinking* about what you're going to do, and all in service of avoiding actually doing something. Tell me it isn't so," with bilious derision. "Tell me one of your little stories, Marandi."

Randi broke a twig from a dead tree, whacked at the surface of the flowing creek, and decided in an instant to go with the flow rather than fight against the current of the conversation. "Sure. After the holidays."

A breathy sigh, the clucking of a tongue. "And?"

"As I keep trying to say," fighting to maintain an even tone. "I'm not on any one particular time table. Maybe I'll think about that dissertation again. Teaching—at Southeastern, or Piedmont Tech, which is across the river in the next county. Write a novel. A series of stories. Write magazine features. Who knows. Right now I'm walking in the woods, and that's all that concerns me."

"By all means, go for the doctoral. But remember that you're sensitive to criticism, and making it through the dissertation process, the research, the writing, the defense," as though Randi didn't know the ins and outs of getting degrees, "is simply a hellish process. And then, teaching? The long road to getting papers published? Playing the political games? Doing the work—I know you don't have the tenacity for it. But yes, that'd represent a tangible goal, wouldn't it? Even if you never finished the degree."

"Something to do. Right?"

"Meaningful work—that's the standard, Randi. And you know it."

The ground leveled out. She leaned against a tree and held herself against the breeze that had kicked up; cloud cover had crept in, and the light in the deep woods fell gray and dim. "Don't remind me of my failures, my weaknesses," paraphrasing an old Jackson Browne song. "I have not forgotten them."

"Sweetheart," an endearment sounding alien coming from her mother, "you mustn't dwell upon the chain of poor decision-making that led you to this point in your life—whether about Denny, or Cullen, or your career. You must only move forward."

"I'd like to know how you and Father would have handled it."

"Handled what?"

"If something had happened to me. When I was ten."

Aylene, quiet at first, then: "Better than you have."

Birdsong lilted from the tree canopy above Randi, unfamiliar chattering and chirping. In contrast to her mother's voice, it sounded delightful. She squinted upwards, but spotted no particular specimens, only faint fluttering amongst the thicket of limbs above her head. "Be that as it may, he always preached about the importance of leading a so-called examined life, didn't he?"

"Until you were fourteen or so, I thought you were going to go out and take on the world. Then for a while I wasn't sure anymore, but no need to rehash the indignities of those days, especially since you got yourself straightened out, or whatever happened. You found a path, or so I thought; you met Cullen. Whatever my reservations about him, or your other choices, for better or worse you seemed to become the person you were supposed to be."

Randi's eyes followed the slow progress of a large sugar maple leaf making its way through a straight, rushing run of the branch; here the land had leveled, the woods thinning, the air cooling. "It felt that way to me, too. For a little while."

Her mother's voice droned on. But Randi stopped listening—she froze in her tracks, holding the phone away from her ear:

The dog.

The dog had begun howling.

And not terribly far away—to her left, away from the creek. She'd now come a long way down into the woods from the relative familiarity of her backyard, and the plaintive wail of the animal seemed to come from above her, somehow. Above, yes, but also downward, toward the river.

But if she kept following the stream, which would continue on at least a slight downward slope until it reached the Sugeree, or else another, larger tributary, how could the poor animal be above her?

Out in the deep woods, sound apparently played tricks.

"—and so, if it were me? That's what I think you should do. I know honesty sometimes hurts. But there it is. If your mother can't lay it on the line for you, no one can."

"You're right, Mommie dearest. You really are. You always were." She had no idea about the substance of her mother's conclusion. Such platitudes might get her off the phone, though—she had bigger fish to fry than going through the motions of this confidence-killing routine of what in Randi's opinion constituted3 psychological abuse. "Got to toddle off, though. As always, I appreciate all your advice," one of the more disingenuous statements she'd ever made. "Take it easy."

"One final thought, if I may: have you and Cullen discussed having—having another—child?"

Randi, furious, flipped the phone shut with a snap, hustled it back into the pocket, fumbled getting the zipper closed. Now there'd been a good place to break it off.

The howling had stopped.

Randi stood and listened, the silence broken only by the branch bubbling through the forest behind her.

Two sharp barks, followed by a screeching yelp of fear—or perhaps pain.

Randi didn't hear anything else for a while, other than the noise she made hurrying through the leaf-strewn forest down the grade, rushing headlong toward the troubling source of all her earthly concerns.

13

FOLLOWING THE CLAY RIVERBANK NORTH, RANDI BEGAN TO SMELL THE dogs—yes, as she now thought with certitude, more than one. Now she could not only hear them but detect the sharp, sour scent of their waste. Feel their presence beyond the trees.

Close.

The dogs she'd seen in her dream.

It had to be so.

However much her concerns might now be multiplied, the proximity of one dog—*her* dog, the whimpering and yipping of which she could identify with clarity—filled her with newfound purpose.

A hindrance: a looming deadfall of rotting tree trunks taller than her stretched from a debris pile at the riverbank back up a steep run of the ridge, disappearing into a dense thicket of brambles impossible to negotiate.

The end nearest the riverbank, easiest to climb.

But as she tried to clamber over, her foot plunged into the malleable, pungent muck of the tree innards, black like the peat of the ground beneath the leaf cover. Disgusted, she pulled out her foot and continued, wincing as a sharp, dead branch scratched her ribs through the thin material of the tracksuit. She tumbled to the soft, damp ground on the other side.

Her hands, black with the stuff of decay. Wiping them on her pants, she cursed her clumsy ass and pressed on.

Delicate and tickling waist-high ferns meant that the underbrush began to thin. The green wall of the deep woods fell away, and through the last of the gum and willow trees appeared the river, rushing swift and deep through a narrow channel on its course to Lake Hollings, fifteen miles further downstream on the other side of the Sugeree River Nuclear Station. Across the roiling expanse of the water, thick forest ran right up to the opposite shoreline; on her side, a sheer face of dried mud dropped ten feet straight down to water swirling swift and opaque.

Randi sat down on the exposed root bed of a tree hanging over the drop. Her legs and ankles felt tired from climbing around on the sloping, slippery hillsides of the forest. She shivered, hugging herself. Listened.

Voices, muffled. Dogs barking. Growling.

And howling, at last, joining together one by one, an eerie, disharmonious chorus of canine voices. The unholy chorale covered her in what the pedant Cullen would call horripilation. Randi felt almost stoned again, a sense of unreality washing over her.

She pinched herself. Not a dream.

Now she felt more than heard a vibration, deep in the roots of the tree, a rumble mixed in with the howling the dogs that were so close, yet still unseen: A train horn blared from downriver, around a bend and out of Randi's sight—a trestle sat nearby, and this, too, she'd heard off in the distant nighttime; the train horn, another complaint to add to Cullen's list about living in the boondocks. The first power bill, about a third higher than what the disclosure documents had estimated, had been another sticking point.

She scrambled down the riverbank so she could see both directions along the rushing river. Free from the canopy of trees overhanging the bank, the curvature of the channel was such that, however close the structure might be, she still couldn't see it. The train's *ca-chunk ca-chunk* traverse of the trestle continued for several minutes.

Otherwise, the river rushed along eerie and brown, its banks shaded by ancient, overhanging limbs. She watched a leaf tumble by in what appeared to be a swift current. Randi, once a teenaged competitive swimmer, had never enjoyed getting into water she couldn't see through, or otherwise have control over. No canoe trips or paddling for her. Not on this river, nor any.

Startled: with the fading of the train and the howling of the dogs, she now perceived a human voice cursing in a stream of jabbering invective indistinct of content, but unmistakable in tone.

Randi grabbed hold of the large roots jutting out from the moist clay and climbed back up, heading along the bank.

By the time she found a narrow footpath following the river, the peat of the deadfall had been exchanged for wet, red clay. A branch tickled her cheek. She rubbed her face, leaving a skid mark.

The voice again—hateful, impatient, and now all too clear:

"I said no, you sorry whelp-ass bitch." A sharp crack, more like a whip than a gunshot.

A dog yelped in pain, the sound high and terrible.

"Esau, don't hit her, don't hit Cleo—*hup*, girl. Hurry on, now."

"Get the other dogs off them chains and back in their runs before this rain sets in."

Whining, childlike: "I'm-a doing it."

"I'm sick to my ever-loving soul of you coddling that sorry old piece of nothing."

"Well, mama says she's my dog, and that's that."

"Mama says, mama says. Sure thing, Julius."

Randi, a quiet snarl all her own. *What are these assholes doing back here?*

She fought her way through thick foliage along the riverbank, found another almost-path, and came upon a clearing nearer her target. Creeping along the tree line, she hid behind a large, mossy trunk. Here a bluff overlooked the river, a cleared area perhaps ten yards square.

Still, eyes slitted, sweeping around. The trees across the clearing again becoming dense, interspersed with more ferns and mountain rhododendron. It had to be close.

In the mud near the riverbank she noted cigarette butts, a broken Styrofoam cooler, beer cans, soda bottles, the fading yellow and red of a Mickey D's sack left exposed to the damp elements, an upside-down metal pail, footprints: She'd discovered somebody's fishing spot.

Randi tiptoed over and looked down. Not as far to the river as the other bluff, a gentle slope to the water's edge, concave in shape.

A droplet of moisture landed on her cheek, then another—she looked at the water and saw the gray sky now drizzling a bone-chilling autumn shower. Already underdressed, the breeze cut against her bony ribcage.

Startled anew: the sound of two dogs barking and fighting, sounding downright savage—frightening growls turning into whimpers at the sound of hands clapping together.

The childish male voice cried out, bidding the dogs to 'quit it' and to 'play nice' and whistling high and sustained.

Again came the voice of Esau: Deeper, adult, a Carolina twang as thick and musical as they came: "You retarded little butthole, get control of Kong, and I mean *now*." Despite his ostensible anger, the rhythm of his voice rolled along like a much lazier river than the Sugeree behind her, his tone emotionless, matter of fact. "That's a lot of money you messing around with, and you ought to know better."

She heard the high whistling again, the hands clapping—once, twice.

The dogs quieted.

"That's better, boy."

Randi crab-walked along the bare forest floor of the pathway. She continued to hear the voices of the two men speaking in grunts and verbal shorthand, their accents damn near impenetrable. The woods to either side of her towered, old growth river trees.

She could hear the dogs shuffling and whimpering. One animal whined with familiarity; the man cursed it yet again.

Why on earth could she not see them?

At last: her eyes locked in on a pattern, like a camera racking into focus: Camouflage netting, a high wall of it.

Only people up to serious business would attempt to hide like this. Ebby Nixon's admonition about keeping to herself suddenly held more weight.

Hiding behind the flaking bark of a river birch, Randi, conflicted, made the decision to bail and regroup. Who knew what these people were up to? Maybe they were cooking meth out here. The dogs and camo netting might serve to keep illegal secrets safe and secure from prying eyes.

Randi's years broadcasting crime stories at WKNO had taught her that mo-fos would kill over money. How many times had her top story on the newscast involved a drug shooting in one of the troubled neighborhoods in the city and the county? Too often—the chief of police himself had told Randi that for a municipality of its size, he considered Columbia to suffer a terribly high instance of big-league drug crime.

With all that in mind, even before Denny had been killed she and Cullen toyed with decamping the city for a place like Edgewater County, if for no other reason than Denny's mythical safety. What a farce it all was, and despite not having the sense to have kept her son alive, much less safe, here she'd found herself moving someplace like this anyway, only to discover she'd moved in next to redneck gangsters and—

The cell phone, ringing in her pocket. Electronic and unnatural in the still of the forest.

Also: LOUD.

She fumbled with the zipper of her tracksuit. The phone's electronic tone sounded again.

Esau, his voice soft. "Julie-boy: you hear'd that?"

Julius asked what his brother meant.

"Boy, don't you mess with me. Who in the hell give you a cell phone?"

"But nobody give me no phone."

"Where is the damn thing? In your pocket? Out yonder by the fishing hole?"

"I ain't *hiding* a phone, Esau. Promise I ain't."

Randi, shitting a golden brick. She struggled to get the device out of her pocket, the Motorola sounding once again: her mother, giving her daughter a few minutes to cool down, had called for round two.

Terrified, she dropped the phone into the leaves with a crunch, bent over to retrieve it, almost lost her balance. Cursed her stupidity, the noise she'd made.

The men on the other side of the netting fell quiet. She heard only the grunting and whining of unseen dogs, and the patter of the rain on the overhead tree canopy.

Julius's voice came gentle, inquisitive. "*Esau:* look."

"Red?"

Her tracksuit: red.

Esau, a combination of anger and anxiety: "This here's private property." Several dogs began yapping. "Who in the hell is that out yonder?"

Julius, screeching: "*I'll run get the rifle.*"

Randi, a split second to decide. *I'm sorry, I'm sorry, I was just hiking around back here. I'll never do it again.*

Or to run. Before they shot her.

Adrenaline squirting into her gut, she hurled herself back through the underbrush in the direction she'd come—toward the deadfall.

14

AS THEY CAME RACING FROM AROUND THE CAMO NETTING, THE footfalls of the men chasing her on the wet earth thundered each with its own rhythm. Over the pounding of her heart Randi also heard sharp whistling to shush the dogs, excited by all the commotion.

Back at the fishing spot, she faced a decision: head into the woods where they would catch up at the deadfall, or else a different tactic.

She chose.

Dropping over the side of the bluff and down to the water, the sole of her New Balance caught on a tree root, turning her right ankle. As the pain shot up her leg, she struggled not to cry out.

Hearing the men approach, Randi pressed back into the wall of wet, red mud, praying she wouldn't be seen. Where else to run now? While she could swim, and swim well, the river, reflecting the ashen sky, flowed cold and forbidding.

Randi, horrified by the brilliant scarlet of her clothing. She castigated herself—no wonder she'd been spotted.

An idea: she rolled her body into the muddy riverbank, coating the tracksuit. Now red-clay red, her big idea hadn't helped, other than to make her more filthy.

The deeper voice—the bastard, as she thought of him—boomed out from overhead. "Where the *hale* are you, woman?" Esau whispered, now, but Randi could still hear him: "Scoot on over there and look."

Julius whined, nasal and distressed. "We got to find that woman."

Esau Macon uttered a short, barking laugh. "We will."

Quiet. She heard twigs snapping. A rustling of leaves. A beer can, trodden upon and crushed.

Clots of dirt tumbled down from the overhang, striking her on the head and shoulders—someone had come right up to the edge. She spread her arms wide, pushing herself into the wall of mud. Her breathing came rapid and shallow; to her horror, her nose whistled like Cullen's did when he slept.

"I see them tennis shoes of your'n down there, dumbass. Show yourself."

Shaking, she did. At the sight of the double-barreled shotgun in Esau's hands, her blood ran as cold as the Sugeree.

"Who you think you is? Creeping around back in here?"

"Guys, I was just hiking, and looking for a spot to sit by the river, and —I didn't mean to—intrude."

Julius, enormous and barrel-chested, but baby faced. At his side two pink fists clenched in fury.

"Hiking?" Esau, incredulous and amused, leveled the shotgun. "Is that what you said?"

"It's not so crazy. Is it?"

"I don't think I believe your little story, mud-queen."

She had to play the hand as it lay before her. "I swear I didn't intend to trespass. I'm your new neighbor."

Esau, grinning. "Why, I had no idea. Howdy, neighbor."

Randi, unable to hide her unhappiness. "Hi."

The gun-toting Esau loomed over her ugly and gaunt. One side of his face offered a pitted lattice of old acne scars, and his left eye bulged beneath a greasy shock of graying, wiry hair. He licked pale lips. His expression betrayed a measure of amusement.

"You didn't mean to trespass. I reckon I can work with that." Squinting, his playful smile fading. "Or maybe I can't," sounding like *c'ain't.* "Now for real: Just what in the hell you doing down here on my land?"

"Like I said, sir, just hiking. Hiking around, and—"

He made no move to lower the gun. "*Who sent your ass back in here?*"

"Nothing, no one. Like I said, I live up the ridge and I wanted to find the river, and I heard, I heard—" She took a step back, her running shoe now full of the gurgling Sugeree, the strong current sucking at her heel. "I heard the dogs."

"You heard the dogs. Glory be."

Courage, dredged up like silt from the rushing river: "And as a nearby homeowner, I wanted to know exactly what's going on down in here."

"You want to know the truth?" He shifted the weight of the gun, pulled back both hammers. "I mean, about everything?"

"Excuse me?"

"Everything under the sun and in the universe? Would you like to know all that?" His coarse features scrunched into a pinched mask. "Would you like to hear it straight from the mouth of the Lord thy God?"

"Please," begging and trying not to cry. "I didn't mean to bother you all."

"Say goodbye, woman."

"No, Esau, don't. She's *pretty*."

Distracted, Esau lowered the gun. "Pretty? That what you said?"

Julius nodded.

"She's pretty dead, is what." He went to aim the ancient weapon, a gun that appeared to have seen its share of firings. Rain, running off the barrel. "Goodbye, trespasser."

The weapon exploded with a flash and a boom like thunder.

Randi, screaming, fell two steps backwards into the water, the depth plunged and the current knocked her off her feet. She clutched herself and coughed up the freezing water, a new shock; sucked in a fresh lungful of air, dove back under and swam with the current as hard as she could.

Choking, she came to the surface to avoid a cluster of boulders, and realized that she felt no pain from her abdomen. Seemed to be whole and alive.

Twisting around, her watery eyes focused on the receding figures of Julius and Esau on the riverbank. He held the shotgun pointed skyward.

He'd fired into the air.

Julius scrambled, graceless, down the bluff and splashed into the river, falling to his waist in the deep channel. Fearful, he called after her: "Lady, it ain't safe—you're gonna get drown-ded."

But Randi, pulled downstream, further advanced her momentum by kicking and swimming away from the men. Feeling more in control and less panicked. Despite the freezing water, a need to escape.

Esau, laughing, hollered down the river: "Next time, it ain't gonna be no warning shot—*neighbor*."

15

SLASHING AT THE WATER WITH ALL THE STRENGTH SHE HAD, RANDI'S already-injured ankle struck a submerged rock.

Going under, end over end. Flashes of green-silver and the white of the sky above. Panic. She thrashed and came up coughing, sucking wind.

The current calmed. She'd rounded the bend, the men on the bluff no longer visible. A hundred yards ahead lay the previously unseen train trestle.

Kicking like she once did back in the clear and safe pools of her high school's P. E. facilities, when all that'd been at stake had been the approbation of her distant father, she swam with the slower current toward the bridge. He'd held such praise close to the vest, like a pokerfaced card shark sitting on a straight to the ace. Since academics hadn't been her strong suit, the teenage Randi hoped a try at athletics would please him. To this day she didn't know whether her stint as a competitive swimmer had meant anything to Professor Montreat. She could remember him dropping her off at swim practice a few times.

Randi grabbed for the ancient pilings made of roughhewn granite and fought for purchase, managing to sink her fingers into the seam between two of the enormous blocks. A hot flash of pain exploded as the abrasive stone scraped her knuckles, but she held on against the tenacious flow of the river.

Squinting over toward the shore she saw a sandy, small beach underneath the bridge pilings and extending downriver a few yards. She pushed off the stone obelisk supporting the iron rails above her head and chopped at the water, a clumsy stroke that would have made the old swim coach purse her lips in rank disapproval.

The aesthetics of her technique aside, Randi's toes struck silt. She pulled herself onto the so-called beach littered with cinders and gravel from the tracks overhead, sharp, angular stones sun-bleached white like chalky shark's teeth.

Freezing, trying to catch her breath. Rain falling, wind. Overcome by full body shivers—from the cold, yes, but also the gun blast. She clutched herself.

Tried to stand, collapsed back onto the uncomfortable ground. Her ankle throbbed; the skinned flesh on her knuckles burned in the cool wind. The rain fell harder.

Processing what had happened: a brush with death.

Randi's mind began to race—she knew had to get out of the woods. Get warm. What if they were making their way along the riverbank to finish the job?

Or had a boat?

How far had she come?

And how far would they go?

Thoughts of *Deliverance* on her mind, and the awful sexual assault on the protagonists by the backwoods rednecks, gave her strong motivation to get her feet moving along the railroad bed. She knew the tracks crossed the road a mile or two from her home. She would survive this.

———

She'd suffered sexual assault once before, back in her Goth phase, at fourteen and a half. Yeah—her virginity had been taken by a fat, older kid named Rufus, who'd gotten her smashed on a bottle of gin the slovenly lout had stolen from his father's liquor cabinet, after which he forced himself on her.

He'd lured Randi, utterly naive, up to his room on some absurd pretense. Once inside, he pushed her onto to his fetid, sour bed. Held her down, yanking at her short shirt and tights. She'd tried to fight him off, but he had been too strong. Had screamed, but the others downstairs had music blasting as they passed the bottle and smoked cheap Mexican dirt weed.

Striding along the railroad tracks and shivering, she recalled with revulsion how, overpowering and enormous, he had taken her. Pushed himself inside with a white-hot, painful ripping sensation before exploding within seconds and collapsing upon her with a corn chip-breath expulsion like a death rattle.

She'd kicked at him until he rolled away. Traumatized, she pulled at her torn clothing and threatened to call the police.

Rufus, hitching up his pants and laughing with derision. "Next time don't fight so hard. You'll like it better."

Aghast and tearful. "I'll cut your dick off if you get near me again."

"Get over yourself." He held up what at first she perceived as a peace sign, one he'd turned into a mocking middle finger. "V-card collected. Bonus points to Rufus. BOOM."

Heartless and cruel.

And while in the end shame and self-recrimination had forestalled her revelation of the incident to anyone, that next week Randi had managed a measure of revenge by pouring an entire bottle of maple syrup into the gas tank of Rufus's shit-box Toyota. After watching his engine lock up in the school parking lot, an event that had reduced the loathsome prig to humiliating, public tears, she still lacked a sense that justice had been done —sex had begun, but not on her terms. At least she'd taken action, and afterwards managed to compartmentalize the trauma enough to go on to a normal sex life with a few different partners throughout high school and college. Until being seduced by her media professor, of course, and worse, falling in love with him.

Randi, strong inside. Rufus meant nothing. Someone else's body function she'd been forced to endure; no spiritual damage. He had not gotten to the essence of her, and she'd moved on with her soul unscathed, prompted by the experience to always make sure her TV station promoted the good works of a local battered women's shelter.

Fuck Rufus. She wrote it all off as a bad dream. Was in no mood to have a new one—not with the Macons, not with anyone.

———

Why hadn't she encountered the road yet? Randi hoofed along the tracks and struggled with the geography of getting back up the ridge to her house.

The breeze knifed through her; she hugged herself.

Her track suit bright red again—the mud had been washed from her clothing and body by the crisp, flowing river—she rested her hand in an empty pocket: the Motorola flip-phone gone, taken by the Sugeree. No help there.

Who would she call, anyway?

The police?

Duh—trespassing or not, she'd been threatened with a deadly weapon.

The tracks angled south toward Columbia, and she worried about how far out of the way staying on them would take her.

She followed the rails until at last coming across a power-line road that cut through the forest and sloped up the ridge. Winded and nearing exhaustion, she climbed until she found the highway, a path to civilization, safety, and reason…unless the Macons, of course, were waiting for her.

16

Limiping along the soft shoulder of a highway littered with debris heavy on beer bottles and fast food wrappers, Randi winced as her ankle swelled, the minutes passed, and rain fell harder. At least she recognized the main road into Parsons Hollow. Heading back north, Randi figured she had maybe a mile or so to Davis Macon Road, and her house atop the ridge.

An engine rumbled behind her, an old pickup truck—Esau and Julius.

Panic turning to relief: benign old Ebby Nixon, frowning with concern, pulled up beside her. "Lord have mercy—what you doing over here?"

Through chattering teeth: "Long story."

Scowling and working his lips, Nixon seemed irked. "Dang it all. I spaced your name, as the grandkids would put it."

"Randi."

"There we go. Did your car break down, Randi?"

"No."

He hesitated before unlocking the passenger door. "Well, climb on in here."

But wait—how well did she know this particular man? She needed his help. Trust would have to be assumed.

Randi got in. Shivering. "If you could—could give me a ride home—?"

"Of course." He pulled a U-turn. "Are you all right?"

What to tell him? "I got lost."

The idea of being lost amused him. "Around here?"

"In the woods. Along the river."

"River don't run but one way, Miss Brandi. Southeast to the fall line." Chuckling. "You can pretty much count on that."

"I've never been that good with directions."

"So I see."

Randi, reticent to tell this ostensible friend what had happened. Maybe he was in with the Macons. Would defend them against the city woman and all her snooping around.

"I was hiking in the woods. Came back up the wrong way. That's all."

"Lot of pretty country to hike around in."

"That's part of the reason we moved here."

The rain stopped, and his wipers began to make a dry, squeaking rasp. Ebby raised a hand as they passed a rural mail carrier driving in a decades-old station wagon with an orange roller on top, vinyl letters reading US MAIL adhering to the faux-wood paneled siding.

He turned onto an unfamiliar road, not much more than a dirt track. She noted a sign at the turnoff. Blocky lettering, hand painted onto a piece of warped, gray plywood:

HOG–DAWG
THIS SATURDAY NITE

"Where are you going?"

"Short cut."

"What's 'hog dawg' mean?"

He cut his eyes at her. "Nothing anybody decent wants to be mixed up in. Tell you that much."

They came to a paved road, and back onto the main highway. Now she recognized where she was, not far from the turnoff to her house. "But what is it?"

"It ain't worth talking about."

She glared. "I'm not a child, Mr. Nixon."

"Why can't you leave it at that?"

Relenting, he motored around the curves and inclines while telling her a sordid tale of the exhibition that the sign advertised, an event in which vicious, trained fighting dogs were set loose not on each other, but instead on wild hogs and other animals brought in as training dummies, in a sense.

Shaking with fury and shock. "I'm sick to my stomach."

Ebby shrugged. "Nothing new around here, I'm sorry to say. Bet your real estate agent left out that part, didn't he?"

"I'm sure it's not his fault."

In her driveway she invited Ebby inside for tea. He declined, again intimating in no uncertain terms that hog-dawging was no business over which a proper lady such as herself need be concerned, nor in his opinion did the subject merit further discussion.

"The Macons, Ebby—they have the dogs down there by the river, don't they?"

"They mixed up in it all. Sure."

"How do you mean, 'mixed up in it'?"

"They're in the dog trade."

"Which means—?" In a flash, she understood. "They train the fighting dogs."

"What they do is breed pit bulls, which is what their daddy and grand-daddy done before them. And I expect they gonna keep on with it, whether you and I like it."

"But it's illegal."

"Raising and training dogs. It's a trade around here, my dear. Always has been."

Outside the windshield of his pickup lay her beautiful home, the lovely view, the rolling hills and the dense, private woods, but Randi, sensing only the sordid secrets held therein.

"Esau fired a shotgun at me earlier."

Ebby put his face in his hands. "Like I been trying to tell you—them ain't boy scouts back in there. I doubt Esau's crazy enough to shoot the neighbor lady, though. He got too much to lose. Was just trying to scare you."

Randi's mortification, complete. "I'll call the deputy who came last week."

Nixon, inquiring as to the nature of her police call.

"They shined a light in my home. The Macons. That's what started all this. Well—that and hearing the dog. And a dream I had. But also, a feeling? Like a presence nearby? A weird vibe?"

Ebby, wearied. "I-ma tell you what: I done lived here in Edgewater

County my whole life, and whatever its ills, you learn to keep to yourself. Places you just don't go, not if you ain't in certain clubs. And if you mind your business, folks'll leave you alone—mostly." He rolled down the window, spat. "You start messing with people's livelihood? Somebody's asking to get their ass whipped. If I may be so crude."

"*Those animals are suffering*," nearing panic. "I can't just stand by and, and—"

An old man's gnarled, tremulous finger, knuckles swollen with arthritis, cut her off. "Get yourself on inside and warm up. Live and let live."

She watched from the front porch as her neighbor drove away down the hill. He offered a final, lazy Edgewater County wave.

Randi, now far past living and letting live. Shotguns and cops and livelihoods be damned, she decided the Macons needed to find out a new era had begun along Davis Macon Road, one of justice, and righteousness, and—

And—

What, exactly?

As a professional journalist Randi had once gathered facts, had she not? She'd do it again. Report the truth to the proper authorities. No fuss, no muss. These barbarians were finished.

17

Afraid to do anything about what she'd seen, Randi declined to report any of what had happened to Cullen, or the cops. After a time, Ebby's words settled in her mind. Her ankle wasn't so bad. She had been trespassing.

Meanwhile, she tried to still her imagination about the dog fighting. Blot out the sounds of the howling with music.

Any way you sliced it, though, creeps lived down by the river.

Next door.

Abusing dogs.

Once hubby arrived—at a reasonable hour tonight, a hair past seven, no committee meetings or class screenings—they sat at the granite-topped breakfast bar in the kitchen eating Randi's thrown-together meal. Gratified about her writing, Cullen had been fine living out of the freezer, or on takeout he brought all the way from Columbia.

Casual, she mentioned needing to air an important matter.

"I hope it's not that you want to move again," with a smirk. "I'm getting into the groove of that hellish drive you've saddled me with."

"No, wiseguy. I'm quite happy out here. I'm settling into my groove, too."

His tone and expression softened. "Honestly? Me, too."

"Yeah?"

"Love this house, love the quiet. It's just the blessed commute. But I knew this," he seemed to be saying to himself more than her. "I agreed to it, and here we are."

"What's that you always say—'Wherever you go, there you are?' Who said that?"

"A philosopher no less esteemed than Buckaroo Banzai, my love."

She grasped his hand. Randi, her lips pressed together, decided how to phrase what she had to say.

She had to tell him, didn't she?

"You're not gonna believe this, but—we moved in next to some real rednecks."

Cullen froze in mid-sip of a fine Bordeaux, one he'd brought home to enjoy with the frozen pizza and wilted salad Randi had prepared. "Do tell."

"I went for a hike. Down the ridge."

"Must be a hell of a trudge coming back up. Steep."

"It's lovely. At least until I got rained on." She chewed the side of her thumb. "And a few other details."

Cullen crunched into his pizza. "What happened?"

The words tumbled out. "There's some kind of puppy mill down in the woods, near the river. It's at the end of the dirt road. The Macons."

"A *what?*"

"Well, I don't know what you call it, not exactly. But that's where the dog—the howling—is coming from."

"The mysterious, howling canine. Let the dog thing go, girl."

"But see, there's more than one dog. That's what I'm saying. I'm not sure what's going on, exactly."

"That's why you went 'hiking,' as you put it?" He forked salad, chewing less with relish than grudging reluctance. He advised her to temper her dangerous curiosity. "How do you know what kind of people you're dealing with?"

"I did some snooping around."

"Dumb. Uncool."

"I have a right to know what's going on next door to my home."

Scowling. "I'd say that's probably a good way to get shot in the ass."

Randi laughed, sharp and unnatural. And again. She sipped wine, felt giddy. If only he knew. "I can handle myself."

"For one so concerned about puppy farms and other nefarious goings-on out here in God's country, you seem oddly elated."

"Just the wine."

His cheeks blazed. "You're making trouble with a bunch of backwoods good old boys? In the first goddamn month here?"

Randi, unmoved by his tantrum. "All I know is that one of them was abusing a dog. I know suffering when I hear it." Now her mood turned dark, determined. "And I'm not going to just live here in this high castle and let it go on unchecked."

Cullen shook his head. "I'm telling you, this is the wrong way to make our entrance onto the Edgewater County social register, honeybunny. Not by sticking our noses into other people's business."

"So I'm supposed to sit on my hands and listen to dogs being whipped?"

Exasperated, a look like *you're not hearing me.* "Randi? Dudes like this will kill you. There's a lot of money in dogfighting. And you don't mess with people's money."

Randi, believing him on all counts. Her thumb had been chewed until it'd bled.

Galvanized rather than deterred: "Stop being a wimp. I'm not going to do anything other than talk to the local humane society. Maybe the cops."

"*Anonymously.*"

She shrugged.

Cullen reminded her it all remained on the level of speculation. "There's no reason to believe there's anything untoward going on back in those woods—hell, they're probably growing weed. Given the opportunity, I certainly would be." He often waxed rhapsodic about a college room-mate who cultivated pot in a closet, that magical senior semester when the herb had never run out. "We should be making friends with them, not sneaking around."

"These guys are definitely not potheads."

"What makes you so sure?"

"A feeling."

"Another in a series," arch leaning to sarcastic.

Randi, sincere about calling the local animal control folks, but consid-ering another path. Another journey of reconnaissance and discovery, a careful, planned one. To gather evidence.

She wondered from whence her newfound courage had sprung, as her father might have put it.

"Those old hound dogs'll be okay. Relax. Let's talk about something else."

Randi held herself so tight her ribs ached. Tried to tamp down the self-righteous anger.

Cleaning up the kitchen she experienced a sense-memory from her old career: of running full throttle up against deadlines, the days full of disasters and shamed civic leaders shoving hands into the lenses of her shooter's mini-cams, floods, fires, fatal car wrecks, and yeah, even kittens rescued from trees. Randi, slipping back into producer mode: driven, results oriented, motivated.

She didn't give a good goddamn how long those bastards had called this ridge home—such a legacy gave them no special license to behave in ways that were simply unacceptable. And now that this land was her home, too?

As she'd said: she had every right.

What she needed next were supplies. Gear. Now, did hunters conceal themselves in red? Nope. Camo. Time to get smart; time to start blending right in with these Carolina crackers.

———

She wondered aloud about riding with Cullen the next morning into town, spending the day in the city on this and that errand, as she put it. "I could keep you company on the dreadful commute, and in the bargain also stay out of trouble. Right?"

Reluctance: "Oh, really?"

"What's the problem?"

"It's screening day for 480," his advanced film criticism lab, the one where his hapless students were expected to absorb *How to Read a Film* and write analyses of a dozen acknowledged classics of world cinema. "We've got *La Dolce Vita*. I suppose you could watch the picture with us."

Randi loved the Fellini, which she'd first seen at age thirteen with her parents at the Nuart in San Francisco. She remembered how her mother had had to drag her husband out that night. How he'd nodded off halfway through the Italian masterpiece. Durant Montreat would rather have been squatting with some Indian tribe drinking mushroom tea in the mountains of Peru. "Sounds like fun."

"What are you gonna do all afternoon, knock around the Old Market?" He crunched into the crust of the pizza, stiff and flavorless like the cardboard circle on which it had been packaged. "Long day."

"Tell me something I don't know. We're barely seeing each other now."

"I came home early tonight. Like I said I would."

"Did you want to, though?"

Randi's spouse stood looking around at the black appliances, the gleaming copper pots, the view out through the large windows at the sloping backyard and the forest beyond.

After a deep breath: "This is a beautiful home, and the more time I spend here, the more I want to make it ours—for keeps. I've thought about taking a sabbatical, even having another go at a screenplay. Or maybe my own novel. I want all these things for *both* of us, not only me. You happy. Me happy. And so, we ought to talk about the future of this family. At some point."

Chastened, she knew 'the future' referred to starting over: Another child.

She choked out the words. "But I can't replace him."

"He was my kid, too. But—it would finally feel like starting over for real."

Randi agreed that it might.

Maybe.

But that she couldn't countenance further discussion.

Cullen gave her a curt, officious nod and decamped for the lower level and his office, or else to 'screen' a movie, as he always insisted on calling it. She didn't care which; talking about another kid, a major turnoff. Akin to telling her she ought to mind her business about the Macons down the ridge.

By the time he came upstairs for bed a few hours later Randi pretended to have already fallen asleep, but her mind raced headlong—not about her dead son, but rather ways of dealing with her new indigenous friends, as well as their dogs.

18

THE NEXT MORNING, A WHISTLING CULLEN ROLLED INTO THE KITCHEN dressed and ready. Randi, a kernel of anxiety lodged in her gullet like indigestion, sat in her PJs nibbling a peanut butter power bar and nursing a cup of cold green tea.

And listening. But outside on the deck earlier, all still and quiet. No dogs.

He tapped his wristwatch. "Well?"

"Aren't you a bright, shiny penny this morning."

"Are you going to come with? Or not?"

"I better stick to my own schedule."

With mild surprise and disappointment: "Suit yourself."

"I'll see you tonight with a proper dinner on the table, as befitting a renowned university professor."

"Sounds good. I should be home by eight, eight-thirty."

Cullen stroked Randi's face. He kissed her, lingering—lips parted, tongues dancing, a moment of intimacy before heading off to work.

Randi, growing warm all over. Cullen's affection seemed to shine on her like the sunlight.

Maybe all would be right between them again.

After he drove away with a cheery wave, she hustled to look up the ASPCA in the Tillman Falls phone book.

But wait—what precise transgressions did she wish to report?

Instead, she copied down the address of the local animal shelter and went to get dressed. She'd go there and talk to someone, a person who might know about this dog breeding business.

———

Once at the Edgewater County Animal Control facility, however, she discovered how little anyone was willing to help. Walking inside and seeing all the faces of the animals, imploring, desperate, and despondent, her gut clenched. A terrible idea, coming here.

An attendant dressed in workingman's khaki with a name badge sewn above the breast pocket—*Coleman*—appeared in an office doorway, wiping his hands on a napkin. "Yessum?"

Again, what to say? "Wondering if you could help me with a problem."

"You looking for a lost pet?"

Her mind raced. "Is there a problem with strays in this county?"

The man, gray at the temples and expansive of gut, sucked his teeth. Took his time. Randi abhorred the pace. "Don't reckon it's no worse than nowheres else."

Her eyes flittered across the cages of furry faces. "What happens to them all?"

Reluctant to answer. "We euthanize. After a few days."

"A few *days*?" Horrified. "That's not enough time. You have to give people a chance to come get them."

"County budget can't afford to keep all these animals alive, ma'am. Wish it wasn't so. Up to me? I'd take 'em all home."

The cacophony of barking dogs made her skin crawl. A cage of cats caught her eye, a skeletal, exhausted female suckling a litter of tiny, adorable kittens, all gray stripes and white paws. Randi, sidetracked by her compassion.

Suspicion tightened his face. "Now I'm starting to wonder who it is asking me all these questions on my lunch break."

"To whom would I report animal abuse? You?"

"What kind?"

"Dogfighting."

The man blinked a few times. His next words came small and brittle.

"That's for the sheriff, ma'am. Not me. Nuh-uh," shaking his head. "Nope. I ain't the one."

Randi, confused and frustrated: "But I don't understand, aren't you the—"

"No ma'am, I ain't got no jurisdiction over no dogfighting mess."

"Are you sure?"

"*Ain't no pit bulls in here.* You go and look."

Flabbergasted. "What's going on in this county?"

"You want to take home a dog or a cat? Well, there they is. That's all I can help you with."

"Who's paying you to protect these people? Are you in on it?"

He held up his hands: *I'm not touching this.* "I got to get myself back to work. Or lunch, I mean. Call Sheriff Truluck if you want to mess with people fighting dogs. All I can tell you."

Randi, squealing in frustration, strode out of the building and tried to leave its stench of death behind. Slamming the heavy door behind her might have muted the aggrieved yelping inside, but the cries lingered as an echo.

Her stomach cramped, and hot tears crept out of her eyes. A common occurrence for the last few years.

In the car she recalled another of Cullen's favorite Italian films, a neorealist heartbreaker called *Umberto D*, about a lonely old man and his small dog, which at one point he loses and must rescue from the animal shelter. The film included a scene, probably quite real, of a cage of dogs being put into the gas chamber and then coming out limp, lifeless.

Randi screamed, raged, beat the steering wheel. She wanted to rush back in and fling the cage doors open and set them all free, free to live and love and frolic along the ridge behind her house.

Fence the back yard.

Create a sanctuary.

What was she saying? A fool's errand trying to save them all, the planet overrun with unwanted domestic animals. Tilting at windmills. Besides, Cullen didn't even want a house pet, much less a menagerie in the back yard.

Getting nowhere, fast. Randi had a specific, localized issue, one she could improve with the right kind of attention. She pondered Coleman's advice about calling the Sheriff's department, in particular Deputy Oakley.

After the spotlight incident, he would at least be familiar with the actors in this passion play.

But the cops, they had to see that hog-dawg sign. And still it went on. Dogfighters openly advertised their disgusting event, with discretion not high on their list of concerns. The animal control officer seemed to know of what she spoke, yet turned a blind eye. Would the sheriff's department be any different?

———

Turning into the driveway, Randi admired the sugar maple in the front yard, its leaves aflame with electric orange, radiant as they fell and tumbled across the yard. She clicked on the garage door opener but froze, jamming on the brakes: a dark mound sat in the way. She lurched the Volvo into park.

As she approached, tentative, the smell hit her, and she covered her mouth: a pile of feces left in an unmistakably prominent place on the driveway. Not the errant leavings of a passing deer or other animal, though: a foot high, this mound, full of dirt, leaves and twigs. It had to be the collected spoor of more than one beast.

She noted a boot print at the edge of the dog-shit pile, the track of a narrow tire from what she supposed had been a wheel barrow transporting its fetid cargo. Other tire tracks on the driveway.

"You assholes."

Head on a swivel, Randi felt exposed, vulnerable, isolated. One or both of them, concealed by the woods, might be watching her right now.

She whirled around toward the dirt road. The chain, pulled across and locked. The hilltop, deserted and quiet as usual.

Randi got back in the car, locked the doors. Turned the ignition. Potted down the radio.

Sat.

Waited.

Watched.

What if they weren't watching from the woods, but crouched inside the house?

She thought through her predicament, tried to quell her fear with logic: *These jacklegs wouldn't have bothered leaving the dog shit. Not if they were going to just break in and wait for me.*

She could call the sheriff's department on them again, as over the spotlight incident. But hadn't she done the same to the rednecks?

Intruded upon their land?

She backed up the Volvo, adjusted the angle, and pulled past the pile of feces into the garage. Once inside, the motor ground and the door dropped behind her, cutting off the afternoon light and the rust colors of the yard. She felt safe—for the moment.

19

Randi, unsettled, tabled the dog issues and stuck to more domestic matters, until hitting snags with her dinner prep. She realized she'd have to brave the IGA in Tillman Falls, a few miles down the highway in the opposite direction from Parsons Hollow, itself not much of a township—a literal bend in the road. A small post office. A convenience store. A pharmacy.

No more quick trips to the market, another downside to the country life: Her preferred health food grocer? Now a brutal thirty-five miles away. A cooler, she'd already discovered, would be kept in the Volvo to facilitate long-distance runs to the more sophisticated stores in Columbia.

Before heading out she took time to shovel the offending offal off the driveway and hosed down the concrete, washing the remaining doggie-do toward the side of the garage where she'd planned to set out decorative plantings. This little joke—or warning, as she well understood—would instead fertilize the earth to yield a colorful and positive bounty, hardly the result those mouth-breathing Neanderthals had intended.

As the foul odor hit her palate, Randi recalled a Halloween in which she and her no-good punk friends, fourteen and high and silly, had pulled the oldest prank in the book on her old man: setting a bag of dog shit alight and placing it outside the Montreat household there in the Berkeley hills near the UC campus, a neighborhood of bungalows as quaint and lovely as a child could have wanted.

At the time, the cobblestone streets and gingerbread cottages overhung with lush vegetation represented, at least under her father's baleful tutelage and impenetrably supercilious demeanor, the equivalent of a cloying, bleak gulag. To Randi, the flaming excrement was more than a dumb prank— the act had been intended as a symbol of her disgust with her father, his impossible expectations, and what to her felt a cloistered and bourgeois life. As many teenagers feel of their hometowns, she now understood.

She and Emily and Raj, what a trio—her best friends at the time. Emily would go on to an English professorship at Berkeley, but poor Raj, one of Randi's first loves, ended up in the morgue with an armful of bad heroin. In these more innocent times they had schemed and scooped several disparate piles from the nearby dog park into a wrinkled, thin grocery sack, and in a time-tested cultural tradition placed it on the front steps of Randi's own home, lit aflame using the same Bic lighter by which they'd sparked up a gurgling bong.

Bumping into each other, giggling and shushing, Randi herself rang the doorbell before all scampered behind the hedges to view the excitement of watching her dignified, stoic father, quick to react and sure to stomp the bag, foul the fine leather of his Florsheim shoes.

Montreat came to the door with thick glasses propped up on a balding pate, a massive, ancient-looking tome held in his hands. He shook his head and peered downward at the bag, crackling with acrid smoke.

Cast a baleful gaze in the direction of the hedges. "Marandi, why don't you be a good girl and hurry back over to put this out? I did see you running past the window just now, you know."

With that, he'd flipped his glasses down and gone back inside, leaving the fire burning on his front stoop.

"Well, that didn't work," Raj commented.

Randi hurried to kick the bag off the porch. "Hard to get one over on him."

"Your dad's a real asshole."

"Don't remind me. He never fails to."

She'd neither gotten his goat nor ever impressed him with her accomplishments and life choices; and with Durant gone to his grave, he would lie disappointed in her for eternity. How he'd blanched at her choice of broadcast journalism for a course of study. Accused her of wasting her potential on being a propagandist. And yet after the divorce and the move to Georgia, Randi had blossomed as a student, and working at her high school's student TV station had been the highlight of her young life so far. Confusing, that man.

The worst part?

Maybe the bastard had been right.

There'd been no real adult fulfillment for her at KNO, and as established, seeing the corruption and collusion between men like Spencer Mathison and the other power brokers in government and law enforcement with whom he lunched at the high rise business club downtown had curdled her journalistic milk but-good.

In truth, after Denny's birth none of her work had held much meaning. The rest of her endeavors in life had taken on a cast of insignificance in contrast to nurturing her child's intellect and soul. She rued the years she'd parked him in daycare while she ran the newsroom. Cursed it all now with bitter vehemence.

———

Randi checked her list and climbed back into the Volvo, willing away a different brand of sadness than that which normally haunted her: thoughts of Raj, her first real lover, made her ache at the waste of his life.

Yes, the overdose had been quite different from the death of her son but a tragedy nonetheless, one of the first losses she had experienced. What needled about Raj was that, like Denny, he could have become anything he wanted. Unlike her son's circumstances, however, a personal decision had led her friend down a fatal path.

Decisions.

The decision to forgive Cullen for his infidelity.

The decision to put Denny on the plane instead of driving him to Atlanta.

The decision to move to Edgewater County, as though relocation would make it all better. Make the pain vanish like smoke in a breeze.

Spiraling into what-if, again.

If only, if only.

Stop.

The Volvo crossed the intersection with SC 217. A green road sign shimmered in the afternoon sun:

Parsons Hollow — 2
Tillman Falls — 10

She'd only been to the local market once when needing milk and eggs, and after experiencing the disparity in quality of products and service in an impoverished area versus her old downtown stores, she hadn't deigned to return. She hated feeling so provincial, but being out here in the sticks often seemed like she'd wandered into another tribe of humanity that in many ways presented as inscrutable—people her father might have studied.

But then again, California, as she recalled in a fit of honesty, had had its own share of so-called rednecks. The only real difference? Their flat beach bum patois rather than the twang of the Southerner, and maybe choice of dope rather than Bud Light as a principal intoxicant. A higher median income. Less humidity.

Class was the issue. Class and money. Not the where and the who.

She drove through an area of shacks, rusted trailers, clapboard houses and churches, more churches than you could shake a stick at, as one of the area's residents might put it. The frequent appearances of sanctuaries and crosses atop steeples made her feel apostate.

Next came better appointed but still modest homes closer to town, but not much so. Finally she hit the bypass around the county seat, Tillman Falls. A small town with genuine character and Southern personality, Randi had grown to understand that its outskirts were ugly and homogenous.

Chilton, a mile from the next interstate exit, boasted fast food and gas stations and a Holiday Inn, but otherwise the local economy seemed driven by a car dealership, with an enormous stars and stripes hanging limp in the still November air.

A couple of new subdivisions, she noted, were under active construction; Edgewater County, as Vince Ellenshaw had insisted, appeared in the process of becoming a true bedroom community for Columbia.

As she'd feared, Randi found herself less than satisfied with the grocer over the availability of the items she needed. Mass market margarine, no tofu, and a spice section offering myriad meat-rubs but lacking in saffron, turmeric and coriander seeds, all required for the korma and saag paneer she'd intended to prepare for Cullen.

She snorted and complained aloud. No one noticed or seemed to care.

Next hurdle: The wine rack at home was stocked, but she also wanted to have beer on hand if that's what Cullen wanted to wash down the spicy food. Coming around the corner in the refrigerator section, she chortled with derision at a fading life-size cardboard NASCAR driver saluting like a soldier at attention. Accompanied by a buxom, bikinied blonde, their brilliant smiles extolled the virtues of the *King of Beers Racetime 18-Pack Special.*

"Buy this beer, and a woman *just like this* will make love to you." Randi pinched the laser-printed cheek of the driver. "You lucky boy."

Finding nothing but the bright reds and blues of domestic lagers, she gave up on any decent beer for her hubby and went to check out.

"Anyplace around here to buy a decent sixer?"

A pudgy, pink-cheeked checkout girl scanned her items as Randi swiped her debit card. "Do what, now?"

"Some imported beer."

"We got Corona back yonder."

"Something more exotic. An IPA."

"Well, la-ti-da." The checkout girl, hooded eyes. "I reckon you'd best ride down to Columbia for all that."

The bag boy, an enormous black kid with thick glasses and rolls of fat around his middle, snickered and muttered: "Beer fills me up. I drink liquor, y'all."

"I heard that." The girl gave Randi the total. "I mix up Evan Williams and Diet Pepsi, then I get *down.*"

Bagging her items, the boy said, "If it was me, I'd go for Crown Royal. Crown is da bomb."

"You *c'ain't* afford no Crown Royal, Hakeem." Glaring at the bag boy, the cashier ripped off Randi's thermal receipt with a sharp snap. "Son, you lie worse than a rug."

"Naw, naw. All I drink is Crown, y'all. Church."

"Bullcrud."

Randi, swinging her plastic sack back outside to the parking lot, chuckled at the banter. Wine would have to suffice.

At first, she didn't notice the pickup truck. In a place like Edgewater County, old Ford pickups were legion. But when the tall man with wiry, graying hair popped out and grinned at her, Randi realized with sudden horror that Esau Macon stood before her.

He spoke into a bulky brick of a cell phone: "The IGA—that's right, here and now. Appreciate it, Wardell."

Esau thumbed off the phone and spat a thin stream of brown juice onto the concrete. Full of insincere bonhomie and quite fake surprise, he said: "Howdy, neighbor. Fancy meeting you here."

20

BLOCKED FROM HER CAR, RANDI CLUTCHED THE SACK OF GROCERIES TO her body. She wished she'd gone to the bathroom earlier.

A quaver to her voice. "Don't you dare come near me, sir."

His eyes twinkled. "Esau Macon, ma'am. It's right agreeable to run into you again—under friendlier circumstances."

"I should say so. Randi Mar—"

"I know who you are."

"What do you want?"

"Lord, you like to worried us to death after you jumped into the river. But here you are. High and dry. Safe and sound. With your little sack from the green grocer. Thank goodness all seems right in your world."

Randi steeled herself, tried to stop quivering. "You followed me here."

"Now ma'am, that's not so. I happened to see that Volvo of your'n in passing, wanted to make sure you were alright. We don't have too many of them running around the county—people buy American around here, usually—but in any case, I took a notion to stop and say how sorry I was."

"Sorry?"

He held out his hands. "Bygones, and all. Since we're neighbors."

Trying to figure out how to play this. "I'm also sorry, then, about being on your land. I didn't know you lived down there. I just heard the dogs, and—"

Snapping his fingers. "Heard the dogs."

"Yes," more cocksure. "And I smelled their *shit*, too. All the way at my house. In my driveway."

Pleased. "I don't know what you're getting at."

"I ought to call the law on you again. Like I did when you were parked outside my home that night."

"You're the one on my land."

"I know I shouldn't have been back there, but: *you fired a gun at me.*"

"No jury around here would convict me of defending my property. And I did not discharge my weapon at you—I did so into the air as a warning shot to an intruder. Same as anyone who felt threatened. We have home invasions in this county, you know."

Randi, knowing all about Southern firearm politics as well as the crime rate in poor counties like Edgewater, couldn't disagree.

But still: "Your response was way out of scale."

"Why did you run, girl?"

"I thought you were dangerous."

"You don't even know me. What give you that idea?"

Meek. "Because of the dogs."

All conviviality, however illusory, now disappeared. Esau's eyes bugged as though they might flop out onto his high cheekbones. "So that's what this is all about. This creeping all round my granddaddy's ridge. You some kinda dog-lover?"

"Who doesn't love dogs?"

A glimmer of a cruel smile. "I know I do."

"Bullshit."

"I'll thank you to watch your language." Esau, jutting out an indignant chin. "But as for malicious intent regarding the discharge of my weapon, it's your word against mine about that. Mine and my little brother's. He knows what's true and real. Do you?"

Randi, disgusted and afraid. "This is ridiculous."

Macon checked his watch. "Mercy—I got to get back home and shave."

"Big date tonight?"

Snapping his attention back to Randi: "I ain't got time for no more of this hooptedoodle. I got church later."

"You must be joking."

"Why you say that? What, are you an atheist?"

"So what if I am?"

Troubled: "Ma'am—ain't you saved?"

"I saved three dollars and eighteen cents inside just now on sale items. Says it right here," brandishing her receipt.

Shaking his head. "My heart breaks for you. You ought to come on by sometime—Gethsemane Holiness."

Snide. "I'll pencil that in."

"It'd do your soul some good."

Randi felt put on—about the cursing, as well as this church business. "Somehow I doubt they'll see either one of us there anytime soon."

"Forever's a long time to be kept waiting outside the gates of Heaven."

"You can't be serious."

"What else is worth being serious about? Than the disposition of one's soul for eternity?"

"I will not endure this. Proselytize to someone else."

"Did you say something about being a prostitute, ma'am? That ain't exactly legal around here."

Randi, shifting the weight of the grocery sack, had had enough. "I want to know why I shouldn't call the police right now. Tell them everything that's happened."

"The po-lice?"

"My phone's right there in the glove box." A lie, but useful. "In fact—"

"Considering I already called the sheriff, I reckon old Johnny Law ought to be here straight away." Esau snickered like a mischievous kid delivering the punchline to a naughty joke. "And presto—here he is."

The Edgewater County Sheriff's Department cruiser, a gray Lincoln Continental with a seal on the door but no blue lights on top, rolled across the empty spaces at the back of the lot and pulled up next to Esau's truck. A gray-haired man of considerable girth extricated himself from the driver's side—nose like a beacon, rosacea-shiny jowls, the stiff-kneed gait of a man who'd rather be sitting down. He slipped on the coat of a suit the color of which matched the finish of his cruiser and hid the gun and badge he carried on his belt.

"Why, goodness me." Esau clasped his hands as though lovestruck. "It's Sheriff Truluck."

Scowling at Esau's display. "You turning queer on top of everything else?"

"Now, now." Esau cocked a thumb in Randi's direction. "But right here's someone you definitely want to meet, a new resident of our fair county."

The porcine cop offered a damp, pliant palm along with his pleasantries. "Ma'am." Back to Esau: "How's your mama and them doing?"

"Fine, fine. We'll have you over for Sunday dinner again real soon, Whardell."

"Looking forward to it."

"So anyways, this here's the *new neighbor* the good Lord done sent me. I think her name is Mrs. Margrave, if I ain't mistaken. Ain't that right, neighbor lady?"

Randi cleared her throat. "The house at the top of the ridge."

The cop scrutinized her. "Didn't realize anybody'd moved in."

Through gritted teeth: "Couple weeks now."

"Nice up there. I remember when that old feller built it." The sheriff remained pokerfaced more so than cordial. "Died of cancer, I believe. Both him and his wife."

"So listen, y'all—I just wanted to apologize to my neighbor in front of the Sheriff, here, for shining my truck light into that pretty house of hers the other night."

Truluck frowned at this new wrinkle. "You done what now, Macon?"

"Shined a light. Me and Julius. We was worried. Truth is, I come down to the old place and picked him up to go eat supper at Mama's, and that big old house up on the ridge, well, it's been sitting there all dark since the other folks passed away, and while I didn't see no cars, I thought I seen something moving around. And so I run that spotlight around the yard. Back and forth," miming the gesture.

"I was *terrified*." Randi, energized. "I called it in. Deputy Oakley responded."

"Yes ma'am—that's right." Esau, pressing palms together in a disingenuous gesture of supplication. "That Yankee boy pulled us over and I explained what happened. I didn't know these good folks had moved in like that, and I didn't want no nig—" He paused, winking. "I didn't want no *n-words* turning that nice place into one of them wicked crackhead houses. I didn't put it that way to him, of course. But that there's the God's truth."

Randi's face had grown hot. "I appreciate your apology."

"Like I told you—just looking out for y'all's interests. Like I'd expect a good neighbor to look after mine."

Sheriff Truluck probed at Randi. "Y'all like it up there on the ridge, ma'am? After moving from the city?"

"Peaceful. Like another world."

"That's about the best spot in the whole county."

She glared at Esau. "I'll say this much: interesting neighbors."

Horrid fish-eyes, shooting daggers.

Randi shoved by him and Esau's smile returned, an expression fraught with guile. Tossing the groceries in the back of the Volvo she peeked over her shoulder, relieved to see her nemesis climbing into his own vehicle.

"You just let old Esau know if they's anything he can do—anything at all. I'll come a-running right over. You can count on it."

The throaty engine rumbled into life. Esau waved to the Sheriff, but as he drove off through the parking lot he offered Randi only a lingering leer.

"Sheriff—may I ask you something?"

"Just did."

"What are those men doing back there in the woods? Do they live there?"

Sheriff Truluck folded his arms across an expansive chest. "You're living on what used to be their land, you know."

"What if I told you he'd fired a gun at me earlier this week?"

"Under what circumstances?"

Randi, admitting she had been trespassing. "I was concerned for the welfare of the dogs."

He uttered a short laugh. "Hell, a good many of us has been fired upon by men like Esau Macon." Odd and reflective: "But them fellas ain't doing nothing the Macons's ain't always done, which is 'defend their honor'," mocking.

"He didn't need to fire a weapon. I stumbled onto their land inadvertently."

"Do you want to make a report about it?"

"And what would that accomplish?"

"Make everybody do a bunch of paperwork."

"And what would you do, if you were me?"

"Mind my own business. The way the Macons do."

"Even if it's—illegal business?"

Truluck scoffed. "They ain't a durn thing going on illegal. Not like them hopheads we busted a while back growing marijuana down near the power line road. Them's the kind of people who's tearing this country apart. It's the drugs and the Mexicans that's ruining this world of ours. Not the Macon boys."

At the mention of pot Randi flashed on their small stash back home. A cold jolt of paranoia. "It's more than Mexicans involved with drugs, sir. I should know—I'm a former journalist."

His demeanor cooled. "A journalist. Really, now."

"Retired."

"Tell you this much. I knowed the Macon's granddaddy since I wasn't nothing but a squirt, and every last one of them go to church and pay taxes and the whole nine yards. Folks who keep to themselves," he added. "That sound like a balance we can maintain here in the county, ma'am?"

"I just keep hearing their dogs. They sounded, they sounded as though—"

"Mrs. Musgrave? I hate to break it to you, but they ain't nothing wrong with a man breeding dogs on his property. Besides, Julius is the only one who lives back in there. And you don't have to worry about him. He might be big as the side of a barn, but up here?" Truluck pointed to his left temple. "Ain't nothing but a big baby boy, still. You talk to him sometime and see for yourself."

"So Mr. Macon, he lives elsewhere?"

The sheriff snorted like a bull. "Now, would you want me telling some stranger where you lived and what all you're doing? Now you do seem like some kind of reporter."

Chastened into lucidity. "I'm not anymore. And you're right—that's none of my business."

"I don't want to sound like one of them old TV cops, but asking the questions in Edgewater County is my job. Not yours, ma'am."

In a small voice. "I'm just interested to know my neighbors."

The Sheriff now sounded more threatening than avuncular. "You heard about curiosity and the cat, ain't you?"

"Heard what happened wasn't good."

"That's one way of putting it." His tone, brightening with a suddenness that further unnerved her. "Now, if anyone else shoots at you, or anything else seems out of order, why, you just take and call me. That's what God put us old Sheriffs here for—to watch over the county and all its decent folks."

"I'm gratified to hear of your commitment to law and order."

"I'm serious as can be. Them Macon dogs is well treated. You can make bank on it." He bid her a good evening. "Now let me get on back to keeping the peace."

She called after him. "How'd you know I moved from the city?"

Without turning back. "Lucky guess."

Watching the police cruiser pull out of the supermarket parking lot, Randi went numb with disbelief. They had her in a bind, Esau Macon and this redneck buffoon of a cop, his corrupt pockets fleeced like an L. L. Bean winter coat.

This had become ridiculous—in what century were these people living?

Her helplessness gradually replaced by fresh outrage, on the drive back to the house—her home, bought and paid for—Randi made a resolution, steely, that frightened as well as galvanized her: These country mice were about to find out what havoc a determined city cat like her, more than curious, could wreak.

21

RIGHT AS THE BASMATI RICE STEAMED OUT AND RANDI TURNED OFF THE flame, Cullen breezed into a home redolent with tantalizing culinary fragrances. She poured glasses of Chardonnay with a hand that still shook.

He hugged her from behind. "Couldn't wait to get home. Smells delightful in here."

She sipped wine and spooned the last batch of paratha out of the skillet, the fried bread glistening with cheap IGA margarine she used in lieu of the ghee for which the recipe called. "It better be good. Rolling out this bread was a chore."

"I assure you it'll be appreciated. My stomach's as empty as a football."

As the piano jazz of Oscar Petersen tinkled rather than Randi's preferred power pop—this kind of music suited the mood, felt to her like twilit autumn should sound—they ate at the kitchen bar and made light conversation. While Randi half-listened, mulling over the Macons and the dogs and the evil fat ugly sheriff, Cullen prattled on about the archival film conference, the upcoming two-percent funding crunch in the Mass Communications program, and finished with a bout of ire over a student who'd been offended by the opening of *La Dolce Vita*, the crucifix hanging from the helicopter flying over Rome, as well as assorted adult content in other curriculum films.

"It's 1999, I said to the young woman. Time to grow up."

"And her response?"

"Made a formal protest to the dean."

"Ouch."

"Farcical. That's the word."

"Aren't there plenty of religious schools she could choose?"

He thumped the bar with a fist. "Precisely. The student has no business making such a complaint at a public school like Southeastern."

"You're a Southerner, you ought to know how people are—they're set in their ways. Sometimes you have to tread lightly," thinking of Esau's sickening smile. "About what people believe."

"Even so, anti-intellectualism's got no place in a college classroom. Not in my classroom, anyway. The girl—young woman—acted as though I had some agenda. As though I was the one who'd come up with the visual metaphor."

"She's shooting the messenger."

"Not that there's a message."

Randi, relaxed and cruising on her third glass of wine, teased him. "Say—didn't the Catholic church itself condemn the movie?"

He put down his fork and rubbed his temples. "It seems every term students are getting more obtuse, more polarized, more doctrinaire in their beliefs—pick a side. It's like we're hurtling toward some kind of dumb-shit critical mass omega point. As though intellectual curiosity's dying out. It's a recipe for a future population that's more servile and malleable than vibrantly independent, I'll tell you that much."

"So I thought about working with the Humane Society." Randi, refilling Cullen's glass and hoping to draw the conversation toward an issue more immediate—the dogs down the ridge. "Volunteering and such."

"Check. And the writing?"

"I'm progressing, but it's—it' s not—"

"Noble; but animal altruism doesn't sound like a lucrative career track. Nor writing, for that matter."

"That Beauchamp guy I heard speak, he said the novice writer mustn't want to write to get rich. She must burn to write for the sake of creation."

"The art life. I get it."

"Also remains to be seen if I can find anything of merit to say."

He dredged Indian flatbread in spicy-sweet mango chutney. "What's not happening with the writing?"

"Don't sweat that part. Whatever else I get into, there'll still be time for tapping out pages."

"Hey, if it makes you feel better, go for it." He killed half of Randi's already generous pour. "I just don't want to come home one day and find you here with a dog."

"I didn't say I wanted to adopt—"

"No dogs, Randi."

Her wine-warmth spread to the top of her head. "I didn't say I was going to adopt. Or even foster. Just help out in some manner. If you won't let us have a pet, at least I can fulfill that desire another way."

"You act like I have allergies on purpose. Just to piss you off."

"Denny always wanted a dog, too. Maybe you've forgotten."

"I thought we were going to have a nice dinner."

"You're the one who's getting defensive." She slugged back her wine and slid off the stool. "Do you want any more curry?"

"Thank you, no. I'll need to chew up half a roll of antacid tablets as it is."

Randi, tossing her plate into the sink with a sharp clatter. "Glad you enjoyed all my hard work."

"I didn't say it wasn't good."

Avoiding his eyes, she hurried out of the kitchen into the great room, flipped off the overhead lights and plopped down in the dark.

"*Guess I'll just take care of all this myself,*" he called after her in singsong.

"I'll clean up later."

She heard the sound of his plate clunking into the sink.

Cullen crept into the living room with a fresh glass of wine in hand and settled into a comfortable position on the opposite side of the sofa.

Randi stared into the opaque darkness of the front yard. Part of her waited and watched for Esau's truck, but again, she understood his introduction to the sheriff served to quell her inquisitiveness about the dogs. Macon himself needed to make no further threats. Clean and neat. Lucky him.

And for most people? Yeah, maybe that would scare them off.

Not her.

Her hubby cleared his throat a few times.

Never a good sign. "Out with it."

"Let me lay something on you."

"Go ahead and buy whatever it is—right? Or plan the trip to the yadda-yadda conference or film festival. As if you need to run anything like that by me."

"Give me a chance, here. I had an idea, and it wouldn't just be for me. It would be for both of us."

Dumbfounded: "What are you talking about?"

"After the Victorian sells and closes, I was thinking how owning a pied-à-terre near campus would make for a good investment property."

"A—*what?*"

"A little apartment. Say, a one-bedroom condo, one of the new ones above the Old Market. And if we decide we're not using it very much, we can rent it out or resell it so fast it'll make your head spin."

"We haven't even sold the old house yet."

"Sounds bizarre at first. Like I said, if we don't use it much, we'll rent it out or sell at a profit."

Her staccato laugh of disbelief returned. "Wait, wait—it's all clear: a swinging pad for you to crash in after a particularly grueling graduate seminar. Or a rigorous screening? Right?"

"After a long enough day? Sure. Don't know about the swinging part."

Another rueful chuckle. "You're as transparent as a ghost. You really are."

Cullen, gulping his wine and choking. "I resent this bullshit. I do. I've made every amends to you, made every good faith effort, but all I get is more of the same mistrust and innuendo. How much penance must I perform? How much effacement and apologies and reassurances and wretched guilt must I endure? What will it take before you fully accept me when I say how much Rachel was a mistake, and how much you're the opposite. How much our marriage—"

"Stop right there. Don't you dare say her goddamn name in my house."

"Calm down."

"No—remember? Remember the deal? Like Brando and that little whore in *Last Tango*? 'No names, no names'." Randi, lisping in a mocking imitation of the legendary actor that, under more positive circumstances, would have made Cullen howl with mirth. "Her name is anathema to me. A spiritual black hole."

"If this marriage is such a sham, and I'm faking it all, why do I bother to stay? Why are we still together?"

Randi, unmoved by the tenor and tone of his remarks. "Call Vince. Go right ahead. Get yourself a pad. He'll put you in the swinging-est bachelor pad in all of downtown. Maybe I'll drop by sometime. To visit."

Hanging his head, he made for the spiral staircase and the solitude of his office below. "A perfectly innocent idea, blown all out of proportion."

"No, I think it's a fine idea. An investment, yes: an investment in your future—*you fucking prick*."

The door to his office, slamming with a *boom* that echoed from below.

While Cullen sulked downstairs, Randi finished the wine and most of another bottle. Passing out on the couch, she awakened only after hearing the grinding of the garage door motor.

Her husband, jerk or otherwise, would now leave her alone for the day, which in this case represented the exact outcome she desired. Randi, a packed schedule: much to decide and do about the dogs.

22

An hour later she drove through downtown Columbia on a grid of streets bustling with workday traffic: motorists, delivery trucks, a screaming ambulance on its way to, or from, some tragedy or random health crisis.

All bright and loud—too loud.

She buzzed inside with discomfort.

Longed for the quietude of her country hilltop home.

Heard a phantom echo: the yipping and howling of dogs.

As she turned onto Main Street, Randi jammed on the brakes at a gauntlet of orange barrels and flag-waving DOT workers. A cement truck spun languid and powerful, disgorging a thick torrent of lumpy, ash-gray material like a defecating mechanical elephant.

The commercial corridor, undergoing another renovation; this, the second such effort in the twelve years she'd lived in the area. *Maybe they'll get it right this time.*

She crept past enormous, centuries-old churches, with atmospheric and densely populated graveyards, relics of a bygone age spared the torchlit wrath of Sherman's shock troops, which had burned over a third of the city proper.

Drumming fingers against steering wheel.

Bouncing a bony knee.

Resisting the urge to go to Denny's gravesite.

Randi endured the delays and inched along until she saw what she'd come for, a venerable, legacy business: The Army-Navy Store. A place for military fetishists, yes; a place for camouflage clothing. She planned no repeat of the Macons seeing her so-called *red* self skulking amid the ferns and thick vines. She'd have to blend into the woods, now, to gather evidence against these monsters.

The store front featured two large, deep display windows to either side of the entrance, an old-fashioned retail building steeped in a mid-century historicity that could be seen and felt in the architecture, the ambience, the smell of the place, and most of all the merchandise packed floor to ceiling on racks and shelves: Military memorabilia, uniforms, outdoors equipment, knives, and a booming trade in Halloween supplies like severed latex limbs, a leering werewolf with a bloody tongue, disembodied heads with grievous wounds, grotesques, monsters.

A zombie, its face half-shredded by an apparent shotgun blast, reminded her of Esau Macon.

Randi, a fit of minor-key PTSD: a panic attack at the memory of that face.

The explosion of the gun.

The icy river water.

A moment in which she could have died.

A near-vertiginous wave of fury swept through her; she scrunched her mouth to the side and gnawed on a thumb. What was there to lose? The fate of those dogs—and her role in it—constituted the first inkling of purpose she'd felt in ages. If she died in the process of helping save them, the world would not miss her. Nor would she miss it, a bleak admission fraught with existential regret.

But while she could, she had to report what she found out to another law enforcement agency, at the state or federal level.

Yes.

But only after she had a charge more specific and concrete. No investigator would take the case on hearsay. Evidence would get her foot in the door.

Randi prowled through the L-shaped store fingering stacks of fatigue pants, shirts, midnight blue pea coats, field jackets, and piles of boots, both used and new. She examined a wall of cubbyholes filled with the accoutrements of military and outdoor life—canteens, mess kits, field stoves, shovels, flashlights, binoculars, first aid kits, mosquito netting, bundles of colorful nylon camping cord, bungees in every size, gas masks and helmets, enough to equip a small army, or perhaps in this case, a scout troop: Among other functions, the shop appeared to be the area's one-stop scouting uniform and sew-on merit badge headquarters.

As for camo items, in a back display area she found an embarrassment of riches: T-shirts, fatigues in both desert beige as well as traditional Vietnam-era jungle green, hats, jackets, waders, rain gear, winter coats, even socks and underwear.

"Help you?"

The clerk, a narrow-shouldered African-American youth, spoke from over her shoulder. Her feet almost cleared the floor. "Oh, *shit*—you startled me."

"Sorry, ma'am." Uncomfortable, he jammed his hands into the pockets of his khakis and avoided her eyes. Sounding rote: "Anything I can help you with today?"

Gesturing to the wall display. "I'm looking for camo stuff. Got to do some—snooping."

"Snooping?"

"Just kidding. I want something that looks—cool."

"You mean for going out? Clubbing?"

"Exactly."

"Word." Chewing on a toothpick, he drawled, "But I don't know— camo ain't in style right now. Not that I seen anybody wearing."

"Kidding again. It's for wildlife photography." Bobbing, weaving, riffing; a swinging bebop improv of falsehoods. Randi marveled at a resurgent penchant for duplicity, a talent first cultivated in her rebellious teen years, but in the time since used only with judicious infrequence. "Of rare specimens, shy specimens. In the wild. I need to be absolutely invisible. For my work."

He brightened. "My sister's studying photography at SEU."

"Fantastic. My husband teaches there."

"You got a card? She keeps trying to get a shadowing gig with one of the shooters from the *Columbia Record*, but they won't call her back for nothing. Maybe—if you could—?"

Shamefaced, she produced a pen and notebook out of her sling bag, a catchall purse from the hippie shop down in the Old Market. "Give me her email. I'll shoot her a note soon as I get back to my office."

The clerk, effusive in his thanks. He scribbled down the info.

Returning to the task at hand, he motioned for her to follow across the store: "This is prob'ly gonna look crazy to you. But I got the perfect solution."

Grinning, he showed her the box, and its picture of a man wearing an outlandish getup called a ghillie suit.

Randi barked her staccato laugh.

"Told you, it looks funny. But it works. You blend right in."

"Sold," digging in the bag for her credit card. "Now show me what you have in boots."

23

BACK HOME, SHE TRIED ON THE SUIT DOWNSTAIRS IN THE SUNLIT REC room. Slipping one leg in after the other, a stinging odor of vinyl and chemicals, like new car with a dash of vinegar, made her eyes burn.

Thinking: *you're really doing this.*

An adrenaline spike lanced into Randi's gut: The target of her surveillance was a backwoods redneck on his own turf, a man who'd gone so far as to send her a further, increasing series of warnings, up to and including a cop on the obvious take.

A fool's errand.

Possibly irrational.

Potentially dangerous.

Would the ghillie suit blend in well enough? Randi imagined herself appearing to a bystander like Swamp Thing tromping around the riverside.

But then, no bystanders out here. Only her, the Macons, and their dogs.

The booklet that came with the suit explained how the astute hunter—or, as intended by its original development, a military sniper—could modify the ghillie suit with materials from the actual surrounding areas in which the wearer planned to conceal herself: Leaves, twigs, soil or mud.

Prior to wearing in the field, drag behind moving vehicle to further season, the notes also advised.

She didn't know about all this seasoning, but leaves and sticks aplenty lay at hand to thread into the webbing of the odd garment.

Gripping the folds of the suit in her clenched fists, flustered and hot all over, Randi considered the few tablets of Xanax she had left. How easy to go take one and float away into a quiet nap.

Later, call in the refill.

Take some more.

Fold her consciousness into full numbness.

No.

Another choice: a woman of purpose taking a small stab at improving the plight of a few of God's fellow creatures, not that she believed in a supreme deity. But still, a mission of service, a quest selfless and just, one with a tangible, measurable result at endeavor's end: to save the dogs from their abusers, an act of heroism as in an arcane legend about which her father might have pontificated.

A father figure. A person of wisdom, of insight.

Ebby Nixon picked up on the first ring. "Well, I be danged if it isn't the pretty city lady calling from up the ridge."

"Mr. Nixon—"

Nixon sputtered and choked with offense. "Mercy, the only folks that call me 'Mr. Nixon' is the ones I owe money to."

She apologized. "Ebby."

"That's more like it."

"Quick question."

"Need me to come help out some horticultural misadventure? Be all over that like white on rice."

"It's not that."

Sounding grim: "Fire away, I reckon."

"I'd like to ask you more about the Macons. And what they're doing down the ridge."

His silence, impenetrable and protracted.

Finally: "You sit still till I come up yonder, all right?"

The phone call dropped.

Reluctant, she put away the ghillie suit to wait for the one neighbor she hoped she could trust.

24

—————

Sipping ginseng tea and sitting at Randi's breakfast counter, Nixon waded through a series of niceties that felt rote.

In getting around to addressing the meat of her questions, he spoke with a soul-weary cadence about many of the same ideas now consuming and motivating Randi: cruelty, compassion, justice.

"But them Macon boys, their daddy and granddaddy before them, pretty much always been in the dog business."

"You mean the dog fighting business."

"I don't mean that a durn bit—they in the dog *breeding* business." He explained that Esau didn't field "them things" himself anymore, only that he prided himself on being a breeder of champions and selling the dogs to others who perpetuated the illegal gaming. "Him and Julius make a right fine trade in the racket. Or so's I understand."

"And you all stand around here in Edgewater County while such cruelty goes on?"

He smiled at the tea. "This is good. My Lipton's seems right ordinary, now."

She sat waiting.

"If something's bound up in money, it goes on, my dear. Surely I shouldn't have to explain that to you about this wicked world of ours."

Randi, agreeing.

"But as for cruelty? It behooves the Macons to present a healthy, strong dog for sale, not one that's been abused. They are well fed and housed and cared for."

Astounded. "Mr. Nixon, I'd like to know how you define cruelty."

"Well now, they are just dogs."

Randi, furious. "Not unlike how plantation owners once thought of African-Americans?"

"True that. Some folks around here ain't changed. But look here—when you spent a year out of your young life loading bodies onto transports out of the jungle, you start to view life differently." He displayed a Vietnam-era Army tattoo on a sinewy forearm. "Overseas, I seen the spoils of cruelty every day. And I ain't talking about animals. Though I seen my share of that, too."

She said she didn't doubt how his tour of active duty had been brutal and trying. "But still, these jackasses make a living off torture. I don't care if it's 'just dogs' or not."

"A living? Well—they got other money, too. Davis Macon owned land near where the interstate runs through, owned land across from the nuclear station that the power company bought off them. Owned the land you now live on. And his granddaddy owned land all around Parsons Hollow, when the new railroad come through during Reconstruction. Old money. But dogs or no dogs, them new subdivisions done made the modern Macon family right well off. None of them got to work like regular folks."

"Dogs raised to be killers."

Shrugging. "Of other dogs. It ain't pretty. But I wouldn't call them killers."

Sickened not only by the depravity, but the semantics. "I can't believe this goes on—it's about to be a new century, people."

"Hardhearted bunch of folks into all that mess."

"So, they fight dogs down the ridge? To train them?"

Sighing. "If you must know, they build up strength and instill aggressive instincts. Tease and bait them with cats, rabbits, little mutts. Now, one sad thing they'll do is use runts from their own litters, ones that ain't coming along. Ain't no different than them poor old wild hogs I told you about. All makes them pit bulls tough and mean. Meaner than any animal ought by rights to end up."

Randi struggled with the implications. "We need to get rid of that damn breed."

Waving her off. "It ain't like that. Pit bull's a fine breed. Raised like a normal dog, he's going to be about as loving and loyal as you could want. But someone who knows what he's doing—like Julius Macon—can flip on a primal switch inside their brains. After that happens, a dog's still gonna be as loyal to a human as it ever was, a danger primarily to other dogs. But not always. Only so much control over an animal that's been turned downright bloodthirsty. Old Esau Macon found out the hard way. That there's another story, though."

"Esau's face—the scars. He was mauled?"

"Long time ago."

"Jesus. You'd think he'd have gotten the message."

Ebby sipped tea, sucked his teeth. "Funny you should mention the Savior. You know your neighbor Esau's an ordained Pentecostal minister, too? Or used to be."

"You can't be serious."

"Esau don't preach no more, not like when he was a boy. I seen him deliver the good word at a camp meeting when I bet you he wasn't but fourteen, fifteen. Fiery, assured. Them eyes of his, bulging out." A small shudder. "I must tell you, though, that I detected a hint of meanness in his oration. Too much admonishment. Not enough charity. Ain't no way to bring someone to Jesus."

"A dogfighting preacher." Randi's head spun. "I've heard it all."

"After he got tore up by one of his granddaddy's dogs, though, I suspect he might've had himself some questions—big ones—that his faith couldn't answer. But that's just me speculating about old Esau. Ain't passed two words with either of them Macons in a long time now, except to raise my hand when they go toddling on by in that truck of his."

Randi, a renewal of determination. "Something's got to be done."

"About the Pentecostals?"

"About the Macons."

"Their argument will be that a man's got a right to raise dogs. And they do."

"I'm calling the Humane Society, or the *Edgewater Advocate*. Hell, I'll get a KNO team out here. *I used to fucking run that news studio.*"

Ebby, troubled, drew away from her outburst. "I see."

"I'm—so sorry." Randi, blushing. "I'm overwrought."

His eyes, moist, found and held hers. "Brandi, I can't say as I blame you for wanting to right the wrongs of the world. All my durn life I've had to scratch around here knowing that, preacher or not, them Macons wasn't worth a durn. That what they do and what they are ain't right. But to tell the truth, I don't see someone like you making the kind of difference that you want to make. Not without—"

"Without what?"

"Grave risk. To yourself. To your family. The folks mixed up in this trade—well."

"I've already experienced it first hand."

His exasperation, palpable. "And you gonna keep on till you step in it again?"

"Am I supposed to sit up here and listen to those poor creatures suffering?"

Flustered, Ebby rose from the breakfast bar and pulled on his tattered Redtails ball cap. "People have different ways of defining what you call suffering, and yes, cruelty, too. Some around these parts—and I'm not one of them, no sir—don't think God give animals souls the way He done us. I don't know one way or another, but I'm not smart enough to try and figure out what God had in mind. Or the way things ought to be. I know what I believe, of course. But one thing I c'ain't cotton to doing at my age is risking what little life I got left going up against Esau Macon and his crazy ass."

Randi, bidding him to calm down, had heard enough. "Thank you, Mr. Nix—Ebby. I'm sorry I upset you. Maybe you're right. I should mind my own business."

"Don't forget something," now standing at the front door. "People like y'all—"

"'Y'all'?"

"Newcomers—some folks don't think you belong here."

"Too bad."

"There's old attitudes around here, old ways, still. And by you, I don't mean you-you, but I mean people *like* you. Sure, they like the money you bring into the county—the tax rolls, the groceries, and the gasoline and fishing tackle you buy. They understand that Edgewater County is changing. But money or not, that ain't going to make them any more amenable to what you think or what you think they ought to be doing with themselves. Some might be moved to do more than just take offense, if you understand what I'm saying."

"So, a Pentecostal preacher's going to cut me up and dump me in the river? For complaining about the treatment of his illegal fighting dogs?"

"Wouldn't put it past him. But these days, I wouldn't put nothing past nobody," a melancholy opinion from a weary old man.

Another one of Cullen's iconic movie lines, from the David Lynch surrealist nightmare about the dark underbelly of small town life, *Blue Velvet*, popped into her head: *It's a strange world, isn't it?*

Perhaps Randi's distracted, wandering eyes—a manifestation of her inner desire to, in actuality, ignore his advice—prompted Ebby to make an offer:

"If you have a few minutes, how about taking a ride?"

"To where?"

"Oh, over that-a-way. Here and there."

"For what reason?"

"A tour. And I don't mean like what your realtor showed you."

Now on the edge of her seat with interest. "Tour of what?"

"Ain't gonna see them old mansions over on Whaley Way in Tillman Falls, no; nor the old Hillsborough plantation house. It's time you, Brandi Margrave, met the real Edgewater County."

25

Ebby's truck rumbled down country lanes as well as city streets, like the main road into picturesque Tillman Falls. Despite her tour guide's assertion, their first stop included the bucolic township rather than what she expected: a tucked-away dogfighting arena.

On the drive Nixon had nodded toward the entrance to an upscale subdivision of brick homes, one she was surprised their broker hadn't shown them. Ebby mentioned in passing that Esau Macon made his home therein.

Randi, shaking her head at the thought of Esau spending his blood money. "Animal abuse pays well, I see."

Ebby shrugged and regaled her by pointing out places where thus and such had occurred in his life, none of which filtered through her haze of ire over the activities of her neighbors.

Once in the heart of Tillman Falls Ebby pulled into one of the angled parking spaces along the curb of the town common, a greenspace of monuments and park benches dominated by the familiar Civil War obelisk as seemingly found in every small Southern town, as well as an undersized statue of none other than Pitchfork Ben Tillman himself.

Randi took it all in: the courthouse and the monuments, the magnolias and live oaks standing strong, ancient, exuding permanence.

It all made sense. A place out of time.

The decrepit business district—most modern retail action took place nearer the freeway, anchored by Hampton Motors and a number of fast food joints—consisted of a greasy spoon diner, the *Edgewater Advocate* news-paper office, the post office, an insurance office, a realtor, a jeweler, an old fashioned women's clothing and wig shop, and two saps to modern times in the form of a payday lender and a mobile phone store.

And, as Ebby pointed out, a watering hole: "Over here's a venerable old juke-joint called The Dixiana."

Randi noted the honkytonk sitting on a prominent corner. She squinted against the glare at the façade of the bar, with its pair of neon signs reading simply LIVE MUSIC and BILLIARDS.

Two old men with flannel shirts and crossed legs, smoking on a bench out front, eyeballed the couple. A word passed between them and they laughed.

"Charming."

"It's a place where folks go to drink, and hear redneck music, and socialize. Not a dive-dive? But neither a more upstanding establishment like you get with a Bennigan's, TGI Friday's, or the Sizzler."

"I think I understand the difference between a dive and a fern bar."

He held up a finger. "Granted, as do I. But I'm telling you a fable, now, if you'll beg my indulgence. So, there's a place called The Dixiana, and it's a place where folks drink and sometimes in the summertime hear bluegrass music out on the back deck, eat greasy hickory-smoked pulled pork barbe-cue, and broasted chicken," said with a degree of fondness. "Maybe have themselves a few beers. Smoke a few cigarettes, and other exotic tobacco products, and all that."

"I'm shocked, I tell you."

"But like in bars all over the world, they also do other things. You see how that building is laid out? The upstairs, there?"

She did, and said so. "And?"

"Well, if you were one of the chosen people 'in the club', there's a whole other side to this honkytonk that ain't open to the public at large."

"Bet they still have poker machines in that joint."

Ebby, mouth downturned as though he'd bitten into a sour persimmon. "That, and more. Cards. Women. You get the drift."

"I do."

"Now turn around. Look back across the town green. Tell me what you see."

She regarded the stately, water-stained yellow bricks of a courthouse approaching a hundred years in age, its columns and ornamentation standing in stark relief next to a glass, modernist municipal government building half a block wide and three stories tall, a silver ice cube looming above the trees and midcentury brick architecture otherwise fronting the streets.

"That's the sheriff's department?"

"No, that there's the Tillman Falls municipal force. Sheriff's department's got themselves a shed further on up toward the river. But the police in town, they all more or less report to Truluck."

"In any case, the authorities, right across the street—"

"—and it's all been going on at The Dixiana for as long as anyone of a certain age can remember. Under everybody's noses."

"You'd think someone would come along who wasn't corrupt."

Nixon, weary but smiling. "There's been a lot of, shall we say, legacies in the various positions of power in this county. That maintain a certain status quo."

Randi, growling with Marge Simpson-esque ire. "Typical."

"Try growing up a black man under such a system."

"Or a woman," she added with an arched eyebrow. "Right?"

"All due respect, but you really have no idea, ma'am."

"This is America for everyone now. All that's in the past."

He squinted at her. "Now I don't know if you think I been kidding, but I can tell you that there's still folks who'd whip my ass for being caught in this truck cab with a beautiful woman like you—a white woman."

"Oh, please."

"Believe what you want. But I'd rather not find out how true it really is." He put the truck in gear and swung around the green, passing the tall neon DIXIANA sign promising live music and suds.

As they turned onto venerable US Highway 1, she sat chastened and thumb-chewing. A half mile out of town he nudged an elbow at the Tillman Chat & Rest, a cottage style motel with perhaps a dozen rooms total, two to a unit and scattered in a semicircle behind the office and the paved parking lot.

"Way before Eisenhower built the interstates, there used to be a whole mess of motels like this. Back then, Highway 1 was the main route between New York and Miami—and good old South Carolina sat right in the middle. Made for a good central location to stop."

Randi had an idea for a documentary: *Tales from Highway 1*. She noted with mild amazement this most creative impulse she'd had in ages. "Too bad they're all gone. At least this one is still operating."

"It's operating, all right. This here's where they run the girls. And the drugs. But you could've guessed that, I'm sure."

"All of a piece." Randi drummed her fingers on jean-clad thighs. "This place is like—oh, what's the Vonnegut thing?"

"Excuse me?"

She snapped her bony fingers. "Unstuck in time."

Nixon nodded. "In some ways, I reckon it is. I'll give you another way to look at it."

She waited.

"Ain't much else for people to pursue but the underground economy. All the mills is shut down."

"You have a point."

"I'm thankful I had my job at the power plant all those years. Had me a good life. And stay duly grateful on a daily basis for my good fortune. But a whole mess of people—the young, unfortunately—don't see many other choices. And that breaks my heart—for the county. For the country."

"Amen."

They drove on, taking a series of turns onto back roads and through shabby neighborhoods of trailer parks and deteriorating ranch houses. Once in the real boonies Ebby pointed out what appeared to be ordinary homes, but explaining how these were actually unlicensed speakeasies that juked and jived on the weekends until dawn, and where, he added, it was said exotic substances well beyond malt liquor could also be obtained.

"So you all have the vices well covered. Check."

Ebby, mournful. "Poverty begets drugs begets guns begets kids running around dirty, fatherless, without values." In the grip of true despair, his eyes became fixed and watery. "I don't know what's going to happen to solve any of it. Except maybe the Lord finally coming back."

"You think that's a possibility?"

"I used to. Sometimes I wonder."

Heading back to the ridge Ebby made one last turn, this time down an unfamiliar dirt track several miles from Davis Macon Road, not unlike the shortcut he'd taken the day he found her on the highway.

"Now what?"

The truck bumped along for a bit through a pine barren, the road flat and sandy, until he pulled over. Ebby pointed to another dirt road branching off, the entrance barred with an all-too-familiar chain suspended between two fenceposts and a *de rigueur,* weathered KEEP OUT sign.

"We not gonna linger. Not out here, not even in the light of day. Back in here's ground zero." Nervous, he started making a three-point turn. "We just all messed up, trying to head back to the highway. Nobody knows if we lost, or what. And that's what we're gonna say, if we need to. But either way, we ain't gonna tarry. Not here on Mr. Rembert's land."

"Rembert?"

"He a bigwig. Organized crime, but you'd never know it. Not from seeing him at the Masonic lodge or the Rotary Club."

Randi thought of her old program director Spencer Mathison hobnobbing with the powerful, quite a few of whom he knew to be corrupt. "Way of the world."

Ebby cocked his thumb back at the dirt road leading away into the woods, disappearing in twin plumes of dust from his accelerating pickup truck. "This don't change nothing about my advice regarding poking around in people's business. But them signs from before? The hog-dawg mess?"

"*Yes?*"

"Back in yonder's where it goes down. Them and all the other —events."

She slapped her knee. "Thank you, Ebby."

"This ain't no kind of gift. But if you do get someone involved— maybe from outside the county, who ain't already bought and paid for— here's a place where bad things go on. All the other stuff we talked about, plus the dogs."

Randi welled with excitement. "A break in the fucking case."

He stopped the truck and grabbed her by the wrist.

"Ebby—what?"

"I can't truly speak for Esau Macon, what he's capable of doing. But I'm here to tell you: Rembert and his mofos?" He released her wrist. "They will kill you just as soon as look at you."

Randi, memorizing the landmarks. "I've got ideas less invasive, let's say, than blundering onto somebody's property."

"Do tell, Miss Brandi."

She nodded, but refused to elaborate. "It's all good."

Ebby drove in silence until turning by his house onto Randi's winding road.

In her driveway: "Now you're a grown woman, ma'am, and I can't tell you what to do. But if I was you, here's what I'd consider: Y'all keep to yourselves and enjoy all this scenery up here."

"Sounds like you want me to go to sleep."

"Far from it. Start working on a winter garden. Roll fresh paint in your new home. The Macons are what they are, and you ain't gonna change that. Besides, look around. Any way you cut it, this here's God's country. And if you pray to him, He'll watch out for you."

Randi, beyond uncomfortable, mumbled her gratitude.

"And so will I."

"You'll what?"

"Pray for you."

Randi got out. A friendly country wave from the window of the pickup.

Once inside, she rushed downstairs and again slipped into the ghillie suit.

Whether he's right or not about waltzing in, this train has left the station. I have to see those dogs with my own eyes. This time, however, it would be with more than her eyes: she'd have a camera.

So she'd be careful. Randi, not an idiot—a capable, professional adult woman in 1999, one who could handle anything these jacklegs might throw at her.

26

Senses honed and nerves frayed, each shuffling step Randi took through the dry leaves and underbrush sounded like a tree crashing. Now she fretted not about being seen, but heard.

Moving with cautious deliberation, she crouched behind ferns, leaned into the bark of tree trunks, once even diving into a pile of leaves after she thought she heard the Macon truck on the nearby dirt road, descending by switchbacks along the downslope of the ridge.

With her heart in her throat, she squatted.

Watching. Waiting. But no truck appeared.

The road cut back and forth twice before she found herself nearing the compound. It troubled her anew how close the Macon property seemed.

Randi's sense of direction, never one of her strongest suits, left her wondering how long it had taken to creep down the ridge. Not as long as the original hike beside the branch and along the river's edge—that much she knew.

While at first she'd been hyper-vigilant, jumping at her own footfalls, as she absorbed the great solitude of the deep woods she found her mind drifting back to a lovely afternoon she'd spent with her son, a golden springtime day a few months before his death. Before Cullen's infidelity. Before the Margrave household had come figuratively crashing down.

Denny had begun to show an interest in the sciences, in particular botany, in which he'd become fascinated the previous spring after they'd planted an herb garden. As the plants sprouted out of the fecund, tilled earth behind the house on University Terrace, his already bright eyes had filled with wonder.

In a nurturing frame of mind—with Denny, when hadn't she been?—Randi had picked up her son from Highland Academy, the esteemed private school into which they'd been pleased to enroll him, and had driven into West Columbia.

She'd read about a park called the Congaree Heritage Preserve on that side of the river, land once owned by a brick-making company and from which dense red clay used in making their product left behind large, rectangular holes in the swampy ground. In the decades since, the now-public preserve had acquired a series of lovely, if artificially shaped, ponds filled with water lilies, chirping frogs, buzzing dragonflies, and abundant flora.

The hike to the first pond had been brief, and in total they looped their way through the preserve in an hour.

"Over much too soon."

"Hard to believe somebody dug out those holes."

"Why, honey?"

"It just looks all natural and—real."

"This is what mother nature—what some people nowadays call 'Gaia,' the living, conscious spirit of the planet—does after we're done messing around." She had rested her hand on his shoulder as they hiked back out to the parking lot. She could feel it resting there still today. "She takes back what was rightfully hers from the beginning."

"And makes it alive again."

"Yes—sometimes even prettier than it was originally."

Indeed, the preserve had been peaceful and serene, the sunlight filtering through the trees in lovely shafts, the springtime Carolina air pleasant, no hint of the cloying humidity to come in the long summer ahead.

The worst summer of her life.

Denny's as well—the brief time he had left, that is.

He hadn't understood what had gone wrong between his happy and loving parents, at least not as far as Randi knew. But the night he'd called out for her complaining of a stomachache while she and Cullen argued downstairs, she realized her son knew an essential *something* had changed.

On her third visit to his room he'd burst into tears, pleading: "Mom—please stop fighting. What's wrong?"

Her heart, already shredded, clenched anew. "Mommy and Daddy are sorry."

"I don't understand."

"Grownups are stupid."

Reliving the moment caused her to fall back against a tree. Choking back tears of shame and loss, she shifted the weight of her bag of espionage gear under the ghillie suit. Tried to breathe, slow and steady.

"Slow and steady wins the race," a mantra her therapist had suggested trying when the thoughts began to gallop in her head.

She wondered if before embarking on this errand she shouldn't have taken a pill, but wanted her senses tuned and sharp. Thus the price she paid, however, whenever she emerged from the narco-fog of the mood altering drugs: Clarity of thought, lucidity of memory. And in her case, as double-edged a sword as had ever been.

———

Pulling herself together, Randi pressed on until a flash of sunlight on metal caught her eye.

Creeping along the tree line, she emerged onto a huge swath of clear land to see tinker-toy electrical towers marching up the ridge like great skeletal owl effigies draped and slung with high tension wires.

Prior to her adolescent rebellion, Randi and her erudite father used to take hikes together, visit areas of natural beauty—the Berkeley Rose Garden closer to home, or Muir Wood up in Marin. Once he had pointed out a string of power lines and mused about the possibility of electricity being the "arms of an archangel, wrapped around the planet in service of this technological miracle unfolding before us. A blessing, Marandi? Or more possibly a curse?" She hadn't known what to make of such talk, which sounded oddly religious coming from a man she knew as eschewing all such issues of faith.

Nothing more to see this far north, but the power lines might offer an alternate route back up the ridge should she need to make rapid egress from the area.

Heading back toward the road, she paused at a shape in the trees she hadn't noticed: a camouflaged tower about three meters above the ground and enclosed at the top like a child's clubhouse, nestled in privacy among the hardwoods and peaty underfloor of the forest. Ahead, as the road curved in the opposite direction, she saw another clearing.

Immobile, she stretched out alongside a mossy log, spooning against the moist, rotting wood like a comforting lover. What was this structure?

A lookout.

Part of the security.

A man with a gun inside, guarding the road.

But the tower sat too far off the road for that purpose, almost hidden, covered with kudzu and other vines. It didn't look as though anyone had used it in quite a while.

Time crawled. Randi, her bladder bursting, tried to be patient and certain.

Convinced of her solitude, she crawled on her belly toward the tower. At the structure she froze, listening—silence but for the riverside birds singing a happy song. She took a deep breath and scrambled up a crude stepladder.

Inside, a repugnant scene—and certainly not that of a lookout for intruders: The angle of the opening faced the oval meadow. On the floor, a mess of fast food garbage and beer cans—like the fishing spot—along with spent shell casings and a small, weathered stool on which to sit.

Sight lines.

The meadow.

A perch.

The tower's purpose, clicking into place: A deer stand. The hunters their real estate agent had suggested might frequent the ridge were quite real. Were the Macons themselves, for all she knew. They certainly had guns.

She pictured the victims: a beautiful doe stepping into a morning mist with her fawns, or else a magnificent buck, proud and strong, a moment of grace and communion between animal and environment . . . but in a wretched flash torn asunder by an easy, gimme-shot from a potbellied redneck's gun hidden within his putrid, lazybones sniper's nest.

Cowards.

The stand didn't seem to have been used in some time. The hamburger wrappers lay crumpled and brittle, leaves had blown in and accumulated in the corners, a short stack of hardcore porn mags turned stiff and waterlogged from what she hoped had been rain leaching in rather than body fluids.

Tired, she sat on the stool. It creaked under her weight.

Weighing the worth of her endeavor against possible consequences, Randi, her bladder aching, tried to justify going on with this dangerous plan of hers. She slipped off her bag with camera, binoculars and a flask filled with water. Wriggled the ghillie suit down around her ankles. Pulling down her trackies, she squatted over the porn magazines, relieving herself —a torrent.

She'd been sweating beneath the getup. The cool air chilled her damp skin.

Her heart seized: the nearby dogs began howling.

Flustered by the proximity of the canine caterwauling, she fumbled with her equipment backpack and the ghillie suit, getting tangled up, struggling.

Calm down.

Now, a low rumbling she felt first before hearing—a train passing on the trestle a half-mile away, which, as before, had agitated the animals.

Randi, figuring the rumbling of the locomotive might obscure sounds she'd make as she crept closer to the compound. It had to be close indeed, and in the opposite direction the deer stand faced.

Listening, she waited at the top of the ladder.

All quiet. The dogs, calm. The train appeared to have passed.

But in the interval of silence that came next, she perceived another rumbling, on a smaller scale, growing louder. Randi, scanning her eyes back toward the road, saw Esau's truck bouncing down the last switchback.

A glacial step back into the shadows, away from the doorway to the deer stand. The covering of vines should have camouflaged her standing in the opening. Or so she hoped.

Randi waited for the truck to pass. Its brakes squeaked and squealed.

But it stopped. The truck, idling mere meters away from her.

"I want you to look at that." Esau's voice came clear and all too close. "That deer stand needs cleaning up."

Randi tried to compose herself—had he seen her after all?

Julius, with his reedy, childlike voice: "I done it the other day. Like you told me."

Esau, his menace quiet but total: "I got a dime to a dollar says you ain't done it."

The younger brother protested his innocence.

Esau laughed. "Son, you the worst liar the Lord ever put on this earth."

Busted, Julius admitted in a cracking voice: "I started, but I ain't finished yet."

Randi's stomach fluttered with panic: Esau, now sure to come inspect his brother's supposed work.

No escape.

"Get it done later today. I ain't messing with you."

"I told you I did. I mean—I would."

"Boy—listen here."

"Uh-huh?"

"You better not lie to me, ever again. Remember, Mama ain't gonna be around forever to take up for your fat ass."

"Don't say that about Mama."

"Well, it's the damn truth."

Julius whined, high and pitiful. "You mean she's going to Heaven. Don't you."

"Esau's gonna take care of you. Don't you worry your pumpkin head about it." Mocking his brother: "There, there. My, my."

"Shut up."

"Watch you mouth, retard." The truck rumbled on down the road.

Tasting bile, Randi wondered if Mrs. "Mama" Macon knew of the wrathful, uncaring cruelty perpetuated by her children upon the dogs, and each other.

What kind of parenting produced this pair of miscreants? Even Adolf Hitler had had a mom, though. Nobody ever blames her... do they?

Randi climbed down, gathered her wits. Now the danger had grown real, but if she got footage of them both in action with the dogs, all the better.

Julius—he had sounded so pitiful and sad. Esau, likely the kind of brother who'd send his own kin to jail, all the while denying he knew anything at all about the dog business there by the river. Knowing airtight evidence presented to the right agency would make all the difference, she had to make sure the correct perps got punished—otherwise, the danger in which she'd put herself would lead nowhere. Esau, the real villain here.

But Randi would fix all that. She only needed to find the path of the hero without anyone else, her husband included, noticing.

27

By the time she came upon a hidden, rusted fence, Randi, frustrated and paranoid anew, fought an urge to cash in her chips and go home. Accessing the property from the bramble-choked north approach seemed untenable, and her attempt to cut around on the opposite side resulted in her ghillie suit becoming entangled within barbed wire concealed by kudzu vines.

A twig snapped—a footfall.

Unmistakable.

She turned. No one there.

Her heart raced. She again feared making too much noise—and now the compound lay close, only yards away through the trees. She could make out the wall of camo netting.

Randi's courage wavered. Coming down the ridge had been beyond foolhardy.

She yanked at the leg of her suit until finally the material ripped with a sound that sent terror through her heart—loud and unnatural, like paper being torn.

Randi froze, listening.

Nothing.

Startled anew: the rumble of the truck, this time exiting the compound.

Ghillie suit or not, she dropped down on her knees, held her breath.

She waited as the vehicle passed, chugging up the switchbacks and away, she presumed, to Esau's comfortable home near the freeway.

But what of Julius?

Had he left with Esau?

That, of course, would be the most advantageous scenario—if the truck returned she'd hear it in plenty of time, and could make haste for the river trail and back home by way of the creek. But no way to know, so she kept her antennae attuned to her surroundings.

Finding a good vantage point from which to observe near the entrance to the compound, obscured by young hardwoods, vines and ferns she peered through her binoculars at a clean view through a gash in the camo netting. Her crouched survey revealed a metal gate hanging askew and needing repair. A chain link fence surrounded the property on the inside of the netting, curving around and disappearing into the trees. Security, too much for such a secluded, ostensibly ordinary hovel stuck out here in the woods.

She crawled a couple of yards to her right, closer to the road, to get a better angle through the netting. The air felt damp. She could smell the river; she could smell the dogs.

Inside she saw a row of outdoor runs with doorways leading into an unseen, enclosed inner space offering shelter for the dogs. The cyclone-fenced runs sat divided by sheets of plywood, each space segregated and private from the others. A building of sheet metal and concrete blocks, like a large backyard Quonset hut, stood attached to the dog runs.

To the left of that structure, a hybrid of a house: an old, decrepit Airstream trailer with a cinder block extension perhaps fifteen feet square built onto the front of it. The block-building part had a rusted, corrugated roof. A window unit AC sat supported by two gray, rotting stilts. The door, like the gate, hung askew. It seemed a bleak place for anyone, even a dog, to live.

Focusing the binoculars, her breath caught in her throat—two pit bulls in their respective runs, both sleeping in a shaft of sunlight pouring through the tree canopy.

She crawled forward through the brush, closer, shifting her angle again. In the middle of the compound, a space of hard-packed clay. A short pole stood with a chain hanging from it; near this grew a huge live oak tree, and from one of its limbs hung an ominous, orange electrical cord tied at the end into a kind of noose. The clay appeared darker around the pole, stained. She pictured terrified, doomed creatures tied there, the bait, as Ebby had said, to train the fighters.

A dog howled, unseen but recognized as the one she'd first heard. This animal had a throatier sound than the others, almost gurgling at times, muffled, coming from inside one of the buildings. Focusing on the sound, *her* dog, the one who had first alerted her to this horrific situation, she barely heard the snapping of the twig again. Indeed, a footfall—a substantial one.

From behind her: "*You better turn around slow.*"

She cried out in shock and whirled around on her knees to face her attacker, bobbling her binoculars and dropping them into the inches-deep leaf cover all around her feet.

Julius Macon pointed a gun, a deer rifle. Gasping for breath, eyes squeezed shut, he seemed more frightened that her. "You better not be one of Rembert's boys."

"Julius: it's—me."

He calmed and frowned at her. "Who?"

With few options, no idea came but a sucker-bet gambit. Busted, yes, but still feeling a modicum of luck in that this time, no Esau around to bring this to a head. "It's the lady from up the ridge."

Julius seemed confused by the sound of her voice. "*I'm calling my brother.*"

"Please. I only want to be friendly. Like—neighbors."

Grimacing and shaking his head at her soft entreaties, he danced from foot to foot like a child needing to go to the bathroom. "Then why you got that thing on?"

The poor dear—his small eyes sitting so close together, a knitted brow, a sick grimace of fear on his pudgy face, Randi wondered where on the autism spectrum Julius fell. "It's so nobody can see me."

"That's scary."

Keeping a sharp eye on the barrel of the rusty rifle, Randi pulled the hood forward and yanked down the rest of the suit. "Remember me, now?"

He announced with wonder turning to suspicion: "*Red.*"

"I'm not here to hurt you, or anyone."

"What the deuce you want, then?"

"I'm here because of the dogs. Because I want to see them."

His demeanor turned icy. "No one's supposed to see them but me and Esau and the customers."

"Well—I might be one. I might want to buy the dogs. From *you*, Julius. Do you understand?"

"I c'ain't."

"Why not?"

"Esau sells the dogs."

"Think how proud he'd be. If you sold the dogs. And made money—lots of money."

"I don't know how to add two-numbers together or nothing." Growing more agitated. "You're trying to trick me."

"You can't do simple mathematics?"

"I done told you, I don't do two-numbers. *You put your arms up.*" His shriek echoed through the woods. The barrel of the rifle wobbled from his fearful tremors.

Randi did as he asked. She kept her words low, her tone melodious and kind. "What are two-numbers, honey?"

He lowered the gun and swept the barrel wide, uncertain eyes darting all around. He ran a huge, pink hand over his close-cropped hair, which glistened in the sun with nervous sweat. "Don't poke fun."

"I'm not. Tell me, sweetheart."

"Like eleven and twelve." *Lebben and twel-buh.* "You know—two-numbers."

Randi got it. Through the icy gut-stab of her fear, she felt a twinge of empathy for the pathetic, lumbering figure. "I could help you with figuring out two-numbers."

"You could?"

"I promise I would, if you'd let me. But first: We have to keep this our secret."

"Secret?" Troubled, glancing back in the direction of the road. "I don't keep no secrets."

"I think it would be best if we did."

"My brother's not coming back," Julius blurted. "Nope."

"Oh—really, now."

At the mistake, his eyes flew wide. "Wait, yes he is. Coming back any minute now."

"Nonsense. He just left."

Julius sighed. She had him. "I messed up."

"No, you haven't messed up."

"I'm in trouble."

"I knew he was gone for the day. That's why I wanted to come and say hello. And meet the dogs."

"Why you sneaking around?"

"Because Esau doesn't like me." Perhaps a stranger with the same problem as Julius would present as no stranger at all. "Can't you tell?"

"Nope. Esau don't like you."

"No, he doesn't. But he's silly."

"But *secret*? I dunno. That don't sound right."

"Julius: I love dogs just as much as you."

A smile, tentative. "You do?"

"More than your brother does."

Julius's face scrunched like a fist tightening. "He sure don't love them the way I do."

Randi, not so certain. As far as she was concerned, Julius, however guileless he might sound, stood equally complicit in the brutality. "Not like he ought to. Right?"

"But that's why it's good I'm out here and he's with Mama in the house over by the four-lane where it's all too bright and loud. Too bright and loud for me. Better. Better here with the dogs."

"That's why you're back in here? Too noisy for you out by the four-lane?"

"That's what Esau says? And Mama, too?" Julius nodded and fluttered his chubby pink fingers beside one temple. "She gets headaches something awful."

"Headaches. I've had a few."

Seeming more relaxed, his statements turned up at the ends like gentle questions from a curious child. "And she can't abide me stomping around? And going in and out of doors, and all?"

"I understand."

Confident he'd explained the situation, Julius smiled and tilted his head. "Besides—that ain't no good place to raise these dogs. With all the houses and cars and whatnot."

Only a monster, Randi speculated, would allow her impaired child to live out in the woods in squalor to tend fighting dogs. "Must be terribly lonely here."

"It ain't. I got Cleo with me always. And I get to eat supper in the big house on Fridays? When we have Mama's fried chicken? And then on Sundays sometimes, too?" Beaming and pleased, the thought of his mother's cooking made his enormous stomach growl. "That's why Esau does the two-numbers, and I take care of my dogs out here by the river, where it's quiet and no one messes with us."

Randi went to drop her aching arms. Julius made a quick nudging motion with the butt of the rifle. She coaxed her quivering hands back into the air.

"Why don't you put down the gun."

Instead, he aimed at her head. "I'm sorry."

Randi thought she might faint—poor Julius, so tenderhearted he'd apologized in advance for killing her. "Sorry about what?"

"About that dookie doo up yonder at your house."

Sounded like what a toddler-aged Denny might have called his leavings. "You mean the mess on my driveway?"

His cheeks flamed with guilt. "I didn't want to. Esau made me. I reckon you can put down your arms."

Relieved, she did so. "Why didn't you want to?"

"I thought it was mean."

"It sure was nasty."

"Yeah."

"But you realize shooting a gun at me is worse. Right?"

Nodding. "He don't make no sense sometimes."

Randi could see how this simple man held no uncertain amount of animosity for his older brother. "He could've killed me that day."

Julius, frightened anew. "You was just hiking around like you said. Wasn't you?"

Not so nervous she couldn't apply psychology: "He's a big jerk, that brother of yours. He's mean to the dogs."

Julius stared at a point far behind Randi. He licked his lips and frowned. Divulged a secret previously held close: "He's real mean to me sometimes, too."

"But especially to the dogs."

Julius, puzzled. He shifted back and forth on his huge feet, frustrated but eager to explain his brother's—and by extension, his—relationship with the fighting dogs. "But that's what you're supposed to do."

"*Be cruel to them?*"

"That's why Esau says God put them dogs here. And what He put *me* here for," adding with pride.

At first, Randi didn't know how to respond. "Well, he shouldn't be mean to them. Or you."

Julius sounded burdened by the necessity of explaining the obvious: "He's all I got, him and Mama. And Cleo, of course."

"We need to do something about all this."

His voice now came as low and serious-sounding as he could muster: "You come here to take my dogs away?"

Randi, quick to answer. "I'm like a customer, Julius."

"No, you ain't."

"Why can't I be?"

"We ain't never had no girl customers."

"It's different with me. I just take pictures. Of animals."

Esau had drilled the photo rule into his brother. Julius's words came harsh: "No pictures. Ever."

Gently, in her most patient voice: "No pictures. I just want to visit with the dogs."

He calmed down. "You just wanna visit? Oh."

She held his eyes. Smiled. "Sure—we're neighbors."

Julius, a slow, spreading grin. "Really?"

"Of course. That's what neighbors do—they visit with each other."

He rolled that around. Worked his jaw. Nodded. "I reckon."

"I can hear the dogs, you know. Up the ridge."

"You can?"

She confirmed she could, including one in particular.

"That's Cleo. She's my dog."

"Yours?"

"Yes, ma'am."

A new wrinkle in what had become a complicated situation—Julius considered one of the dogs a pet. "So it's okay with you? This visit?"

Uncertainty written across his wide moon of a face, Julius began whining and grimacing.

Birds singing, sunlight glancing at a sharp angle through the trees, she made one last entreaty: "*Please.*"

143

Julius nodded down at his filthy work boots. "Maybe for a minute or two."

Releasing several minutes of pent-up breath: "Wonderful."

Mulling it over. Shuffling his feet. "But secret, though."

Randi smiled and promised. Another lie.

28

INSIDE THE COMPOUND NEAR THE BLOCKHOUSE, RANDI, NOTING THE attentive, disciplined behavior of the dogs for Julius, their obvious master and caretaker. After the two lying in the outside runs sprang awake, barking and howling at her presence, he implored them to settle down:

"*No,*" accompanied by sharp whistling, a downward motion of his palm.

Without hesitation the dogs sat, looking to Julius for further instructions.

Impressive degree of control.

One of the pit bulls appeared monstrous, with an enormous head, a thick muscled frame of rippling flesh, battle scars on his snout. Another dozen runs in all were connected to the rectangular structure with its tin roof, but she didn't see any other dogs.

"My goodness." She tried to make herself sound like a nurturing kindergarten teacher. "How many dogs *do* you have?"

"They's my only ones right now. Them and one-nother. He's done had some kind of stomach mess, and I got him caged inside so he can't give it to them. That's Malachi. That brown one with the spot under his eye is Willie Wonka and the other'n," he said, prideful, pointing to the bigger pit bull, "is King Kong the Strong."

She tried not to become distracted analyzing the mix of pop culture and biblical names. "How very impressive."

Julius blinked, his eyes wet. "He's done been bought, though."

"And what does that mean?"

"He's going to his new daddy soon."

"How does one become a customer?"

"So if you're a customer? And all? I don't know how many dogs you wanted? And all? But them's the only ones till springtime, when we gonna breed again." He seemed nervous at performing the salesclerk part. "It's not our busy season," as though the Macons were in retail over at Edgewater Towne Centre, the strip mall in Chilton that held the IGA.

"So, you have 'seasons'?"

"We put King Kong out to stud last week? When we was going past your house? And Esau shined that light and you got mad and called the law on us?"

Dry. "I remember."

"Anyway, you ought to wait till springtime to visit. That's when the little pups start growing up. If you did want one—like Cleo—you'll have more to pick from." He nodded with vigor, pleased and relaxed at describing a process about which he felt confident. "More pups. That's when it's the funnest."

She changed the subject. "Where's Cleo?"

Sputtering, incipient panic: "She ain't for customers. You can't, you can't—"

"Calm down, now. I just want to meet her."

"She's inside my house on her bed. Where she's comfortable."

"Well—let's go, then."

At the doorway to his dilapidated home, Julius stood waiting for Randi to go in.

Wait—what if he were conning her into a more vulnerable position?

No. Julius Macon didn't seem capable of such duplicity. She took a deep breath and pushed the door open, stepping inside.

The interior wasn't quite as bad as she was expecting, maybe fifteen feet square, with a doorway leading up a set of wooden steps into the carved-out Airstream trailer, which served as a second room.

The kitchen, such as it could be called, sat tucked into a corner like a cobbled-together version of a beach motel's efficiency unit: A hot plate, a small fridge, a sink with a mirror. A couple of loaves of bread sat on a TV tray next to a large, industrial-sized can of peanut butter as one would purchase at a wholesale club. Bags of cheap salty snack foods. Candy bar wrappers everywhere. A giant jar of M&Ms about half full.

As Julius shut the door behind him, the first move he made was to the jar, where he swept a handful of candies into his mouth, crunching happily. An ancient, minuscule television set with aluminum foil rabbit ears sat at the end of a bed that looked too small for Julius's bulk. The stained mattress sagged in the middle, especially since a dog, curled and asleep, lay upon it. A well-fed, nearly all white pit bull.

"*Cleee-o*," Julius sang-spoke. "Somebody done come to see us."

The dog moaned and rolled onto her back, exposing a pink underbelly.

"Get up, Queen Cleopatra." To Randi: "That's her real name."

"That's a special name."

"I picked it out just for her."

Cleo stretched and smacked her jowls. At first the dog struggled to turn over, but managed to get up and face her visitor.

Randi gasped: The dog's right ear was missing, one eye sewn shut. Scar tissue went down the side of her neck and onto both front legs. She knew the source of the injuries—a bait dog.

Blazing with fury, she fought to keep cool. "You poor sweet thing."

Cleo smacked her lips and stood, wagging a wiggly nub of a tail. The dog jumped down from the bed and padded over next to Julius, leaning against his legs and looking up at her master. Julius's meaty fingers scratched Cleo's head; the animal seemed to enjoy his attention, especially as he concentrated on the area where her ear had been.

"This is *my* dog." Julius, again with his prideful tone. "Mine."

Cleo sported an affectionate, innocent expression of canine happiness.

Even so, Randi thought, the scars indicated the dog had experienced more than life as a pampered pet—in fact, quite the opposite.

She bent down to pet Cleo, who nuzzled her outstretched hand. In a ragged whisper: "What happened to her?"

"We don't remember that mess. We done forgot it."

Randi forced eye contact. "So it was bad."

Julius, his face a sour mask. "Cleo was the runt in this one litter?"

"Yes?"

He shook his head. "So Esau, he says, since she ain't worth nothing, we got to make her good for something."

"I think I understand."

Julius, fists clenched. "I tried to stop him, but he wouldn't. He don't never listen to me."

Randi seethed. Tears, hot and unexpected, crept out of the corners of her eyes. She tried to wipe them away without Julius seeing.

His gaze became faraway. "You know what I done?"

"What—?"

"Afterwards, I made Mama and Esau pay to fix her. I hollered until they said they would." He blinked and nodded as if in a trance. "I cried, too."

"You must've been yelling pretty loud."

"I held Esau down." Now for the true confession. "Sat on him until he turned blue. He cried, too. Mama was beating me with the broom, and hollering to let him up. But I didn't. Not until he promised I could keep her. Made Mama promise, too."

"And that's the story of Miss Cleo, eh?"

"You know what I think?"

Randi asked what.

"That Esau's been mad at me ever since."

"Maybe you scared him."

"I'd-a done more than scared him. If he'd've took my Cleo away."

"You did right—you saved Cleo."

His eyes sparkled with affection. "I tried to tell him she was mine. Isn't that right?"

To Randi, the dog seemed to ruminate upon the question. Yawned. Panted.

"Yes it is," her master answered.

The daylight outside began to fade, which meant she needed to get her skinny, trespassing ass home. But having now observed more humanity than she'd ever expected from the Macons, Randi's mind felt jumbled.

"Why does she howl?"

A bright smile appeared. "That's her singing. Singing to the woods and the river."

"Singing? About what?"

"How she's happy I'm her people-person. That's what."

One man's singing was another woman's aggrieved howling, she supposed.

Julius's devotion to this animal amidst all the others he spent his days training to fight to the death presented a paradox. Still, the mission remained unchanged.

He's not innocent in all this. Don't forget that.

"Julius: May I come and visit with you and Cleo again?"

A flash of fearful skepticism. "I'm not supposed to."

"Our little secret. Remember?"

Julius whined, shook his head.

"I don't mean you all any harm," hating herself. "We all have to live together here on the ridge."

In the silence that followed, Julius's stomach again rumbled.

A new tactic. "How's this: I'll bring treats. For all of us," scratching Cleo's good ear. "Sound good?"

Julius, mute and uncertain. His gaze flickered over to the rifle he'd propped by the door through which a cool autumn breeze flowed.

"Go bye-bye now."

"And so I can come back?"

Julius didn't answer.

"With those treats," she reminded him. "Okay?"

Julius turned away. "Please go on, now."

"Okay. Bye-bye—for now."

She didn't wait for a reply. With the sun setting on the far side of the river, the deep woods had begun growing dark already.

As Julius thumped the door behind her, Randi rushed to retrieve her camera and managed to snap off a few photos—the compound, the pens, the ominous electrical cord, the rusty pole. Next time, she'd get images from inside that blockhouse. She suspected that inside the building lay more than enough evidence to shut these guys down.

A sense of urgency, gripping her.

To get home.

To get safe.

If that were even possible here anymore in bucolic Edgewater County. Randi hustled back up the ridge.

29

Winded and flushed, Randi made it home in time to hear the creaking garage door opening—Cullen had arrived, and early for him.

She hustled into the laundry room, threw her backpack and ghillie suit into a cabinet and stripped off the tracksuit, damp with sweat. She'd planned to shower before he got home, but instead a quick change would have to suffice.

Rummaging in the dryer she found sweats and an olive-green *Dr. Strangelove* T-shirt of Cullen's she had inherited. Randi remembered his anger at having discovered the shirt, one hundred percent cotton, mind you, had shrunk. The way he'd pouted for hours. She'd tried the old *ignore it and just be sweet* routine, but he continued to glower until blurting out about how stupendous and satisfied he'd been to have even found a *Dr. Strangelove* T-shirt in the first place, how remarkably obtuse on her part for having not given the artifact its due. Would always cut his eyes at her whenever she now wore it around the house.

"*Honeybunny?*" Cullen's voice, echoing from the spiral staircase. "Hi-ho."

"Down here."

He started to clomp down the curved metal steps, but she'd already begun her ascent. "Hold on, I'm coming up."

Trying to scheme a reason for her red face and tousled hair, she emerged on the main level to receive a peck on the forehead.

"You're salty. Have a run?"

"Tromping around in the woods again." At least this part wasn't a lie. "Hell of a workout."

"Not the woods." Yanking at the knot of his tie, a J. Garcia of floating, vibrant colors, suspicion clouded his smile. "Really, now."

"Just down the creek to the river and back."

"Randi—"

"You've got to hike it with me one weekend. Isn't that part of the reason we're here?"

Cullen yawned. "Hiking doesn't sound too hip to me right now. Groggy. My hands are clammy, my gums seem swollen. Feels like my teeth are being pushed apart." He stuck a finger in his mouth and rubbed around. "Swollen gums, swollen gums—is that the flu? Or a sinus infection?"

Randi, gripped with annoyance. If Cullen had the flu, she'd have him knocking around the house all day tomorrow and maybe the next as well, right as she'd made a breakthrough in what she now thought of as her official Macon Boys investigation.

Covering her mouth and nose, she backed away. "I don't want to be sick, not now that I'm finding some energy again. Feeling better. Et cetera."

"You mean better-better?"

"Sure. I kinda do."

"You're hedging."

"I'm feeling a little spark, here and there. I'd prefer not to count unhatched chickens. Or some other hoary old aphorism."

In truth she felt like she had a job again, tasked with rescuing those dogs and shutting Esau Macon down for good, if she could. She fantasized about seeing Esau's disgusting face on her old newscast, the redneck frog-marched in a jumpsuit and leg irons across the Tillman Falls town green, with Cyn-Anne Goforth chirping away in voiceover:

"*Macon, seen here following the verdict, received the harshest sentence available to the county court judge . . .*"

A daydream—Randi, far from naive enough to believe they'd put a man like Macon away for this crime. Not for training dogs to fight.

Julius Macon presented a more complex matter. Equally guilty, yes, but the innocence of his affection for Cleo, along with his mental condition, mitigated his culpability.

Didn't it?

She couldn't decide.

She wondered if she should try to protect him. Pondered if Julius could be persuaded to come to the authorities with her. Get him to testify in exchange for immunity. This had been the grand idea coalescing on her long trudge up the dark ridge:

That Julius, impressionable, could be turned.

Alongside that galvanizing notion, Randi also wanted to learn as much as she could about the family to document how well they'd been living off the suffering of those canines. This new surveillance included the "Mama" to which both Esau and Julius had referred, but how many more Macons were there? Esau gunning for her was bad enough, but for all she knew a dozen bugeyed brothers and sisters and cousins also lay in wait to fend off her efforts.

Perhaps she could press Ebby into giving her more details, but she knew he'd wearied of her curiosity. To Ebby's credit, his warnings about the Rembert gangster and the cops and the underground economy here in rural South Carolina had thus far not only proven true, but had given her some degree of pause. As she'd already demonstrated, though, his advice fell on all-but deaf ears. Randi knew she couldn't change the entire world, or stamp out a depraved subculture, but by putting Esau in his place she could make a small contribution.

Cullen, his nose shiny and eyes two puffy slits. "I'm going to go crash for a bit, if that's okay. My head feels like a basketball."

A stab of pity for her husband. "Get some sleep. Feel better tomorrow."

"Thank god it's Saturday."

Randi, realizing the weekend upon them, now accepted that Cullen would be home anyway, her investigation tabled no matter his condition.

She gave him a hug, but held her face away from his germ factory. "Let's get some chicken soup in you."

Nuzzling her neck. "Say, 3M—I think I've contracted flu bug hornies."

Randi, smiling at his cutesy, standard joke: hangover hornies, neighborhood cookout hornies (in the kitchen after everyone finally leaves), exams-are-over hornies, Sunday Night *Simpsons* hornies, Truffaut-double-feature hornies.

But rebuffing him in the style of the sitting President, she brandished a finger of admonishment. "You need rest, not jostling around."

"We need to make up for the other night."

Randi, with a new mission in life, now far less paranoid about Cullen and other women. "I agree."

"You do?"

Nodding. "That was some kind of bad-news flashback of mine. But still—raincheck?"

"Boo hoo," with a protruding lower lip. "Raincheck, then."

"You got it."

Happiness bloomed inside her, a sense of duty and fulfillment she had all but forgotten. She'd seen what was going on down the ridge. She'd met Cleo. Now when the dog howled, she would be able to see her sweet, scarred face—a troubling image.

In any case, Randi knew the score in a more complete manner. She'd interacted with Julius without being killed, and found out that if she moved with haste—before the spring breeding season—only a few dogs needed rescuing.

Ramping up into her old producer mode, she lay out an ideal schedule in her mind, and decided to get this project wrapped before the holidays, when Cullen had invited family from the upstate to enjoy their new, gorgeous home. *Guests? Really?* Randi felt better, but maybe not that much.

But hey, she'd gotten over her anger, if only because of bigger Sugeree River fish to fry than the irritation of an extended visit by in-laws: She had matters of justice in her hands, which as she stood at the granite kitchen island preparing her sick husband's dinner felt clean, virtuous, and purposeful. Maybe she'd talk him out of the family gathering. Who knew what might be happening around the ridge then?

30

AFTER DINNER, A PUNY-FEELING CULLEN ANNOUNCED THE ARRIVAL OF 'movietime,' code-speak that the sofa in the now satellite-ready home theatre should prepare itself for occupation.

But first, he helped Randi clear away the dishes as he listed a litany of typical complaints—essays, dunderheads, Southeastern U politics—all now compounded by the exponential burden of having picked up a dorm-incubated flu bug from one of the students.

The conversation took a typical turn with a question about what she'd done with her day. She fended this off by fibbing about working on a short story.

"You gotta let me read something soon." Blowing his nose on a dinner napkin. "Earlier I was thinking about how much I loved those teen-angst melodramas you showed me."

She smiled at the memory of finding a stash of short stories composed during high school junior year, the season after her mother divorced Durant and left California for her own sociology associate professorship at UGA. Randi's overwrought, purple prose had left her and Cullen in stitches.

"When there's something of merit, I'll print it out."

"Tree killer. Just make a PDF and shoot it to my email."

"Why don't you write your own?"

Wistful. "I know, I know. That was my dream as a kid—a novelist. Before the space operas turned me onto movies."

"Nothing stopping you now from writing fiction. Or screenplays. Or anything besides the scholarship."

"I need to keep publishing."

"The price of tenure." She kissed him on the forehead. "For now, relax while I fart around in the office—movietime, remember? Student papers, childhood dreams, and most of my scribbled nonsense, all that can wait."

"Bring me some tea." Sniffling and pitiful, a sick Cullen could seem as childlike as Julius Macon. "If you make some later."

"How about a juice box with a bendy-straw?"

A cute smile. "Nah. Tea time sounds better."

Tromping down the spiral stairs, he shuffled to the left into the rec room while Randi cruised into the laundry. She intended to start a load of washing to stall for a bit on the short story question, in hopes that before long he'd fall asleep.

After dumping dye-free detergent into the washer and twisting the dial, she yawned and eased into her desk chair. Exhausted, her day's adventure seemed to catch up to her all at once.

She closed her eyes, decided to try meditating. The soundtrack of Kubrick's *Eyes Wide Shut*, a DVD that had arrived in the mail from a new online retailer called Amazon, would no doubt be a distraction.

The spell, broken before it could take hold: Randi's replacement cell phone, a Nokia brought home the previous day by Cullen, vibrated on the desktop. A number she knew as Cyn-Ann's flashed on the screen.

"Hey, girlfriend." Randi, answering without enthusiasm. "What's shakin'?"

The news anchor, her natural effervescence a given, here all but bubbled across the digital connection. "Guess-who's-been-sniffing-around."

"Do tell."

"Freaking CNN."

The broadcast colleagues let out a mutual squeal of delight. Randi brightened—Cyn had chased this chance for as long as they'd known one another. The big time; network news or bust.

"You must be anxious as hell. Anyone else know?"

"Spencer, of course. I had to tell him."

"It'll get around for sure, now."

Coy. "I'll just have to deal with all the attention—somehow."

Randi suspected her friend would survive the ordeal. "You've sent your reel?"

"Oh, honey—they've seen it. That's why they called." Her voice quavered and she sniffled, seemed to need to collect herself. "I'm gonna hit Atlanta next week. My agent says face time, that's what'll put me over with the execs."

"I'm happy for you. Dreams are coming true."

"What about you, 3M?"

"Me?"

"Was it your dream to live out in the boonies on a hilltop? Surrounded by pine trees?"

Musing. "Probably not. But, I'm here; I'm making it work."

"To what end, though?"

"Been getting some writing done. Sure." Staring at the blank slate of the dark computer screen, Randi winced at the pervasive and profligate lying now informing all her human interaction. "Short stories. Maybe the Denny book."

"That'd be lovely. And healing."

Now for idle, catching-up small talk—the house, the countryside, Cullen's state of mind, and after a question regarding neighbors, a sanitized description of the local yokels.

Cyn's question filled Randi with quivering anxiety. "A quaint place, Edgewater County. That's for sure."

"So why don't we lunch to celebrate? After my interview, we go on vacation. We're flying to Rome straight from Atlanta."

The thought of Hartsfield airport caused Randi's heart to clench. "Aren't you the lucky lady. Lunch on Monday it is."

"*Sounds-like-a-plan.* I'll buzz you."

Randi closed the phone. Her friend's news, already fading. Fully documenting the Macon's place of work, her only concern. Only so many more chances.

Before Esau took action. If not Julius himself, whose confidence she may, or may not, have gained.

While already courting danger, she mulled a more brazen act: tomorrow night, and only a couple of miles away from where she now sat, the hog-dawg would happen.

Randi, repulsed by the circumstances, as well as the risk of what she considered: capturing evidence of that depraved circus out in the woods. But the thought of exposing every last one of these atavistic Edgewater County rednecks in a manner that would stick—maybe even the Sheriff himself—caused a wave of elation to roll through her. Much careful work lay ahead.

31

THE NEXT MORNING, RANDI STEELED HERSELF TO DIG OUT THE camcorder.

The one they'd bought a few years ago.

To record Denny's growth.

The 8mm tapes, the hot new format at the time, had all been packed away with Denny's things out in the storage shed. Since his death they hadn't bought any fresh cassettes, but the journalist in her knew unimpeachable video and audio would offer a rock-solid case.

A jolt of inspiration: Julius, describing his methods on hidden camera. Difficult, but possible.

On the breakfast bar sat the camcorder, an ugly black object like a threatening, mechanical insect. Light from the kitchen windows glinted off the singular black eye of the polished lens, a piece of dark glass through which so many images of her darling boy had passed.

In a daze, she drifted out of the house and into the mild autumn air, bright and sun-drenched as Carolina mornings tended whatever the season. She drove out to the main highway, through Chilton and onto the frontage road by the interstate.

Where they'd decided to stash the remains, so to speak, of their boy.

To keep from tainting the new living space with his achingly troublesome presence.

The storage facility, rows of orange sheet metal buildings, gray rolling steel gates and dangling padlocks. Driving between the rows her breath drew razor thin into constricted lungs.

Randi sat outside the shed for a long time listening to the faint signal from the Columbia classic rock station, with its rotation of Aerosmith, Skynyrd, the Stones, the Who, the Dead, the Floyd. Denny had so loved that stupid *Wizard of Oz/Dark Side of the Moon* mashup, his youthful mind blown by the odd synchronicity between ostensibly disparate artworks.

In a rush, Randi fumbled her seatbelt undone and tumbled out of the car. At this end of the units, tucked into a corner, windswept detritus had accumulated ankle-deep.

She kicked a path through the leaves, paper fast food cups, and cigarette cellophanes. Stood at the steel gate, the key in her trembling hand. Chewed a thumbnail.

At last she fumbled the lock off and yanked open the heavy door, hurting her shoulder. Despite having stashed the boxes only weeks before, dust billowed as though entering an Egyptian tomb. She coughed until she wretched sputum, wiping her eyes and cursing.

Inside, shadowy stacks of boxes and disassembled furniture, but no musty smell of decay as in a forgotten basement, nor any immediate shock of recognition—again, it had only been weeks. And yet, here she stood.

Already.

On the day in which they'd deposited the boxes she'd eaten Xanax like breath mints. Horrid; a gut check. But she had done it. Packed away his things. Sickening, but also a relief.

Her staccato laugh of disbelief bubbled up—she'd ventured out to the shed? For what? Surely not to waste the afternoon looking through boxes for a cache of videocassettes containing images over which to cry and heave until sick-drunk with self imposed grief.

Surely not. These objets d'art were not meant to be seen; were strictly time capsule material. Required a much longer rest before disturbance by heartsick, amateur archaeologists bumbling around clueless about what artifacts they truly sought.

Randi pulled the door back down and futzed with the lock. She scraped the knuckle of her thumb, an injury noticed only in a cursory, instinctual manner.

But she did not retreat from the storage shed in tears, no; shaking her head at her weakness, perhaps, but not sorrowful. She had a job to do, and to deviate from the forward course she'd undertaken—a sacred undertaking, as she thought of her calling to save the dogs—would be a grievous disservice not only to Denny's memory, but to the living: Cleo, and the others awaiting rescue. Instead of watching old Denny videos, she drove instead to the Walgreens near Tillman Falls and purchased a pack of fresh, blank camcorder tapes.

———

The afternoon faded into the hazy gray of a twilight that fell oppressive and forbidding. As the hours ticked by, Randi grew agitated, antsy. The hog-dawg exhibition would be underway soon, if not already.

Satisfied that Cullen, full of meds and cough syrup, would sleep well into the night, Randi assembled her gear on the floor in front of the high windows of the great room. She plugged in the camcorder to charge its battery. Loaded high-speed film into her Canon AE-1. Made a statement into an Olympus voice recorder that brought matters up to date and outlined her intentions for surveilling the dogfight.

Questions consumed her. How could she gain entrance? What was the process for admission? Was there a secret word?

She remembered *Eyes Wide Shut* from the night before, which after awhile she had watched with Cullen. No more uncomfortable filmgoing experience had either of them ever known. Perhaps she should try "fidelio."

In any case, she doubted being able to waltz onto the property and watch. If Macon caught her, she shuddered to predict what he and his cronies might do.

Earlier, she'd heard the rumbling of his truck engine. Had watched as Esau rolled down into the woods, the tarp covering what she now knew was a cage for one of the dogs. A last chance to show off the prowess of King Kong the Strong, she speculated.

Forget the subterfuge—even if she didn't attend the dogfight, Randi would still follow them. Let the Macons know that she knew the score. That they were as exposed as novice thieves breaking into a car in broad daylight on the town green. And most of all, how she would not be deterred.

She turned off all the lights and lit a candle, watching and waiting for the pickup, as well for the green battery-full light on the camcorder to appear.

A thump—Cullen, stirring in the master suite.

She slid her electronics under the coffee table and tiptoed down the short hallway to the master.

The bed, empty. She could hear a splattering from the bath, along with a tuneless humming: An unconscious trait that meant Cullen stood urinating while still all-but asleep. At least most of the pee usually ended up in the toilet.

Sure enough, he shuffled heavy-footed out of the bathroom in a medicated fugue state, rolled straight onto the bed without so much as noticing Randi observing from the dim of the hallway. Within thirty seconds, his snoring returned. She closed the bedroom door with a gentle click.

Back in the silent family room she heard what she'd been waiting for: Esau's truck, coming up the road. Randi hustled her gear together and bolted for the garage.

32

RANDI, CATCHING UP TO ESAU AT THE TURNOFF TO THE HIGHWAY. AT the stop sign he jumped out and flipped on the truck spotlight, blinding her by turning it back toward the Volvo.

Through her fingers, she saw Macon peek into the dog cage before turning his blazing gaze back toward her.

His arms straight and chest stuck out like a rooster—the cock of the walk—Esau strutted up to her window, which she rolled down a couple of inches.

"May I help you, Mr. Macon?"

"I didn't just wander in out of a turnip patch in Cracker County, woman."

"Your subtext escapes me."

Running fingertips across narrow lips. "Feels like you're following us."

"I'll have you know, sir, I'm going to that shitty IGA over 'yonder' for a six-pack of PBR. What else is there to do around here for kicks on a Saturday night?" Heart pounding, she feigned courage and arched an eyebrow. "Are you telling me I can't come and go from my own property as I please?"

Aggrieved: "*Lady, why are you acting the fool like this?*"

"Step away from my vehicle." She showed him her Nokia. "Or I'll call the law right here and *now*."

Esau's face, craggy and scarred, flashed unbridled disgust. But then his expression softened and he snickered. "Ain't no need to get snippy."

A roadside standoff. Randi, silent, drummed her fingers on the wheel. "I'm really just going out to get my husband some beer."

"Ain't you the good and proper wife. But you got to know that store'll close before you can get over there."

"Then I'd better be on my way." Shooing Esau back to his truck. "If I may."

"'If you may?' You got some smart mouth on you."

"I'll take that as a compliment, sir." Adding under her breath: "Fuckhead."

Back at his truck, Esau snuffed out the spotlight.

Once her vision adjusted she could see Julius peeking back at her from inside the truck cab. His eyes, terrified, floated over the top of the dog cage.

Randi put the Volvo in drive and followed Esau down to the highway, almost all the way to the turnoff she knew he'd take to the Rembert property, and the debauched spectacle awaiting.

At 217, Randi faced having to turn toward Chilton as she'd claimed, or following on behind Esau.

She knew exactly where they were going. She could drive on her way and backtrack.

If she really wanted to take such a risk.

Now it all seemed ridiculous—she wouldn't get within a half mile of the place with her old Canon dangling around her neck. They had to have guards, or some other admission process. At least she'd managed to fuck with Esau's head a bit, which alone had been worth leaving the house. *You have to give me that.*

Esau pulled across the intersection, but on the other side of the highway he stopped, the truck idling.

She sat, hands at ten and two o'clock on the leather-wrapped steering wheel. He waited, she knew, to watch her go in the opposite direction.

And so she did, driving down 217 with her eyes locked on the rearview, Esau's taillights sitting immobile until she rounded the first bend.

She drove for a mile or so before turning around in a church parking lot—Gethsemane Holiness, Esau's church. The paradox presented by the twin poles of the man's existence further confounded and unnerved her.

Her stomach in a knot, Randi wished for one of the mythical beers she'd had no intention of buying.

Was this a serious investigation, or not?

At that thought, she headed back toward Mr. Rembert's land, and the exhibition.

33

AT THIS HOUR, THE FOREST LOOMED AS DARK AND MYSTERIOUS AS IN A child's fairy tale. Who knew what monsters lurked therein. Randi, imagining one of Cullen's students turning in a paper on idiot horror movie victims making stupid and risky decisions, who put themselves and others in grave jeopardy.

Fortune favors the bold, a voice said. Her father's voice.

Deep breath time. She threw a sweater over the camera and drove down the dirt road. Tried controlled breathing in anticipation of what she hoped would be a steady voice when confronted. Perhaps knowing she was onto them at this level would persuade these cretins to cool it with the dog stuff.

She came to the fork off the rutted track Ebby had shown her—and as she feared, a corpulent man sat in a lawn chair with a lantern at his feet, a golf cart painted up in camo parked at an angle on the dusty shoulder of the road. He didn't seem to be armed with anything other than a flashlight, however, which now pointed in her direction.

She rolled down the window. "Hi there! May I ask a question?"

"I'd say you already asked one."

Wisecracks—a familiar routine with this crowd. "Another one, then?"

Despite standing well away from the window, she could see a change in the man's face, shifting from mild annoyance at having had to get out of his chair to squint-eyed suspicion.

"What can I do you for?"

"I think I'm lost."

"That much I already know."

"I was looking for Pecan Ridge? Or Pecan Ridge Road? Something like that."

"What you hunting that road for?"

Randi stammered about looking at property for sale.

"Property for sale? On Pecan Ridge?"

"That's the address I—I wrote down. Off the internet."

"You house hunting on a Saturday night?"

"I work all week."

The gatekeeper rolled a toothpick around in his mouth. "Back on up toward the Westside Highway to Red Mound."

"Oh—I came through that way. It's so dark out, I must have missed it."

"Ain't far."

Randi rolled her window all the way down. She could hear dogs barking. Voices, laughing and hollering. Twanging country music, the smell of charcoal burning—a real party underway.

"So: what all's going on back here?"

A long pause. "Camp meeting."

"Like a tent revival? Wow, I'd love to check that out."

"You got to be a member of this here church to come."

"How do I join?"

"You ain't already got a church?"

"No."

"Then what you want to join one for?"

He had her there. "I'm a historian. Southern history."

Unimpressed, he swept his flashlight the length of the car. "That a Volvo?"

"Yes."

"Been seeing a lot of them around."

Toying with her—Esau had told the guard to watch for the blue import wagon.

What a fool she'd been.

The man took a step toward the car. Reached into the pockets of his jacket. "Heard tell them Volvos ain't nothing but trouble. That if you had one, you'd be smart to get rid of it."

Panic.

Randi jammed the car into gear, making the same awkward three-point turn as Ebby had on his tour, if a touch more desperate and hurried.

The beam of his flashlight bobbing, the guard jumped aside. He hustled to try to block her way, but with a final wrenching of gears she gunned the engine and spun sand in his face. Randi caught a glimpse in the rearview of the guard coughing dust.

Back at the fork, she slowed. Stopped. Turned off the car. Listened.

Crickets. The ticking of the engine.

Then she heard a call echo through the woods, a high voice:

"*Hup*—!"

Julius.

Her guts, flooding with icy-hot adrenaline. It was happening—right here, right now. Sounds of brutality came wafting dreamlike through the trees. A high, squealing horror. The cheers of excited monsters on two legs. But images of the dog compound would have to do.

She cranked the engine and got the hell out of there. How right, she now knew, both Cullen and Ebby Nixon had been: if she hadn't left when she did, who knows what they would have done to her.

Stakes of such gravity, she now understood, meant that this situation begged for resolution sooner rather than later, if in fact Randi Margrave wished to stay alive here in Edgewater County.

34

RANDI, UNWILLING TO SLEEP.

Instead, she stretched out in the dark on the couch before the huge windows, watching the stars and waiting for Esau's truck—for him to come for her, rifle in hand. She quivered, worried about Julius's ability to keep their secret. The house phone and her cell, both close by her side.

After midnight, a shock: the room exploded into light. Randi screamed. "Holy shit, dude."

Cullen, yawning and tousled, had flipped on the three frosted globes suspended from the high beam above Randi's head. "Jumpy tonight?"

"I thought you were passed out."

Shuffling over, stuffy and miserable. "Did I run you out of there snoring? My sinuses are fucking wrecked."

"You're fine. Turn off the lights."

"Why?"

"Please."

Whining and puffy, his eyes swollen like Stallone's at the end of any given Rocky Balboa picture, he did as she asked, plunging them back into darkness. "But you know, maybe I do feel on the mend, now. Sweated it out."

"Glad baby's all better."

"Real better, in fact—why don't you come to bed?"

"Gracious. Still wound up?"

He flopped down on the couch, nuzzling her and growling like a beast. "Cough syrup hornies."

She begged off. "You're contagious. And I'm exhausted."

He pawed at her breast. Sported a half-mast flagpole in his pajama bottoms.

"Honey—I'm tired."

"Come to bed anyway." He rolled off the couch and floated back down the hall. "You won't catch this."

She stayed on the couch.

Watchful to the point of hallucination—hearing phantom noises, images jumping in her peripheral vision—she finally drifted off around two. Unless she missed them, Esau and Julius never returned to the ridge all night. But Randi knew they would.

.

35

THE REST OF THE WEEKEND PASSED WITHOUT INCIDENT; NO MACONS, no retribution, and no further espionage.

On Monday Cullen toddled off to work honking and blowing his nose, while Randi also made the drive to meet Cyn at an upscale seafood place in the Congaree Vista commercial district, an old favorite lunch haunt for glasses of white wine and the best she-crab soup to be had this far inland.

They were seated by the manager himself, obsequious, attentive, and dispatching servers who scurried with smiling enthusiasm. On local TV for a decade now, Cynthia-Anne Goforth sported one of the most recognizable faces in the city. She beamed at her many well-wishers, who either called out in passing or otherwise approached to chat.

"People get so starstruck." Cyn, whispering as though Randi couldn't see it happening since their arrival in the parking lot. "All for little old me?"

"When they find out you're leaving, your fanbase will weep and rend their clothing."

"Not a done deal." The news anchor's pancaked brow crinkled. "Don't go and jinx it."

During their soup and salad lunch Cyn-Anne's face shone at describing the possibilities her future now afforded, but with her, t'was ever thus.

Dessert came, a mango sauce-drenched cheesecake wedge accompanied by two forks and a garnish of mint leaves.

"Want to. Shouldn't."

Randi, more eager. "But you know you want to."

Not an act—TV personalities suffered urgent worries about matters of weight. "I simply cannot."

"More for me." Randi forked off a thick wedge with a chunk of graham cracker crust she dredged through the golden, sugary glaze. "So tell me: know any good private investigators?"

Cynthia's face darkened. "Oh, dear—not Cullen. Again."

"No, not Cullen."

"Thank god. Why, then?"

While eliding most of the details about the dogs, Randi explained how she'd discovered illicit activity only a few hundred yards from her new home.

The newscaster reacted with grave skepticism and worry. "Why don't you call the local police?"

"Believe it or not, the county cops are on the take."

Flabbergasted. "And you know this how?"

"It's just good old investigative journalism. I have to document things myself. To take matters higher up the cop food chain."

"I smell a story here: crusader takes on small town vice?"

"No publicity, please."

"Ever see this old 70s drive-in movie called *Walking Tall?*"

Randi had never seen the film, but remembered Cullen talking about it after a student had turned in a paper on a sub-genre designated *Redneck Revenge Cinema.* "I don't think we're talking that level of drama."

"So what are these folks up to?"

Randi chewed the side of her thumb. "Just some animal abuse."

"What kind?"

"A puppy mill."

Cynthia, relieved. "I heard you were getting into some kind of Humane Society work. Right?"

Randi, curious—she knew damn well she hadn't said anything about the dogs, not on the phone, nor here. "I'm concerned about some people with dogs, yes. But, how would you have known about that?"

"Cullen must have mentioned it. He said you were concerned about some animal mistreatment—"

"—but that I was being hysterical?"

Her cheeks, coloring. "He only said you were concerned."

"When did you talk to him?"

She folded her hands on the tablecloth. "Oh—when was that? Last week?"

"On campus? Or—"

"It was nothing. We ran into each other. Had lunch. Like this."

"I just hadn't heard."

Cyn, composed and nonchalant. "I didn't know lunches were state secrets."

Randi, studying her friend. Cullen and Cyn, always best pals. Bumping elbows. Swatting each other on the forearm.

Shit—could it be?

Cyn dabbed at her lips with a linen napkin already profaned by frosted-rose lipstick. "I remember now. We were in the Old Market shooting a PSA about a holiday food bank donation drive. Cullen pulled over on his way to the coffee shop, where we grabbed a cup and caught up. I'm sure he must've mentioned it to you."

"Oddly enough, he didn't."

She could see it on Cyn's face. Not guilt. But a shadow of duplicity. Perhaps not recent. But real.

Damn. How Randi hadn't seen it before, she knew not.

The news anchor blew out her lips, waved manicured nails as though fanning gnats. "Now look here," whispering. "I'm not boffing your man."

"I didn't mean to interrogate you like that."

She reached across to squeeze Randi's pale hand. "I understand. What woman wouldn't worry?"

Randi fretted. No reason Cullen shouldn't have mentioned seeing her friend, unless he simply didn't want his wife to know.

Wait—it all clicked into place.

Not for an affair, but to discuss her still-fragile mental condition. Check.

"Don't doubt him—I know how much he loves you. You need each other, more than ever."

"There's still so much to heal," her voice cracking.

Gentle, but firm: "As if you need to explain that to me."

"On most days? I'm still only at about a quarter speed."

"I should probably get back to the station." Cyn, a plastic smile splayed across her cherubic face. "Lunch is on me. Or somebody, anyway. Watch this—"

The restaurant manager, a pudgy, aging frat boy, approached with pie-eyed supplication. "Ladies, your meals today come compliments of the Bluefin Grill. Always a pleasure, Ms. Goforth."

"But we couldn't."

"I insist."

"This is just too much."

"It's our honor and duty—you serve us all by keeping the community informed."

Amusing—the bullshit reminded Randi of the pile she'd shoveled off the driveway.

Outside, Cyn hugged and held her close. "Don't get too lost in those woods of yours. You and Cullen heal. Figure out the future together."

"That's the plan."

Watching her friend drive away, Randi tongued a last smidgen of mango sauce from the back of her teeth. She pledged to let Cullen off the hook for dishing to Cyn, as well to get her paranoia under control before she undermined all her remaining close human relationships.

36

RANDI ARRIVED BACK IN EDGEWATER COUNTY TO FIND A FEVERISH, flushed Cullen bundled into a comforter on the bed, a fan of bluebooks arrayed beside him waited to be graded.

Touching him on the shoulder with a gentle hand: "You canceled afternoon class."

"Nearly passed out during 521." He cracked open one eye. "Should've stayed put today."

Nodding. "That's right. Just sleep."

"You and Cyn had lunch—right?"

"Yep."

Cullen, pulling himself to wakefulness, asked about Cyn-Anne's wellbeing.

"We talked about how CNN seemed poised to start kissing her feet."

"Good for her. I know she's happy."

"You do? How's that?"

"Oh—we chatted last week."

"So I heard. What else did you two discuss?"

Cullen became fully engaged. Met Randi's eyes. "Mostly about how much she missed seeing you."

"That all?"

"All I remember." Troubled. "Hey—you aren't worried—about —I hope."

"About what?"

"Nothing."

"Want the fire on?" Unlike the one in the great room, the bedroom fireplace offered a convenient, gas-log design, with heat and atmosphere available at the flip of a switch. Modernity; no fuss, no muss.

"You bet. Bring me a juice box?"

She laughed—poor Cullen, needing her. "With a bendy straw?"

A crooked, lascivious smile. "Yes, please."

Startled by her own frank admission of affection, she blurted how she loved him.

Hair corkscrewed, he sat up on one elbow. "I've been waiting a long time to hear you say that again."

She came back to the bedroom to again find him bleary-eyed and groaning.

"You really have the creeping crud."

"I want to find out who gave me this. Get some blood-soaked retribution like out of a Tarantino." His bluebooks and red marker remained untouched on the floral-patterned comforter, a gift from one of Cullen's upcountry yokel aunts. Randi found the design gauche and unappealing, but for him it held sentimental value. "Speaking of crud: staring down a dozen terrible papers makes me want to puke. I feel like I'm showing these films and lecturing to the fucking wall."

"What's wrong this term?"

He didn't know. "Are they taking notes? Are they listening?"

"This is the real media generation coming in now. You'd think they'd be more engaged."

"Not one of them's mentioned Godard's assertion that his films were just like any others—beginning, middle, end." Cullen kept a small framed portrait of the French auteur on his desk the way some people displayed pictures of their kids. "Basic stuff."

"'Just not necessarily in that order,'" by virtue of hearing him recite it a thousand times.

"A key tenet of the artistic philosophy."

"I get it."

"But again, taking notes in class isn't rocket surgery," a familiar Cullenism. "Feckless little nitwits."

"My father always said a classroom full of failures includes the one behind the lectern."

"So now I'm not living up to your deceased father's expectations either? He was a tough one."

Smiling. "We should form a club."

He mocked himself in a stentorian voice: "Professor Margrave, how you got to teach a class in anything is beyond me."

They shared a warm chuckle.

Cullen, holding her eyes.

Her husband.

She hugged him; held on tight. It felt right and true.

———

The ridge lay quiet.

No dogs howling.

No Esau in his truck.

No nothing.

A relief.

Reclined on the bed beside her groggy husband, Randi skimmed a volume she checked out of the downtown library after meeting Cyn for lunch.

Cullen, squinting at the colorful cover of the large paperback book. "*Shadowing and Surveillance Techniques?*"

"Check this out: I've come up with a private eye character."

"Crime fiction?"

She noted how a decade of news-gathering had given her plenty of material. "Besides, we want to sell some books, right?"

His delight, palpable. "My wife is writing a freaking thriller."

On campus Cullen's rep came cemented as the erudite, snobbishly discerning cineaste, but behind closed doors his private shame included a fondness for 70s grindhouse and drive-in fodder like *Race With the Devil*, low budget, cheesy action films, science fiction epics, Japanese stunt men in rubbery monster suits. As for reading, while his bedside table groaned under the weight of lofty academic texts it also held innumerable pulpy mysteries, entertainments through which he'd page on most nights before drifting into slumber.

"Dying to hear the logline. Lay it on me."

"We're in pre-search, here. Character-building. World-building. I don't have a plot yet."

"What kind of tone are you going for? Campy, or straight noir, or—?"

"Slow down, cowboy." She found herself running short on fibs. "I'll bang out a synopsis soon. Let me educate myself first, and my character. Then we'll talk story."

"What's the private eye's name?"

Randi, feeling impish. "Kat Furlick, Dog Detective."

Cullen's delight dimmed. "Amusing, semi-colon, but I think Jim Carrey might have milked that one." His face hardened. "Now listen: no more of this OCD dog foolishness."

"Isn't being OCD considered a mental disorder?"

"I mean it in a more casual usage."

"It's not crazy to want to make the world a better place."

"Pardon?"

"If I'm worried about the well-being of an animal, how is that compulsive?"

"It's the finger in the dyke problem—it's a fool's quest trying to change cultural tropes and behaviors endemic to this region. Look at that Confederate flag flying atop the State House in Columbia."

"We must be the change we wish to see," an assertion self-assured. "I've heard you say those very words."

"I'm concerned about you pissing off some rednecks we don't even know."

"I suspect I know them well enough." Struggling to keep her voice steady. "All that's under control."

"Please tell me you're not sneaking around again."

"Forget the dogs. It's none of my business—right?"

"Of *our* business."

Randi, chilled as though she'd picked up his flu bug. "I'm being careful."

"Now that we've fixed some problems, I don't want a crop of fresh, shiny new ones. That's all."

She understood. Said so.

"A private eye mystery," lightening his tone. "Can't wait to read it one day."

She risked eye contact and found Cullen beaming at her, hopeful and alight with a twinkle like out of the past. She didn't believe he could fake a look like that—despite his passion for the arts, Cullen, far from accomplished enough an actor to pull off such a performance.

In retrospect, the entire time he'd been cheating Randi had sensed a difference in him. Not so much a coldness as a subtle change in demeanor, a dimming of the love-light in his eyes: His affection for her subsumed by carnality, by submission to the ministrations of the lower brain.

The worst part, of course, had been the deception, the betrayal of both her as well as their son. Cullen was neither the first man to behave this way nor the last—the understatement of all time—but as he'd said in repentance even before the tragedy of Denny: look who he ended up choosing. He'd come home to his wife and family, recanted his profligate indulgences, reproved himself, and most of all, stayed.

A shocking fullness swelled inside: Before this moment, Randi realized she'd never forgiven Cullen. Had blamed him for Denny. Had made her husband's marital transgression the instrument and focus of all their destruction, when it truth she would have made such a decision—putting him on that goddamned plane—regardless of Cullen having had an affair with his grad assistant. They'd talked about sending Denny to her mother's one summer. Having a getaway just for them.

She allowed herself to remember.

Exhorted herself to forgive.

And glowed inside.

It wasn't anyone's fault. A bad draw of the cards—for us, sure. For Denny most of all.

Randi felt a warmth in the air of the bedroom going beyond the simmering fireplace: she could see the set of his jaw and droop of his eyes. He'd given her the look not long after they'd met as teacher and student; seeing this face again these many years later, and after all they'd been through, flooded her with desire and anticipation of a comfort available only through the deepest of true intimacy.

Cullen—you do love me, don't you? I think that you do. She didn't want to say it aloud. She wanted her partner to sense the truth of it.

To feel.

To know.

"I'm so glad this move seems good for you—good for us. Screw the commute, the whole pied-à-terre bullshit. After you write this book, we'll collaborate on the screenplay version. Together, out here in the woods. Team Margrave."

Randi flung the covers back, exposed a pale leg. Skinny, all right. But not bad.

She tickled his shin with her toes. "How's the soap rash? All better?"

He peeled off his gray *SEU Redtails RULE!* T-shirt. His voice came breathy. "Could always be better still."

Snuggling, but skipping the deep kissing due to the cold germs. Instead, she traced her fingers all around—face, neck, chest. The burgeoning peak at the fly of his boxers.

They got into it.

Exploring angles and opportunities with aplomb, as in the days Randi had feared might have passed for good, her body thrummed and burned. Her responses to his touch came vocal and insistent, at times downright febrile. She bucked up against him, primal and urgent. Rolled him over, ground with pleasure until she roared with release, a flood.

Cullen slipped in behind her. Blazing and drenched, he stroked now with his own fervidity until at last erupting with an intensity like she hadn't felt in ages.

The sheets a wreck, a glass of water knocked over, Randi's book and Cullen's schoolwork scattered across the floor, they lolled like two bundles of raw, satiated nerve endings. Randi, sighing. "Now that's more like it."

Cullen groaned and hummed. "Were you fantasizing that you were Kat Furlick trying to force information out of me?"

"Were *you?*"

Nodding. "Yeah. A little bit, there."

Randi moved to nuzzle and draw close, but he rolled away to go turn down the fireplace—indeed, it now felt a thousand degrees in the bedroom.

"Gonna grab some fresh sheets and a glass of water."

That was Cullen—not much of a snuggle-bunny. Liked to rinse off and get back to whatever he'd been reading. The sex had always been good. But afterwards?

It was what it was.

Soon Randi drifted into a dreamless sleep lasting until dawn, a day that started out as rested and ready as she'd felt in years—perhaps ever. Absent the dogs down the ridge, life felt as though it had begun anew in the Margrave household. At last.

37

TUESDAY.

Once she got a sniffling, grumpy Cullen bundled off for his campus commute, Randi assembled her various investigatory materiel on the dining room table, the catch-all for mail and paperwork rather than the place where they broke bread together. As the synth and shimmering guitars of 'Just Like Heaven' filled the house, she tried out a couple of camera lenses, especially the telephoto, aiming it out of the great room windows. She focused on individual leaves, the mailbox, the skinny limbs of the sugar maple, other details.

Running the same exercise with the camcorder, she inserted a tape tiny and fragile compared to the bulky Betacam SP cassettes they used in the WKNO minicams. After Randi pressed down on the wafer-thin transport housing with a trembling fingertip, the mechanism whirred as the tape clicked into place.

The sound tried its best to remind her of Denny. All those videos boxed up and collecting dust.

Pushing it all away.

Focusing on the mission.

What else did she need? Her surveillance book recommended changes in hairstyle and/or color and wardrobe for tailing subjects who might recognize the snoop at work. The same held true for vehicles, which she would address through a rental agency; as for her appearance, she'd get a couple of wigs from the little shop in Tillman Falls. Wear nondescript, neutral color clothing. Fade into the background.

No big whoop.

As the song ended, all plans forgotten: In the silence before 'Lullaby' began, Randi heard a dog yelping, but this time close:

Cleo wasn't howling from down the ridge—this had come from right outside.

Randi rushed over to the kitchen window. Nothing in the backyard, or around the toolshed. As the next song kicked in, she stabbed at the countertop stereo and silence returned.

Yip.

And again.

Close.

She flung herself down the spiral stairs to the lower level, racing through Cullen's home theatre. One of the first acts he'd performed in the service of making the house his own space had been to replace the vertical blinds in the rec room with heavy, theatre-style drapes for blocking out the light from the patio, so that one could enjoy a hypnotic Herzog or Ozu indulgence at any time of day without the annoyance of light leakage.

She yanked open the heavy curtains. As daylight flooded in, Randi sprang back in surprise—

On the other side of the sliding glass door stood Julius Macon, caught in the act of peering against the glare into the darkened room; he jumped as well. Cleo yipped again, the dog sitting at its master's heel and wagging with canine pleasure.

Julius's startled face melted into a nervous smile. He flopped an uncertain hand in salutation. Muffled through the glass: "We come to visit."

Randi hesitated. Couldn't hide her concern.

Julius's smile withered. "Now we done gone and scared you."

Sliding open the door. "You took years off my life, but it's all right."

"We're sorry."

She squatted down. Cleo, a downy-white dog butt wiggling with enthusiasm, sprang over and licked her face.

"Well-well. Look who's here." Randi asked to what she owed the pleasure of such a surprise visit.

Julius, sheepish. "We was lonesome down there. Nothing to do right now but fish, or walk around or look at TV. Getting colder. Esau don't come round as much in the winter."

Good to know.

"What do you do when you're busy?" Randi, hopeful for candor, wished she had snagged her digital voice recorder, one like novelist Cort Beauchamp had advised carrying for purposes of note-taking.

"When we ain't working dogs? Ain't nothing for us to do."

"Sounds boring."

"I reckon it is."

Now what? Randi, on guard, not yet willing to trust Julius. Perhaps Esau had found out the truth. Had sent his brother to make some kind of trouble.

Perhaps Esau himself lurked nearby.

Glancing around, however, she saw nothing out of the ordinary. Only the woods, the birds, the creek gurgling.

The way Julius discussed 'working' the dogs indicated a high degree of comfort with her. In any case, she doubted he possessed the mental capacity for being put up to much other than manual labor.

Like, say, dumping dog shit on her driveway.

She searched his eyes. A kindness, lurking within. Innocence. She knew the look. Julius might have been in his late thirties, but had the bearing and demeanor of a prepubescent child.

Smart enough to reference their previous visit's contentious elements, he said, "And I wanted to tell you? How I didn't say nothing to Esau about our secret?"

"You didn't, I hope."

"No sir, not me." Nodding with vigor. "I kept it real good."

"I think that's best."

"I was laughing to myself one time thinking about it? And he asked what I was laughing about? But I didn't tell, which made me laugh harder for a while. Till he hit me with his hat and said to put a sock in it. I still don't know what he means by that. I wouldn't put no sock in my mouth if you paid me."

That brought up an interesting point: "Julius—do you get paid anything? Do you have your own money?"

He busted a gut. "Shoot, no. I get took care of by Esau. He brings me everything I need."

"Speaking of him, what about the other night?"

"When?"

"Saturday. On the road."

"Lord—he was cussing you up, down, and sideways. But I just set there all quiet, and pretended like I ain't seen you since he made you jump into the river. It wasn't till later that I got the sillies about it."

"I was just going to the grocery store. Like I told him."

Julius nodded, satisfied. "See? I knowed you wasn't lying. I says to him, I says, wellsir, maybe that's all she's doing. Oh, but Esau." Julius, shaking his head in pity. "'Don't nobody go to no IGA on Saturday night,' he kept saying. But I said, if their stomachs was hungry, they would."

"That's exactly right, honey."

"Later on, old Harlem Waugh told us you had come down Mr. Rembert's road? But Esau said for Harlem not to worry none about you? That you were our neighbor lady? And that we would take care of you?"

"That doesn't sound good."

"It ain't like that. Esau wasn't mad then."

"What was he, if he wasn't mad?"

Julius grinned. "That's when he started laughing, too. I was glad. That I liked you. And how nice you was. Not that I had talked to you again, or nothing."

Randi's stomach plummeted. So much for the secret.

But more to the point: Esau planned to 'take care' of her. Maybe everyone had been right, the time ripe to back off a bit.

The dog's sweet and scarred face regarded her with expectation. "I wonder if I might not have a treat for Miss Cleo here."

Julius's stomach growled. Embarrassed by his noisy, unhappy belly, he tugged on the tail of his 3X fleece work shirt, its buttons straining against flesh.

"Would you like a snack as well, young man?"

Meek, he nodded. "Hate to bother you? But—yes, please."

"It's no bother." But limits remained. "Wait outside here."

A pinched face. He gazed over her shoulder into the comfortable house.

An excuse: "Oh, it's not you. My husband's allergic to dog hair."

"What's 'allergic'?"

"Dog hair makes him itch and sneeze. Yuck."

Julius, perplexed. "I ain't never heard of nothing like that."

"I wish I hadn't."

Another stricken wave of disappointment. "I reckon I best wait out here."

Pausing at the sliding door. "Why did you really come to see me?"

His innocent smile returned. "Cause when I woke up it was cold? But still so pretty out? That's why we come walking in the sunshine." He scratched Cleo's missing ear. The dog ground its head against his hand with affection. "We thought you was nice, Missus—Missus—I can't remember."

"Randi. Mrs. Randi."

Excited: "I had me a cousin named Randy. He was a boy-cousin, though."

She found herself touched by Julius's apparent lack of guile, but forced herself to remember: Here stood the trainer who taught the dogs to fight and kill. "Turkey sandwich?"

Julius leaned against the hot tub cover. "With yellow mustard, please?"

"Mustard *and* cheese. Does Cleo like cheese?"

He frowned. "Esau says not to give none of the dogs my people food. Says it makes them fat and slow."

"You know what?"

"What?"

"Fuck Esau, and what he thinks."

An impish smile of complicity. "Lord have mercy, but that's a bad word."

"And what does Cleo think about some people food?"

"*Yip.*"

Randi bent down, scratching the dog where it used to have an ear. "That's what I thought. Hang tight."

38

JULIUS, FULL OF TURKEY SANDWICHES, SAT SLEEPY-EYED IN A CAMP chair from the garage. Cleo, her belly full of cheddar cheese chunks and cold cuts, also reclined in satisfaction on the patio bricks. Randi had broken through to her neighbor, now, on the most elemental of levels—to feed an animal is to befriend it.

Sitting on the sharp edge of the decorative brick ledge and pulling her sweater tight, she turned the conversation toward the particular field of expertise in which Julius excelled, but not before thumbing the micro-recorder concealed in a pocket. "So, now, tell me about the dogs—the pit bulls."

"What you wanna know?"

"If I wanted to pick one of the dogs that you train for sport, how would I know which one was best?"

Julius squinted, ground his gears. "There's three kinds of dogs? And you don't know what they are until they get growed up and trained some?"

"Tell me the different kinds."

"Well, there's neck dogs. There's leg dogs. And then there's dogs that are real scrappers. That just won't let go? Them's the kings. You can't hardly beat one like that."

"Could Cleo be taught to be a leg or a neck dog?"

Disturbed, a shadow fell across Julius's face. "Cleo don't get taught none of that."

Randi explained how she didn't mean Cleo herself, but rather, any particular dog.

Julius continued as though reciting. "A neck dog, he's gonna snap and dance around and run away. But he's pretending. Pretending until he's got that one good chance to get at the other dog's throat?"

"Go on."

"A leg dog, now, he attacks right straight out. That fella runs in, grabs himself a leg and starts to roll over like a big old alligator flopping around in the river."

"And then—?"

"Once the other dog's leg is broke, the fight's done."

Randi, appalled, kept her fake smile frozen. "Goodness gracious."

"I know—the dog that won't let go, it don't matter if it's the neck or the leg or whatnot, he's what you want. Dog like that, you can sling him around, bite him, kick him, roll over on him, but he won't never let go. Not until the other one quits."

"Dies, you mean."

"Usually you got to put one of them down. That ain't no fun."

"So that's what happens to the loser. At the end."

"Not always. It depends."

"On what?"

"On how bad he's the loser."

"Meaning what?"

Julius regarded his pet, stroked her head. "Whether he's worth fixing."

"Who does the killing?"

Downhearted. "Mostly Esau."

Of course the cruel bastard took joy in that part.

She had to keep the interview on course. "And how do people wager?"

"Do what, now?"

"How do they make bets to see who'll win?"

Julius, troubled, shook his enormous pink head. "Dang if I know."

"Why don't you know?"

Embarrassed, he shrugged and grimaced.

"Esau doesn't let you deal with money at all, does he."

"Done told you, that's two-numbers stuff." Getting back into his comfort zone. "But as for the dogs, some folks think that a neck dog can always beat a leg dog. Others think a leg dog can beat a dog that won't let go. It ain't just seeing which one is the meanest or the strongest, though that's pretty important stuff, there."

"What's more important than strength?"

The huge, pitiful man grew faraway. "Sometimes you get one that's all the things at once. Them's the smart dogs."

"How smart are they?"

"Durn near people smart."

"How do you mean?"

"Them dogs know to watch for what-all the other dog's trying to do, and from that, they figure out how to beat them?"

Randi, horrified—what if one of these beasts got loose?

"That's like King Kong—he's the best and smartest we ever had. We done bred him a hundred times, I bet. But he's still the king."

"He must be a—champion."

Not only pride, but affection: "Besides Cleo? He's my bestest buddy."

Randi, touched by the devotion on display toward the animals, but confused as to how this gentle spirit could bring himself to train them to slaughter one another.

Still, she had begun to believe this man could be redeemed. Could be set free from this depraved lifestyle. With this in mind, she not only planned to shut down the pit bull factory, but also rescue Julius from a life he didn't fully understand. Arrange remedial adult education. Find a way out of the woods for him as well as the dogs. No one had ever cared enough about this human to help him become more than he was. Her revulsion with the Macon family now felt complete.

And while wicked Esau to blame, sure, thoughts turned to Mama Macon: What monster sired this dysfunctional family? Another brand of curiosity now burned.

———

Randi decided to use some of her newfound clout by attempting what she hoped would continue to appear as innocuous rather than interrogation. "Julius, listen to me."

"Yessum?"

"What do you think about what you people—I mean, *y'all*—are doing down in the holler?" Randi tried to speak more like Julius than her flat California patois. "With the dogs down yonder, and all."

He belched. "Lord, but them was some good sandwiches. I thought that bread was funky at first? But dang if that didn't leave a good taste."

Randi had served him wheatberry slices, exotic to one raised on peanut butter smeared on squares of ordinary mass-market white bread.

Pressing the issue. "All those dogs—if you didn't train them to—you know." Choosing her words with cautious precision. "Be mean to one another?"

"Yessum?"

"Mightn't they all turn out sweet like your Cleo?"

"I ain't never thought none about it."

"Why not?"

"We do what we do with the dogs. S'all I know."

"Isn't that right, Cleo? Aren't doggies supposed to be sweet? And loved?"

"Esau says—well." Recalling her lack of enthusiasm about his brother's opinions. "It don't matter what he says."

"Tell me."

"That the Bible teaches how the animals was put here for us to use? Like cows and pigs to eat? And birds to fly, and fish to swim and beavers to build dams and cats to chase mice." He cleared his throat. "And our dogs?"

"Yes?"

Eyes shining, the truth self-evident: "Our dogs was put here to fight."

Her guts twisted. "But don't you remember how much it hurt Cleo to fight?"

"She wa'n't supposed to fight."

"I know this."

A flash of anger tightened Julius's soft features, a darkness Randi found frightening. "Esau was wrong to do what he done. He knew I didn't want him to use her for no bait dog. I had done told him not to." Mad enough to bite nails. Breathless, like a child trying to hold back tears. "*But he done it anyway.*"

Encouraged by the rage she'd glimpsed, she realized this long-simmering disagreement between the brothers could be used to her advantage.

But she also found herself in competition with a man throwing holy words around in defense of his immorality and hypocrisy, and knew that extremists believing God at their side could be the most dangerous of all.

She wished she had her father close at hand. Durant Montreat would have picked Esau's pious bones clean. Certainly the late anthropologist held the utmost respect—at times awe—for the societal constructs that had allowed fervent religious belief to flourish over such a comparatively long period on the timeline of modern, recorded history. At the same time, though, Prof. Montreat's patience had been gossamer-thin when faced with literalists who worshipped and cultivated their faith in what he could never accept beyond his well-considered understanding of the difference between mythology and the supposedly inerrant, divine word of God so many followed.

"Indeed, what humanity calls 'God' might be in a sense 'real'," Randi's father once said, "but there's bugger-all solid evidence that He or She's yet to author any actual books. Or certainly that such a creature would take any notice of what we're are up to, crawling ant-like on our sphere as we do, with a lifespan in cosmic 'time' that begins and ends in a flash-frame—the human lifespan is but a blip of energy, a droplet of water evaporated by the sun up into the boundless ether. Such a God must surely have bigger fish to fry than to micromanage our base and grubby behaviors—or otherwise be enriched or gratified by the same.

"But if there were once a prime mover, I suspect that the essence of whatever it was has moved on to other projects, leaving us to our own ruinously mortal devices. Or else in the gnostic sense, left to be the play-things of malevolent spirit-bodies existing in complete envy of our ability to enjoy this mostly delightful material experience."

She had paraphrased the hippie philosopher Alan Watts: "Maybe we're all the eyes of the universe—of God—cracking open to have a look at itself."

Her father, having none of it. "Humanity, a manifestation of the over-mind? New Age rubbish."

"But dad—how do we know?"

He'd always begged off by telling her she wasn't ready for a discussion of matters epistemological. By the time she might have been—now, let's say—her father had passed away.

Randi, growing up influenced by such a sober and skeptical vision of organized religion, hadn't spent any undue time wondering about the existence of God, except perhaps after Denny had walked away from her into the howling void of nothing. After the tragedy she'd held many 'conversations' with her current version of God—hateful, one-sided excoriations projected up toward the high popcorn ceiling of their old bedroom. These diatribes had neither made the deity any more tangible, nor in a modern-age miracle of divine intervention, managed to resurrect her son.

———

"Esau is free to believe that God approves of all this with the dogs." A jet from the airbase east of Columbia shrieked overhead, causing the dog to sit up and cant its head. "But that shouldn't have happened to Cleo."

"No." Julius, his shoulders tense. "But Esau knows a lot. He used to be a preacher."

Randi had almost forgotten that historical tidbit about her nemesis, a fact she'd had a hard time swallowing. "He doesn't seem like any preacher I ever heard of."

Again beaming with pride. "Esau used to preach on Sundays at Gethsemane, back when I was little. But don't neither one of us go to church no more."

"Why not?"

"Mama says I'm just too big and loud."

"I meant Esau—if he was a preacher, why doesn't he at least attend services?"

"I asked him that before. Says he knows enough about what God wants without having nobody else tell him."

Oh boy, Randi thought.

Her next question, a notion with which she held considerable facility. "Did Esau get mad at God about something?"

A look of amazement. "That's exactly the way Mama told it to me."

"Mad over what?"

"After he got tore up that one time."

"Tore up—?"

"By a bad dog."

"A bad one? How so?"

"One that wa'n't trained right. One trained to go after people instead of other dogs." He'd gone pale, his voice hushed as though describing a type of fairytale monster. "Granddaddy used to train dogs for that, too. Back when people wanted white dogs."

"White dogs? I don't——" The implication hit home. "Oh, my god."

"But we don't do that, not no more. No ma'am."

She shuddered. "Esau was hurt pretty bad, I guess."

"He durn near like to got his guts tore out. Sure as I'm sitting here. I was little."

And yet he still breeds these animals. "A lucky man."

Julius, faraway. "Granddaddy, he had to put the dog down."

"Maybe God was trying to tell Esau something. About the dogs."

His mouth frozen into an O. His wheels, turning. "That don't sound right."

"What if, though?"

Mulling it over. "Naw, I don't think so."

"You ever wanted to do something else besides raise dogs down in the woods?"

"Lord, no. That's the best place for me."

"Why do you feel that way?"

"It's what Esau says."

"And what about your mother?"

"That's what she says, too, all right."

The humming HVAC unit kicked off. In the silence that followed, Cleo sat up. The one good ear, unclipped like those of the fighting dogs, stood aloft. She sniffed the air.

Cleo began to howl, her high lonesome call.

Randi perceived a low-frequency rumbling from around front—a truck engine.

"Julius—do you hear that?"

Puzzlement sliding to concern. "*It's Esau.*"

"He must be sitting out front. Did he follow you?"

He struggled out of the camp chair. Cleo yipped, sharp and staccato. "He can't catch us up here—he'll get super-mad."

"I'm sure. Here——"

She hustled them inside, slammed the sliding glass door.

Cleo barked. "Hush," Randi ordered.

Julius shushed the dog.

She pointed to the sofa. "Sit down. Do you understand me, young man?"

With Cleo huddled at his feet, Julius sank back into the plush, L-shaped couch. He stared at the gray rectangle of Cullen's projection screen television. "What in the sam hill is that?"

Randi, pausing on the spiral stairs. "That's the TV. Now stay quiet, please."

Hushed reverence. "*Can I turn it on?*"

She implored him to remain still and quiet. Forging the connection: "Wait here—I'm going to go have a talk with that brother of yours about all this sneaking around on us."

39

Esau sat in his rumbling truck, but not in her driveway—he'd stopped in front of the chain on the far side of the cul-de-sac. Why he drove an old beater like that, Randi hadn't a clue.

Fists clenched and arms swinging like a power-walker, she charged off the front porch right as he climbed from the cab of the rickety old pickup, a relic of the mid-70s still running she knew not how.

Glancing her way, he blabbered on his bulky, older model cell phone in the midst of what seemed a contentious argument, barely registering that he'd seen her. "J.W.—settle down. I don't know what to tell you, beau. God picks winners and losers."

He listened, grunting. Shaking his head.

"Son, you been in this game longer than anyone around, and ought by now to know how to lose with a little grace." Listening. "Don't tell me you ain't never seen odds-on favorites get their butts whipped like that."

Randi, waving to get his attention. "Mr. Macon—if you don't mind."

Holding up a digit to shush her—his middle finger. "Smart dog them fellas brung in—big and smart. Warned you them mo-fos was starting to crossbreed with mastiffs."

He stood staring into the trees, lips working in silence as he listened and waited for his chance to speak again. "Cajun Rules is Cajun Rules, and neither you nor me can't—no, no, now, that don't mean our deal with that old boy later this week is off or anything. Kong's still for sale. He's prime time, prime choice dog-meat. He's—"

Randi, waving her arms: "Hey, asshole—*stop talking*."

Esau fully faced her. Grinned. Blew a kiss.

"Well look, J. W. Rembert can stand to lose once in a while. I hear tell around The Dixiana that it's happened more than once."

Esau thumbed the disconnect button, cutting off a torrent of tinny invective.

"Howdy, neighbor," a greeting lacking in goodwill. "Hiking around much these days?"

"Hanging around my property, are you?"

"This here's a public road, little lady." He pulled a tin from his back pocket, shoved a chaw of tobacco into his mouth. "And besides—you done it first."

A lightbulb went off. "After everything that's happened, how do I know you're not spying on me?"

"Now here's my big idea," sounding like *idear*. "Ain't no reason we can't start over. That y'all can't fit in here on our little ridge."

"I don't plan on leaving anytime soon."

"Everybody living, and letting live. All that righteous and godly behavior about which we've been taught by our elders since time immemorial. Together."

She made a gag-me gesture. "Spare me."

"I'm game to try. What say you, citygirl?"

"So it's 'our' ridge now?"

"Legally? Yes."

"And that's okay with you?"

He snorted. "It all ought to be 'my' ridge, and a fair chunk of the rest of the county, but my great-granddaddy took and started piecemeal-ing it off—first to the railroad, and the power company, then when I was a boy my granddaddy and daddy sold parcels to them greedy pencilnecks building houses all up and down the interstate. Now, it made the family a whole pile of money—but money ain't permanent. It ain't even real, not when you think about it, least not since Nixon took us off the gold standard. But definitely not real like land." He sighed, weary. "Nothing was ever the same for us after the war."

It dawned on Randi that Esau meant the Civil War, not one in which he'd personally served. "I think I'm starting to understand all this better."

A reverie: "The Macon house—besides Hillsborough, of course—was the grandest in this part of the state. Had many folks living and working there," with a psychotic yet wistful air for the days when humans, treated like property, were subjugated to a life of bondage and toil. "A productive, industrious plantation it was. But burned to cinders."

"You're proud of this history?"

Ignoring her. "And the Macons continued to fare poorly afterwards. Much of what we had left was took from us—by our own people, or vagrants and drunkards, and before long came the carpetbaggers of Reconstruction. But not everything was lost. The part of the family what stayed here still had one thing: land."

"Somewhere Scarlet O'Hara must be getting a tingle down her leg."

"Don't mock and profane what you couldn't ever possibly understand."

"Some say nobody really 'owns' land."

"Want to see the deed? The originals lay in the county archives."

"That's the point. It's not like you'll always be around to possess it."

"That's right—not even if they bury you on it." Esau, thoughtful. "Question."

"What."

"Why ain't there any young'uns?"

"None of your damn business," her fists clenching anew. "And you?"

"I never married. What's your reason?"

"Like I said. None-ya."

He dropped the chain to his property. "Now there's a good *idear*. As in: You mind your business, and we'll mind ours. Like we always done."

Arms folded. "And what business are you in?"

He ignored her pointed query. "Lady, it's like this: I don't mind you living on what used to be my land, because you ain't the first nor last to do so. Long as you understand that, to come here and live you must bend to our ways and not us to your'n, no reason we can't go forward on what Navy boys call 'an even keel'."

I don't think I can do that. But she couldn't find the courage to say it aloud.

"And one thing I surely suggest you refrain from doing? Bothering other people on their private property—your little case of Saturday night fever." Snickering, amusing himself.

"I must've gotten lost. All these little dirt roads around."

"Lost—a good word for you." Back in the truck, he rolled down the passenger window. "Mind fixing that chain back up after me, ma'am? I would appreciate it." Throwing the pickup into gear, he rolled away without waiting for an answer.

Randi, putting the chain across the road. Perhaps a symbolic act—keeping the evil down the ridge blocked from consuming her.

Back inside, disgusted and unnerved, she didn't care who owned what land, or if the Macons had come over on the Mayflower and ridden mules all the way down to settle and tame the wilderness of pine barrens they now called South Carolina: In America a citizen had a right to have a voice in the community. And as a property owner, no way in hell Randi Margrave would allow one more dog to suffer for the sake of a depraved family tradition.

Downstairs, she found the patio door wide open. No sign of Julius or Cleo, only evidence left in the form of mud-tracks on the carpet: Julius's boots, and the pads of Cleo's white paws. At least he'd seemed afraid of his brother. She worried now, however, just how secret their relationship would stay.

40

Knowing Esau would be down the ridge for an indeterminate amount of time, Randi went back to packing her gear into a canvas gym bag for future surveillance and sat tight. Plugged the DVR into her laptop and pulled over the file with her recording of Julius describing his work. Listenable but muffled, especially when she would move and the fabric of her sweater distorted the microphone.

Damned near useless. Proved nothing.

To stay busy she began poking around on the internet for more surveillance tips; dogfighting info; legal statutes covering animal abuse. Tapping her fingers, squinting and waiting as web pages crept their way into a viewable state, she became consumed by a feeling of time being wasted, and learning nothing she didn't already know or suspect. The problem of dogfighting didn't seem to be getting enough attention. That much had become clear.

All Randi's goals remained theoretical. She needed evidence, better evidence. The shots from her visit to the dog compound had been developed at the CVS in Chilton, but turned out as blurry as the audio had been distorted.

Furthermore, she needed the whole story—photos of Macon going and coming from his nice house in the subdivision. Where Mama Macon lived with her favored son, Esau.

Logging off, Randi mulled advice she read in her private eye manual: a clandestine stakeout required a number of tools, none more important than a reasonable cover story. She needed an excuse for snooping around Esau's suburban neighborhood.

Going through the mail she considered renting the quintessential, nondescript unmarked white van, or perhaps a uniform of some kind. Envelopes, folders, flyers, mailers; a backlog after the change of address to Edgewater County kicked in.

But a large white envelope stood out:

CENSUS 2000
INFORMATIONAL PACKET

That was it—a census worker.

Back online she searched for an example of an old census form. Printed out copies, attached them to a clipboard to which she also affixed a couple of ballpoint pens. Next, she clipped out a colorful Census 2000 logo, taped it to the back of the clipboard.

Voilà: instant census-taker.

She dug out a thin Edgewater County phone directory which had been left on the front stoop one day. There he was—*Macon, Esau*. One would have thought a badass dog gangster like him would keep a lower profile.

And yet not a gangster—a citizen of the county, a man of the church. When you're good buddies with the sheriff, what does discretion matter? But really, after Ebby's vice-tour of a couple weeks ago, nothing about her adopted home surprised anymore.

She jotted down the address, searched on Mapquest—five miles away, closer to Tillman Falls—after which she planned a new mission: a meet and greet with Mama Macon.

41

THE WIG SHOP IN TILLMAN FALLS SMELLED MUSTY, THE LONGEVITY OF the business concern apparent in the fading paint on the walls, the wear and tear on the fixtures and displays, a general 1950s vibe. For whatever reason, Columbia's Main Street featured three similar businesses, all on the same block the downtown suits called Wig Alley. The shop here felt like a place out of time—like the rest of the community.

Randi's entrance, signified by a jangling strand of bells tied to the aluminum door handle. The aged proprietor, coiffed and made up as though going out for an evening on the town, struggled to a standing position from behind the counter.

"How may we help you today, my dear?" The woman's voice, cracking and ancient.

Randi explained how she desired two wigs, each distinct from the other.

The old woman, giving her the once-over through rheumy, wet eyes. "For fashion?"

Randi frowned. For what else one would one require a wig? "I'm a secret agent."

"We'd better find you a good secret agent wig, then."

The women shared a bloodless chuckle.

Randi, pointing: "Let's try that auburn-colored bob cut over there. And, how about blonde—long, and blonde?" Maybe she and Cullen would try some role-play after all. Worn under the right conditions, either wig might possess an erotic charge for him.

The proprietor's tone turned piteous. "Well, darling—you just go ahead and give yourself permission to look pretty. Don't you worry about a thing," patting Randi's bony hand. "It'll be fine."

Confused.

All became clear: As the woman gathered the wigs for her to try, Randi caught a glimpse of herself in a countertop mirror—wan, thin, pasty. The wig lady thought her a cancer victim preparing for hair loss.

"Here you go, angel," handing over the auburn bob. "You're going to look beautiful and whole again."

Randi slipped on the wig, tucking under her sandy, stringy hair. With wig and sunglasses, no longer the nosey neighbor lady, only an average woman of the county.

She tried the blonde number. Satisfied by the quality of pretense the wig lent her appearance, she said, "I'll take them both—and, I'm not sick. It's for a fashion show. I'm a consultant."

"A fashion show. I see." The woman's powdery countenance turned skeptical. Randi's rumpled house-clothes—jeans, and Cullen's *Dr. Strangelove* T-shirt—were hardly the mark of a fashion plate. "Bless your heart."

An elaborate procedure commenced: the boxing of the wigs, an entry into a handwritten ledger, the punching of heavy keys on the cash register, which looked as old as the proprietor, and Randi's "charge card" as the old lady called it, imprinted on an old-fashioned, multipart carbon transaction slip. The wig lady would weather Y2K just fine.

Concluding the transaction, she rested her wrinkled hand atop Randi's. "May the lord bless you and keep you."

"I appreciate that. You have no idea how much."

"You have challenges ahead. But one way or another, it's all going to be fine. Just you wait and see."

"I hope you're right."

42

PINE HAVEN, AN AGING SUBDIVISION ON THE OTHER SIDE OF TILLMAN Falls, sat convenient to the interstate offering passage to the inhabitants to their workaday lives in Columbia and elsewhere. The streets—clean and curving and Spielbergian in their suburban comfort and order, as Cullen might describe it—lay in weekday autumnal quiet. The kids all in school, moms and dads away at work, as with Cullen in jobs situated closer to the capital city.

Randi, concerned for the condition of the local economy—a retailing giant had opened a regional distribution center, and the Sugeree River Nuclear Station from which Ebby Nixon had retired employed hundreds, but with the curtain drawn on the golden age of Southern textile prosperity, local, good-paying jobs in this part of South Carolina had become scarce. You could tell by downtown Tillman Falls—it had no energy. Dirty, cracked sidewalks. Shuttered storefronts. More peeling paint on buildings than fresh. A stupid Confederate flag mural painted on the side of the local honkytonk.

To Randi, the Macons—landholders and legacies that they might have once been; gentry, as Esau had suggested, an idea filling her with scoffing disgust—didn't seem like bedroom community types. But here they resided.

And yet as she rolled by the house, did a U-turn and parked down the street on a curb, all made sense: Esau chose to live in a two-story brick behemoth because, she supposed, he could afford to do so: a legacy of the family real estate windfall, of their two-century reign as the inhuman elites of Edgewater County, and who knew what else.

The dogs, for one.

Slave owning; dogfighting.

Most impressive—not.

At the car rental down closer to the lake country above the city, Randi had selected a white LeSabre, a common sedan, but also because of its modest but concealing window tint. She snapped off a telephoto shot of Esau Macon's lovely home, landscaped with azaleas and decorative trees, not a leaf out of place but for a gardening hose waiting to be rewound onto its yellow, plastic spindle.

Randi's zeal for justice sizzled inside her. Made her want to punish the Macons, every one of them. Perhaps offer a lesson in healthy mothering to the one who'd begat these monstrous humans.

Yes: for all her guilt and self-blame, Randi *had* been a good mother to Denny—an accident, unforeseen, had taken him from her.

Nothing more.

Random. Blind, cruel chance.

What was someone to do? Never leave the house?

Never get on a plane to go and visit grandma?

Worry instead, she reminded herself, about the matter at hand: Esau, his old Ford in the driveway rusting before her eyes, sat inside right now. Who knew what perverse hobbies he pursued in his spare time.

In the days since her last visit with Julius, she'd had good success thus far in tailing Esau around without being caught. What she'd learned so far was a bit of a prosaic letdown, however—ordinary visits to the post office or the bank or the home improvement warehouse, which based on his purchases made it look as though he might be about to embark on some painting.

He'd also bought holiday decorations. She doubted they would be for Julius out in the woods, though. Randi wondered if they let him come stay in the house with them on Christmas Eve, or if such a kind gesture to their own blood seemed too humane a favor to grant.

———

Randi adjusted the auburn wig, shifted on the seat and took a sip of the water she'd been hitting with restraint so as to avoid bathroom breaks. She hadn't taken to the boredom of the stakeout, made to look so thrilling and intrigue-filled by Hollywood, but also hadn't expected Esau to stay put all day like this. She needed to document the man up to his nefarious misdeeds, not sit in the street accomplishing nothing.

Furthermore, she'd grown chilly. Thanksgiving week had arrived, and with it a Canadian arctic front. Randi should have layered. After all, one couldn't sit all day outside somebody's house or building with the car running:

A dead giveaway; cover, blown.

The stakeout, a failure.

Failure, not an option.

She rubbed her cotton gloves together. Wondered if she shouldn't call it a day. Make the trek back to the rental place, dump the car and start anew another time. What was all this sneaking about supposed to accomplish? She needed to catch Esau with dogs, but also in the context of the gambling—the fighting itself. That, she understood, would take more than sneaking around.

These people will kill you soon as look at you, Ebby had warned. And as Esau pointed out, her aborted attempt at crashing the hog-dawg had been an abject and foolhardy failure.

She glanced down at her camera, at the newspaper she'd brought along in strict violation of surveillance protocol—no reading to distract from the job at hand. All the news did was remind her about Y2K anyway, and other societal ills destined to cause pain and suffering and horror well into the new millennium.

It occurred to her that she'd been a complete nitwit about this dogfighting crap, a child with a hyperactive imagination and no sense of consequences. Following people around who were mean enough to fight dogs to the death, all the while laughing and wagering money as though the brutality no more consequential than a mere card game.

She regarded the Macon house, a suburban manse of comfort and taste. Ordinary and serene, but a domicile underwritten with blood money, harboring a barbarous secret. Risk or not, she couldn't walk away. Not now.

Not after seeing Cleo's sweet face.

———

Cold and distracted, Randi found herself jolted into full attention: Esau, in a heavy jacket and knit cap over his unruly hair, trotted out of the house and jumped into his truck. In her reverie, the asshole had gotten the drop on her.

She sat ready with her hand on the keys, forcing herself to wait before starting the LeSabre.

Esau cranked his truck, but instead of backing out he went back inside, slapping and rubbing his hands together.

Randi, getting that he was only warming up the vehicle. Monster or not, he felt discomfort like any normal person, she supposed.

But unlike her confusion over Julius, she'd begun to feel no empathy for, or kinship with, the human trash named Esau Macon. For all she cared, he could freeze to death.

Blessed now with foreknowledge, Randi pulled away from the curb. Only one possible exit existed from this point in the subdivision, and a cul-de-sac sat a few streets over into which she could relocate to wait for Esau to pass. That way he wouldn't see her pulling out right at the same time, only an ordinary sedan parked in another part of the neighborhood.

Once repositioned on the block of older, ranch-style homes—the first phase of the subdivision, dating back to the mid-1970s—she buzzed with anticipation.

And waited.

And waited; but at least in warmth by keeping the LeSabre running.

Finally the pickup drove past, and this time Esau had a companion, a large shape in the passenger seat Randi thought at first was Julius.

A woman, elderly.

It had to be the matriarch.

Randi's excitement, tempered: to what benefit could surveilling Esau carting his mother around possibly gain the intrepid investigator?

Her mind open, she pondered a scenario: that the old woman was the power behind the throne, a backwoods Ma Barker with her finger on the pulse of Edgewater County vice-peddling. Randi wouldn't put it past her. Not having raised a son like Esau.

———

She followed the Macons through the typical highway interchange of Chilton—gas stations, a strip-mall with the IGA and other small shops, two car dealerships, a smattering of fast food, and as it happened, also a plaza of medical offices, an outreach facility of the county hospital. This little 'township' possessed none of the Southern charm of Tillman Falls or Parsons Hollow. Here lay only homogenous, generic America.

This could be anywhere; this could be everywhere.

Randi pulled into a burger joint and rolled around back, positioning the LeSabre to observe Esau's truck across the way in the parking lot of the doctor's office.

Watching through her birding binoculars, she saw as he helped his mother out of the truck. His movements and body language bespoke patience and deference.

Mama Macon, indeed a large woman, one from whom Julius had inherited the genes, leaned on a thick-handled cane and seemed to berate Esau, who gestured for her to enter the building. Wearing a floral-print, blowzy housedress, slippers on her feet, and a long overcoat, she moved on bloated ankles at a shuffling pace. Aging and debilitated, here was a woman well past the point of bowing to feminine vanity, a condition to which Randi, in the torpor of her grieving period, could relate.

Mrs. Macon seemed to calm down. They went inside through doors that opened and closed behind them with automated efficiency.

Randi sat in the parking lot of the Wendy's for over an hour, waiting, she suspected, with as little patience as the people inside the doctor's office. She risked an indulgence by power-walking inside for a pee break, a sack of fries and a soda, not so much for hunger as to explain her continued presence.

She ate a few limp, undercooked fries, which tasted like a mouthful of salty chemicals. Crumpled the bag and tossed it onto the floorboard.

Waited.

Finally the sensor-doors in the medical building slid open and Esau appeared, this time pushing his mother out to the truck in a wheelchair. After he opened the door and helped her to her feet they paused. The son and mother exchanged words; Randi could see that Mama Macon was sobbing. Esau hugged her, patting her enormous shoulder.

After helping her into the truck, Esau paused at the tailgate. He leaned on the frame, head down, a hand on his hip. And if Randi hadn't known better, she'd have sworn Esau brushed an errant tear from the corner of one of his bug-eyes.

Ditching any further pursuit of the Macons back to their home, she returned the car to the rental agency. Her sleuthing today had done nothing but reveal how Esau Macon, for all his vices, suffered the same real-world problems as anyone else: aging parents, a special needs sibling, Esau's own old debilitating injuries, and the task of putting up the Christmas tree for his infirm mother, who for all Randi knew may have been told this holiday season would be her last. Driving back to the hilltop house in her own car, the intrepid dog detective felt more confused than ever about how to proceed.

43

Thanksgiving.

She sat in silence the whole drive back from Athens, where they had enjoyed her mother's warm, lively all-vegan Thanksgiving spread. Randi had talked Cullen out of the in-law visit after all.

He hadn't seemed to mind. Cullen, not only a tenure-track full professor but the first from his upstate family to attend college, had little in common with his blood relatives, neither politically nor intellectually. "Not that I don't love them, bless their hearts," as he often said. "We'll catch up over Christmas."

After the Margraves crossed over the Savannah River into South Carolina, he asked how his wife had been feeling.

"Lousy."

"You and Aylene have words?"

Randi said, not-exactly. "But her continued disapprobation of me rankles, honeybunny. Her notion that I'm wallowing."

"You told her about the writing?"

Shaking her head, a curt gesture. "A hobby. A passionless lark."

"How unfair."

Randi, mocking her mother's upper-caste, New England accent. "*Don't you realize how formidable the task in forging a meaningful career writing fiction, for pity's sake? Marandi, you have neither the tenacity nor the insights necessary to make it work.* And blah-blah."

Cullen chuckled. "But—is there any writing?"

"What the hell's that supposed to mean?"

"Nothing quite so aggressive."

"Of course there's writing."

"Would just love to see—"

"As we bargained, I'll let you read when it's ready."

Less than impressed. "Sure, sure."

He switched on the radio, scanning. Finding nothing but tinny country music and radio preachers, he settled on a feel-good NPR Thanksgiving report about the apocalyptic amount of edible food introduced into the waste stream every day in the United States.

Next came one of myriad, inescapable features about Y2K prep, now hurtling into critical phase for companies and governments both large and small, a boon for certain corners of a tech sector already enjoying massive stock valuations and profits, but worrisome for everyone else—would nuclear power plants go down? Would planes fall from the sky? The year 2000, the announcer intoned, would be a New Year's like no other in human history.

Right: let the end come. Then she'd get to be with Denny again.

Maybe the Esau Macons of the world were right—that God watched after us. Made a place for us in which to dwell, but only after our earthly works had been achieved, whole and complete.

And for Randi, that meant buttoning up her investigation. And saving those dogs, who cried out for her help both in dreams and by day. Her actions represented concrete endeavor they'd all be able to recognize as worthy—her mother, Cullen, Cyn-Anne, and maybe even Prof. Montreat, her father dwelling somewhere in the great beyond. Randi would show them all.

44

On Sunday morning—she'd found that Esau almost never came to the ridge on Sundays—Randi set out with pluming breath on a brisk morning hike, but with a difference: this time, she strolled down along the switchbacks of the dirt road like she owned the joint. Forget the ghillie suit. Now to begin the real task of evidence-gathering. This foolishness would be over in a matter of days.

After she called for him from the compound gate, Julius emerged from the blockhouse through a doorway near the outdoor dog runs. Bouncing on the balls of his feet with childish anticipation, he smiled and yelled to her: "You hiking today?"

"Took a notion."

"Well come on in, if you want."

In the compound she handed him two sandwiches in wax paper and a Zip-lock of cheese-cubes for Cleo. "How's our girl today?"

"Inside having her nappy time. You want to sit with us for a spell?"

"No, I don't want to wake her."

Disappointed. "Oh-kay, Miss Randi."

"You go on in and eat, and feed Miss Cleo. I'm going to go sit by the river—is that okay?"

"Can I come out there with you after I eat?"

"Only after you finish all your sandwiches, and Cleo her snacks. And then clean up." Randi felt more confident. "Do you understand me, Julius?"

"Yessum."

Timid, half-fearful of her authority—perfect.

"Very well. Now, go inside and shut the door so you both can enjoy your lunch."

"Yessum."

He disappeared into his hovel, the door shutting behind him with a thump.

Randi leapt into action, yanking out the camcorder and sweeping its lens all around the compound. She zoomed in on various details like the pole in the yard, the stained dirt, the electrical cord, which had been taken down from the tree and rolled into a neat pile, all the while whisper-narrating the images.

Cutting her eyes around and listening out for truck engines, she trotted over to the blockhouse and crept inside. The smell alone had been enough to tell her that this was a place of death—of suffering.

A worn, old treadmill. More hooks. Two whelping boxes where puppies would be born. Shelves of dog food and what appeared to be supplements and nutritional items.

At her appearance inside, the three other dogs went ape.

Heart pounding, she swept the camera around. Whispering: *"This is where they breed the dogs. And then train them to kill one another—sometimes even unwanted puppies."*

Double-time, she fumbled and stuffed her camera inside her bag, and cursed the dogs for being noisy. Sure Julius would now catch her, she steeled herself for his appearance. Tried to think of a reason for snooping around in there.

Instead Randi heard Julius's whistle, long and persistent, which he held until the dogs quieted. His voice, muffled: *"Y'all hush and let us eat our lunch."*

The dogs, now silent and still.

Randi waited until hearing the door of Julius's house again slam shut. As though goosed, she exited and made for the river.

Hurrying along toward the riverfront trail, she tried to erase the images in her mind—the bank of small cages against the wall.

The dark stains on the floor.

The stainless steel morgue-table.

And most of all, the scarred faces of Julius's dogs staring at her, snarling, and capable, she suspected, of tearing Randi Margrave to pieces.

With what she now had to show the world, though, they'd never get the chance.

45

As the Sunday sun fell glinting and glimmering on the rushing water, a few minutes went by before Cleo and Julius joined Randi at the peaceful fishing spot.

From his demeanor, she knew he didn't suspect her. Had only thanked her for the delicious sandwiches with the special bread and spicy mustard. Belched. Smiled.

The wind off the water cut right through her jacket, but felt cleansing rather than uncomfortable. Julius squatted on the ground while Randi perched on the old fishing cooler, hands clasped between her knees.

"A beautiful afternoon, isn't it?"

"Long as this wind don't give me a sinus infection."

"It's good to sit, and be quiet. Just be present."

"Well-sir." He wrinkled his nose. "Reckon it is."

Randi bade Julius to look at her, but his eyes wouldn't hold hers. Taking a chance, she dug deeper: "Are you happy living out here?"

Julius shrugged and frowned, which Randi read as: *You mean there's another choice?*

She glanced at faithful Cleo, who watched with interest as a gray squirrel foraged among the fronds of rustling riverside ferns.

"What about her?"

Suspicious. "What about Cleo?"

"Is she happy, too?"

"I make sure she is."

Randi assured him she had no doubt. "But do you get everything you need?"

His passive face tightened. "I dunno what you mean."

"That's all I needed to hear."

Julius now surprised her: Bursting into tears, rocking back and forth and weeping *huh-huh-huh*.

She asked what was wrong. He mewled and mumbled nonsense.

At first she thought this outburst was his way of telling her how envious he felt about the rest of his family—of their life in the 'big house,' as he called it. But Randi was wrong:

"King Kong—he's going away." He pounded his meaty thigh. "For *good*."

"To a customer?"

Wiping his pink, tear-streaked face. "When he was little? I used to hold him and rock him to sleep. Now he's done been sold, like he wasn't nothing but a thing."

"It's not right, is it? This business of yours?"

"I'm-a gonna miss him, is all. He was the best dog ever. Well—next to Cleo." Julius sniffled. "Esau don't let me cry like that. I'm sorry."

"Don't be sorry." Randi, having acquired a key bit of intelligence, had but one more question: "When is the customer coming?"

46

THE DAY OF THE TRANSACTION, RANDI, BEWIGGED AND DRIVING another nondescript, rented sedan, caught up to Esau in downtown Tillman Falls, where Julius had said his brother would meet the customer. Not long after he parked in an angled space on the town common laid out in front of The Dixiana, she pulled into a space across the green.

She noted with interest the distinct absence of the dog cage: If he were meeting King Kong's buyer for the handover, she assumed it wouldn't be happening out in the open—but then, little about her new home would surprise her.

She held her Canon and waited.

Adjusted the blonde wig.

Willed herself to be not-Randi.

Esau ambled across the street in his down jacket, waving to an old man sitting on a bench by the miniature Pitchfork Ben Tillman statue on its mighty pedestal of polished red granite. In front of the tavern Esau greeted a younger man rolling his stout body out of a Mercedes SUV, a vehicle appearing as though it had been driven right off a showroom floor.

Randi noted Esau's customer's bulk: Broad shoulders and thick limbs. Pinholes for eyes. The kind of asshole who'd watch a pair of dogs fighting each other to death. For money.

The men shook hands and exchanged words, folded arms and chatted for a few minutes before disappearing inside the opaque rectangle of The Dixiana's corner-facing entrance, all the while Randi snapping off shots.

She shook her head with disgust—as she'd already noted, the far wall of the honkytonk along Common Street featured an offensive, ridiculous mural of the old Southeastern University mascot called General Reb, marching and waving the Confederate stars and bars, a bygone relic like the business on the other side of the wall. The university had long switched to the "Fighting Redtails," a muscular aviary figure modeled on a hawk, but The Dixiana had yet to catch up. Randi had never quite gotten used to seeing Confederate flags flapping everywhere.

Now what? She felt reckless and moved to action.

Why not let Esau know how brave she felt. Go inside and have a beer? The sign said OPEN, after all.

Her plans changed once she noticed a deputy coming down the front steps of the courthouse across the green: Oakley, her savior the night of the spotlight-rape, strode with an officious gait toward his cruiser parked in a reserved cop-spot at the curb.

Randi hurried across the town green. "Deputy Oakley—hi there."

Oakley raised a tentative hand. "Hello?"

"Remember me?"

"Not sure that I do, ma'am."

She realized not only had he met her for about five minutes, but at present she happened to be wearing a freaking disguise. She lowered her sunglasses. "Randi Margrave—from the top of the ridge."

"The spotlight-shining incident."

"Thank you again for checking on me."

"Your hair's different."

"Good observation."

"Part of my training."

"I can only imagine."

He asked how she was doing. If there'd been any other problems.

"A little excitement here and there. Some gunfire."

"Gunfire? Hunters?

"No. Not hunters."

He produced a small notebook from his breast pocket. "Ma'am?"

Randi felt exposed. "Could we talk somewhere else?"

"Why?"

"Because it's cold." She gestured over to Louella's, a diner that held down the opposite corner of the green from The Dixiana. Her head pounded at her notion to march inside and confront Esau—she might not have come back out of that creepy honkytonk alive. "How about lunch on me?"

"Have to take a raincheck on that." The deputy raised his hands together in front of him. Fingered a gold wedding band. Worked his eyebrows. "Sorry."

Oh, for heaven's sake—he thinks I'm hitting on him. "Don't misunderstand me. Not like that."

"Still. Another time."

"Deputy, do you realize what's going on in this county?"

Oakley swept his eyes around the quiet, dusty old downtown, which on this deserted weekday looked like an outtake from *Last Picture Show.* He put away his notebook. "What's your specific point?"

"Look: you're not from around here. Right?"

"I've lived in places not too different, though."

"Military background?"

Clipped and dry: "I'm told it isn't hard to tell."

"No."

A church bell chimed the noonday hour. Another police cruiser rolled by, a female city cop. She blipped her siren. Oakley offered a curt wave.

Randi collapsed—not into hysterics, more like the breathy whoosh of a deflating balloon. "I come from a background very different than Edgewater County. So different it's kind of beyond explanation. And I can't countenance how there's things happening here that people seem to be okay with."

"Again—meaning what?"

"I'm talking about dogfighting. That's what I'm specifically saying. And I don't understand how—"

A raised hand, cutting her off. "Change, ma'am, is slow in a place like this. Neither you nor I are gonna tip the scales, Mrs. Musgrave. Not overnight. We can make a difference in our own small ways, of course." He patted the pocket with his notebook. "So—is there something specific you want to report?"

Randi, aghast: why did she have to be the messenger? "Do you drive the back roads, sir? The ones near where I live?"

"At one time or another during my shifts, almost certainly."

"Remember seeing those 'hog-dawg' signs a few weeks ago?"

Oakley cocked his head. Reached up to scratch the side of his nose. "Not sure that I noticed."

The hesitation, the touching of the face—these were tells. Of course he'd seen the signs; he knew. Ex-military or not, outsider or native, Oakley was one of them.

Randi, crushed. She knew he could see the pain and conflict on her face. But he didn't ask about the source of her distress.

"Anything else?"

"I suppose not."

The cop tipped his trooper's hat and went to climb into his cruiser. "Something like what you referenced, it's not for you to get mixed up in."

"So everyone keeps telling me."

Conspiratorial. "Leave all that to us."

"Oh? Do tell."

"I can't discuss ongoing investigations."

Trying to throw her off the scent. "Terrific to hear."

"The Edgewater County Sheriff's Department is your friend."

"I'll keep that in mind."

She watched Oakley drive away.

Back in her rental car, she drummed fingers and regarded the dingy old honkytonk. She imagined herself trapped inside with Esau and who knew what other toothless, atavistic souls—a grave risk indeed. Her nemesis would present her with future opportunities by which to hang himself, of this she felt certain.

Without King Kong, no case to make anyway.

But even if the dog were with him, what were they doing? Only selling a dog. No dogfight about to happen across from the Edgewater County Courthouse; no case to make.

She'd been a fool. Time-wasting nonsense.

And it *was* cold today—bitter. The meteorologist at KNO had called for a possible December dusting of snow in the upcountry. Such weather was rare in South Carolina, which tended to remain temperate and fall-like all the way through New Year's. Remarkable.

She pulled off the wig. Cranked up the heat. Craved a glass of wine.

But Randi, dissatisfied and hungry for information: she had an inkling she should use this time on another thread of the investigation, finding out more about the other player deserving further scrutiny, in a location where damning evidence might also be gathered: Inside the Macon McMansion.

Was she nuts?

No—the old woman had never seen her. Esau would be otherwise engaged. And in her bag, the Census 2000 clipboard.

She'd go for it.

Yeah—while Esau the holy man drank and smoked and traded in dog flesh, Randi would defile and profane the sanctity of his own comfortable home, the one in which poor Julius could only dream of living. Who knew what dividends a peek inside would yield. Randi, deciding to go for broke, hopped onto the bypass and headed back to the suburbs, and Mama Macon.

47

THE INFIRM, CORPULENT WOMAN REGARDED RANDI FROM BEHIND THE safety of a glass storm door. "What on earth you want?"

"Mrs. Macon—Estelle?"

"Don't nobody call me that. Not who knows me good."

"What do they call you?"

Glaring through the storm door, Mrs. Macon swayed on bulbous ankles. She blinked at Randi through thick, enormous glasses. The crepe of her flesh hung loose from pale arms peeking out from a floral print housedress expansive enough to cover a queen bed. Her breathing ragged, a clear tube feeding her oxygen, here presented a woman unwell.

And disgusted. "You would have to come knocking soon as my boy left to go downtown. I got a bad hip. I got a bad everything."

"I'm terribly sorry."

She relented, telling Randi folks called her Stella. "What're you selling?"

"No selling. It's a simple survey, Stella." She displayed the faked census form. "A way to serve your country."

"I don't wanna do all that mess."

"It's a civic duty."

She scoffed. "I don't give a rip."

"Mrs. Macon—Stella. You can't give me five minutes to serve your dear old country?"

Randi, feeling guilt at making the woman get up and walk around,

225

another inkling of *What am I doing?* But she had to find out: Did the mother understand about the dogs? And Julius?

Moreover: Did the woman approve?

After this last task complete, Randi planned to spend the evening typing up notes, assembling photos and video of the dog compound, ending with images of Esau meeting the customer in town, for what they would be worth, which wasn't much; but she still felt that, if this information wasn't sufficient to get the state police interested enough to conduct an investigation, nothing would. She didn't need to document the depravity of an actual fight—she could lead interested authorities right to ground zero where the dogs were bred.

All that remained? Certain nagging, philosophical questions.

"I know it's an inconvenience." Randi, speaking like a polite young professional. "But with the year 2000 right around the corner, this represents a crucial census."

"Crucial, is it?"

"These questions will only take five or ten minutes."

"Why ain't they sending it through the mail? This don't make no durn sense."

A good question—did this make sense? Randi, in too deep now to withdraw.

First thought: "This area—rather, Edgewater County—has been chosen as part of a pilot program for old fashioned, door-to-door canvassing. To make sure the mailed-in forms provide us with a legitimately representative sample." The bullshit flowed. "Won't you help us make sure your community—including the Macon family—is counted with accuracy?"

Stella's eyes shone, and her voiced dropped to a hush. "Y'all's expecting them computers to quit working after New Year's. *Ain't you.*"

Her invocation of Y2K gave Randi chills. "Not at all."

"Don't tell me you ain't scared."

"I'm sure it's all well in hand."

Snickering at Randi. "I don't blame you for not thinking about it, sugar. But that's what my boy says is going to happen. That it's one of the signs of the end times."

"What's a sign?"

"All these computers is nothing less than the Great Sword of Revelations." She worked her pale lips in disgust. "Once the Lord comes back, all you liberals is going to find out y'all ain't as goddurn smart as you think."

226

"Professionals are working with diligence to prepare the computer networks."

Back to the subject at hand, Stella tapped her knuckles against the storm door toward Randi's clipboard. "I ain't gotta tell you nothing."

The sky loomed low and heavy, layered with gray pillowy clouds. "It's awfully cold out today."

Stella relented and opened the door. "Come in. I reckon."

"Thank you."

"I'm telling you right now: if you start trying to sell me anything, I'm gonna wring your scrawny neck. Don't think I won't—or can't." The sick woman mimed Randi's potential strangulation with the plastic oxygen tube. "You hear?"

"No, ma'am—nothing for sale."

Bypassing a more formal living room at the front of the house, they settled into the expansive open air of the two-story family room. A fireplace crackling and her clipboard clutched close to her body, Randi perched on the edge of a sofa while Mama Macon collapsed onto a La-Z-Boy set at an angle to the projection TV blaring a garish game show, the studio audience going apeshit as some lucky contestant triumphed and won big. Mama Macon muted the program with an enormous universal remote like Cullen's home theatre control.

"Well? Get to it."

Checking off the woman's answers on the faux-census form, Randi hurried through the boilerplate address-age-sex questions. Running out of material, she ached to poke around. See what could be seen. Maybe there were dogfighting trophies to photograph with a miniature digital camera nestled in the coat pocket of her black business jacket. She kept waiting to be offered tea or coffee, which might offer a chance to snoop.

"I tell you what, it's colder than a witch's brassiere out today. I wonder if you'd turn up the fire," fire sounding like *far*. Mrs. Macon extended a tremulous finger to the wall beside the inlaid-stone fireplace, a gas-log version similar to the one in the Margrave bedroom. "See that little wheel over yonder?"

Randi adjusted the setting and the blue flames burned brighter. "How's that?"

"I thank you kindly, honey."

Randi scanned her eyes across the photos arrayed on the mantle, fading Macon portraiture going back decades, if not into the previous century. Cullen would have suggested getting the treasured images better preserved, but Randi noted not the condition of the photos but rather the details of the faces, common traits like Esau's unappealing, walleyed countenance, which as it happened afflicted him no worse than many other Macon family members.

Even before his mauling, boyhood photos depicted an unhappy, wild-haired beanpole, including Esau's high school senior yearbook portrait, a color-shifted 16x20 in a gilded, golden frame. The image contained a sallow face with a rug-burn case of acne, and offered a grimace of a smile with joyless eyes, as though the expression had been made under duress.

Another, more candid snapshot depicted a group of teenage Macons standing on the riverbank of what she presumed was the Sugeree. Grainy, the photo had been enlarged to portrait size—a gangly Esau, nearly squeezed out of the frame by Julius's prepubescent bulk, scowled and squinted, but the others appeared happy and carefree. Then as now, the face of a troubled soul, Randi opined to herself.

Another yearbook-style portrait hung beside Esau's, a girl with the bulging Macon eyes, which on her looked deep and striking—a beauty who also appeared in the riverside snapshot.

"I see you have many lovely family photos." Randi went back to fake-scratching on her clipboard. "Do you live by yourself, ma'am?"

"My firstborn boy lives here. Takes care of me."

"Your firstborn—so there are more children? Grandchildren?"

Stella wheezed and scratched at the small tubes poking into her nostrils. "No, I ain't got no grand-babies," pitiful. "There's also my boy Julius, but he don't live here."

"I see."

"I had me another young'un." She pointed with her cane at the mantel. "A girl."

That explained the other portrait. Poor Julius didn't rate one. Perhaps he hadn't attended high school long enough to get his senior picture made.

"And where does your lovely daughter live?"

"Ruthie-Lynn passed on. She wasn't but a child, still."

Aghast and surprised, she could but whisper: "What—what happened?"

"Drown-ded in the river."

Randi's blood ran as cold as the water had been. "I can't imagine."

But she could.

228

"I told them young'uns it was gonna happen. Told them till I was blue in the face." At this distance from the tragedy, she seemed more angry than sad. "Terrible waste of a young life, over nothing but cutting the fool like a bunch of you-know-whats."

An awkward silence. Randi could hear the oxygen, wispy, flowing through the tube.

"Mrs. Macon: I'm so sorry."

"Ruthie-Lynn was going to college. Had her whole life yet to live."

"At Southeastern?"

Mama Macon shook her head. "Up at Foothills State. Smartest one that ever come outta this family." Stella, glasses hiding a pair of eyes gone dewy, gazed over at her late daughter's portrait. "Had a scholarship and everything."

Randi's gut clenched with a pang of genuine empathy: a flash of Denny's angelic face on the jetway, walking away. Forever. "What a tragedy."

"Lord, but they used to fight like cats and dogs. Worse after Julius come along."

"She fought with your son?"

"Even though Esau was older, Ruthie-Lynn used to whip his butt, I tell you. And it wa'n't always just playing and hollering, neither. They like to kill each other. Give each other bloody noses, like a pair of colored boys boxing in the ring."

"Oh—my."

"That was her problem, you know."

"What was that?"

"Being so smart."

"I don't consider that a problem."

"Thought she was smarter than anyone else. Especially that brother of hers."

"Children will be children."

The Macon forebear snorted. "Not like Ruthie and Esau."

"He resented her?"

Faraway. "No, no—he loved his sister. Bless his heart."

Randi's mind reeled. What if he'd hated his kin enough to kill her? To drown her in the rushing Sugeree? She'd thought that no further brutality from Esau would surprise her, but such a crime seemed beyond the pale, even for him. Perhaps she rushed to judgement.

A dark revelation wrenched her mind back into focus, a question with measurable relevance neither about the dogs nor Julius, but one cutting her to the quick:

"After all this time, do you still miss her?"

"Miss who?"

"Well—your daughter."

The woman's jowly face hardened into an aggrieved mask. "You must not have children to go and ask a hateful question like that."

"I'm sorry," with enormous honesty. "Of course you do."

"You don't got no young'uns?"

Her breath drew ragged and thin as Mama Macon's. "No, I don't."

Mocking. "'Do I miss my dead daughter?' Mercy, but you ain't got good sense, girl."

Randi recovered. "So: tell me about this Julius."

Mrs. Macon spoke now with a weary cadence. "Julius is one of them who come out touched, but in a good way. You never seen a bigger heart on a boy than him. He would've made a good doctor or a preacher—if he'd been born whole, of course."

"Julius is developmentally disabled?"

The woman smacked her lips at Randi's modern nomenclature. "Precious, but slow. Too slow for this fast-turning world."

"Is he institutionalized?"

Mama Macon, now at ease, conversed away. "Oh, my, yes, yes. He stays up in Columbia. Where they can help him look after himself."

"Columbia?"

"At a—hospital."

Randi tried to digest this information. "What hospital would that be?"

A shadow fell across Mrs. Macon's face. "These is starting to feel like mighty odd questions, young lady. I'm wondering if you ain't from the census at all. Say."

"Of course I am, it's just—these questions—"

"You're from the goddurn insurance company," with biting vitriol. "That's why you asking all this about Julius's hospital and whatnot."

"That's not so."

"You get your skinny ass out of here, missy, before I drag you out by your hair."

Randi no longer cared how much the woman knew about the dogs. Her beloved firstborn had his own mother convinced that Julius was off living in a nurturing environment, when in reality used as slave labor down in the woods. Esau's duplicity sickened her anew. "Mrs. Macon, there's something you should know. Julius, he's not in—"

A thump caused Randi's words to freeze in her throat: The enormous front door, slamming.

He had returned. In the house. Leaving no way for Randi, verging on panic, to escape.

A voice—Esau's—boomed out from the foyer: "Mama, you been watching the news? It's gonna snow. You believe that?"

"Come in here, son. There's somebody I want you to meet."

48

DOOMED.

Randi fumbled the big sunglasses onto her face with a hand that trembled. Maybe he would be clueless enough not to recognize her under the blonde wig.

"Son, it ain't gonna snow no more than there's a man in the moon."

"Who the hell's this?" Esau, clutching plastic grocery sacks. A shock of recognition widened his eyes further than normal. "Well—I be dog. You."

Randi, the gossamer veil of her disguise falling away. She tried to smile, but her facial muscles would only quiver.

"This here's the census taker—or so she says."

Esau's mind seemed blown. He stifled a laugh.

"Hello, Mr. Macon."

"Census taker?" His mirth withered. "You are something else, lady."

Mama Macon said, "You know who this woman is?"

"Sure do—the friendly neighborhood census taker. Right?"

"Part-time."

That made him laugh again.

Randi, sensing an opportunity. "Look, this is all a crazy coincidence. I started the job only this week."

"Co-inky-dink? The Lord does work in mysterious ways, I tell ya what."

Esau's mother, spitting mad. "*Now, what are y'all talking about?*"

Chuckling, Esau did a silly little skip-step into the kitchen to put down the bags. Calling over his shoulder: "Y'all should've seen them fools lined up at the IGA. They was snapping up every loaf of bread and jug of milk in sight. You'd've thought it was the end of the world."

Back in the family room, he adjusted the greasy trucker's cap he'd had pulled down to his eyebrows. "Oh, look, y'all—it's already starting."

Outside a wide picture window Randi saw enormous flakes drifting down onto a manicured lawn, a picture-postcard little slice of suburban heaven.

"I always did think snow was pretty." Mama Macon, wistful. "You just don't see it too often round here. Better get on home, girl."

Trembling. "Yes, I'll be going. Thank you so much."

All pretense of cordiality falling away, Esau stepped between her and the hallway to the foyer. "Just what in the holy hell are you doing in my house, woman?"

"Esau, hush that filthy mouth. I'm tired of you embarrassing me in front of folks. You act like a cussing fool, make me look like—like—"

"Mama? Hold onto all that."

Randi, steely. "I have all the information I need for today."

"And as for you—just hang tight."

The game, long over. "I'm sorry about this. I'm not with the census."

Mama Macon didn't seem to hear. "Yeah, son—she said they normally do it through the mail, but this here's a pilot program we got picked for."

Esau exploded with laughter. "City-girl, you got a keen imagination. About a lot of things," he added with emphasis. "What's all this nonsense?"

"I know exactly what's going on here."

"You don't know shit."

"*Esau Macon*—hush that mouth."

"Mama?" Gentle and loving. "The doctor said for you to sit still and stay quiet."

"That's what I was telling this woman here, how she was talking me half to death. And how I am not well, and need my rest rather than be bothered with her foolishness." Haughty. "And yet here we sat, blah-blah-blah."

His cheeks deepening in color, Esau loomed into Randi's face, close enough for her to smell his rank breath: "First you come messing around on my ridge, and now here? With my mama?"

Hissing. "You're lying to your own mother about Julius."

Mama Macon, shouting from over on the couch: "I can't hear a word you little smart-butts are saying."

"What about Julius?"

"The truth."

"Woman—you have lost me. Completely."

She didn't know how to assuage his rising fury. But then: "I won't tell her about Julius. Not being at the hospital. Deal?"

"What you're not gonna do," he said, "is walk out of here on them skinny legs."

Randi, feral and accusatory: "What you've all done to Julius is inexcusable—*he's a human being, not an animal.*"

Coarse like that of a manual laborer, Esau's hand brushed her cheek, from which she recoiled. "Bless thy heart, neighbor. As pure and innocent as that snow outside."

Dredging up courage. "I'll be missed—soon."

"Don't matter. I'm gonna deal with you, and make it stick."

"Please—let me go. I'll—leave you alone."

"Sure, sugar." Esau now spoke in a tone loud enough for his mother to hear. "Can you believe it, Mama? We ain't had snow this early in years."

Mama Macon, urgent: "You better go help Julius get them dogs squared away."

Randi, flabbergasted. "The dogs? Where? At the 'hospital?'"

Stella sucked in her thin breath. Held one chubby hand to her mouth: *Oh-shit.*

"Yes, she means Julius and the other patients at the hospital. At her age, she's been getting confused lately." He grabbed Randi by the arm. "Now leave my mama alone."

"She lied to me." Struggling with Esau, the clipboard falling with a clatter on the gleaming, hardwood floor. "About her own son?"

Mama Macon cussed her. "He's happy living down there with them dogs."

"How could he be?"

"You ask Esau. He'll tell you. Besides—what difference does it make to you?"

Randi wrenched her arm away and made for the front door. She shouted and spun around. "I know all about Julius and how happy he is. I know everything."

Mama Macon, icy and menacing: "Boy, you better tell me what's going on here."

"I don't know." Esau's voice broke with frustration. "She's a reporter, or something."

An order: "*Well go after her, then.*"

Randi fumbled with the lock on the heavy, ornate front door, pushed against the glass of the outer storm door.

Felt his hand on her shoulder. An iron grip that took her breath and yanked her back inside.

"Hold on now—I just wanted to apologize."

Elbowing him in the ribs, she tried to spin around. "You're going to be sorry, all right—"

A hot, heavy thud fell against the side of her head; a blinding flash of white-red. And with that, Randi Margrave, census taker and concerned mother of none, winked out of existence.

49

Randi awoke from a fogged dreamworld. She gagged on the biting, metallic taste of a rag shoved in her mouth.

Her head, throbbing.

Vision blurry.

Missing her shoes and the jacket of her suit.

Lying upon rough, dirty concrete.

Leaning against a shaft of rebar jutting out of the floor, her torso constricted by one of the insidious electrical cords, this one heavy and green and giving off a musky smell like mildew as though stored outside in the soft river-land peat, Randi tried to pull herself to full consciousness.

But before the pain in her head thrummed fully into life, she felt only cold—biting, painful cold.

Eyes focusing: the blockhouse in the dog compound.

Ruthie-Lynn's face from the faded portrait came to Randi. Dead in the river. Her ultimate fate as well.

And here, so close to home.

Unlike in the movies, the bound damsel refrained from trying to scream. Randi, sagging back down into the finality of her predicament. What an idiot she'd been.

She drew in a tortured breath through her one good nostril—the other seemed clogged. One eye felt crusted shut, and her cheekbone itched; she began to realize her face was covered in sticky, drying blood.

On the verge of again passing out, she glanced around and saw the circular 'cat-mill,' with its thick orange cords hanging in two nooses used in suspending the tortured bait animals. Twisting her body she could see the dogs watching in silence from their kennels at the other end of the building, their passive faces reminding her of the dream-dogs staring up at the bedroom window.

Now hit by the familiar smell of blood and death permeating the building, a yawning despair overcame her, an emotion beyond fear, beyond words. No, this wasn't some ridiculous, 70s B-movie from Cullen's collection—Randi now found herself held hostage in a kind of dog-abattoir, deep in secluded Carolina woodlands. By a madman, depraved and dangerous.

With a measure of detached amazement: *I'll never leave this place alive.*

No—she couldn't give in to this sorry fate.

Coughing against the filthy rag, she thrashed and bucked against her bonds, which held her to the rusty stake of rebar.

A flood of white light, cold air, and snowflakes blowing in from the doorway. A man standing there. "I wish you'd settle your ass down."

Randi, shouting muffled epithets through the greasy rag.

Esau, puffing on a foul-smelling cigarette, entered and perched himself on a stool in the shadowy corner. "You see how angry you done made me?" He exhaled blue smoke in her direction. "I've picked up the devil's weed again over your shenanigans."

She tried to shriek *FUCK YOU* through her gag and thrashed to no avail.

She couldn't let it end this way.

Not by his hand.

"You'll get your chance to explain yourself. Don't worry, I got a whole mess of questions. Like you did for my mama."

His gait stiff, Esau slid off the stool and ambled over to the cat-mill, spun the tread around. Fingered one of the hooks by which the bait animals were hung. Musing, "I wonder how my dogs would respond to pieces of a pretty yuppie woman hung up here on this here exercise machine. Hell, they might run slower—your meat looks mighty stringy, old Brandi Graveyard, or whatever your name is. Grave something, though, that's what I remember most. Missus Graveyard. Sounds about right, don't it?"

How are the dogs going to respond when your crooked redneck dick's hanging from that hook? Perhaps it was better, Randi thought, she remained silent.

Esau lunged and grabbed her chin in his rough hand. "The main question? I know your name and all, but who the hell are you? Or maybe better: who sent you? Maybe that's the right question."

Randi, mumbling: *The cops are already looking for me.*

He seemed to misunderstand. Shoved her face away. "You ain't no cop, not one like I ever knowed. You'd have some kinda ID or badge. And a sidearm tucked somewheres. But you don't got none of that. Not on you. Nor in your vehicle." Hands on hips. "Who put you up to all this?"

No one, she vibrated through the gag. *This is me—just me.*

A calloused finger across her neck and between her small breasts.

She recoiled, tried to kick at him.

"What—you don't like to be touched?"

Randi, staring daggers at her captor.

"Too damn bad. That's only the beginning."

Randi, staving off the feeling of *oh my god, it's actually going to happen.*

To me.

Again.

And yet she'd sworn never-again.

The idea of violation by the hand of a man like Esau, beyond abhorrent. She'd rather he go ahead and kill her.

Her gut empty, the gesture futile, she prayed and pleaded for mercy. Begged a God in which she'd never truly believed to deliver her. She at last understood the old saw about atheists and foxholes.

As though he could sense her specific fear, Esau launched into a ridiculous, profane monologue, one sprinkled with invidious double entendres and threats, using terms that should have been foreign to the ostensibly pious man. But his profanity had the feel of familiar language—the tongue of a hypocrite.

"I'm gonna take you all the way, lady. Show you how a real man does things. Fill you up with the spirit, and something else, too, like how they say you got cake and you got icing on top to boot."

He paused, held his finger aloft. "Now of course, I want to reassure that you ain't got to worry none about Julius. He don't do nothing. But we might let him watch. Learn him something."

Randi, her gorge rising. Despair.

"As for me?" He sucked snot back into his sinuses. "If you think this is just gonna be over soon, without me teaching you a lesson? You're wrong, way wrong. But that much we already knew. Born wrong—that's what you were."

Randi's terror ebbed, replaced by the continued tug of the survival instinct: she twisted her wrists back forth, but produced only self-inflicted Indian burns.

Noting strange, small shadows creeping across the floor, she glanced up to the wire-meshed window to see fat snowflakes continuing to fall, which meant she probably hadn't been out too long. Under better circumstances, the snow might have seemed as magical to the California girl as it did to the Southerners.

But right now? No magic. No happiness. No hope.

The ache to survive, flooding back into her.

To get this bastard.

"Oh, hell." Esau, stepping around and putting the crotch of his khakis right at the level of her face. "This ain't hardly no fun at all. I reckon what I ought to do is get that old shit-rag out of your mouth so we can, like, interact better and all."

He reached behind Randi's head and yanked the rag from around her mouth, a blessed occurrence even with the handful of hair he pulled out with sharp, fresh pain.

Up close, Esau's scars proved beyond grotesque. Acne on one side, streaks and mounds from injury on the other. His nose, hairy and greasy; a bug-eye thrusting out.

She coughed, gasped for breath. *"My husband's already missing me."*

"You bet he is. Fine filly like you." Esau laughed, high and silly. "But I got that all covered."

Randi spat blood onto the concrete. "What are you going to do—get rid of me?"

"Anyone else out looking?"

"Not yet," a painful admission. "Probably not."

"Who you work for?"

"I'm not a cop."

"Duh. Who, then? Ebby Nixon said you was some kinda TV person."

"I used to be, but not any more. Let me go and I'll just forget all this." A lie—she lusted to come charging back down the ridge with a phalanx of police in tow. "We'll keep to ourselves. No—we'll move."

Esau frowned at her apparent desperation. "They ain't gonna come looking for you down here. Not after I parked that car by the interstate, over at the motel them punjabbis bought." He made a mocking, gape-mouthed face, exaggerating his own accent. "'Gosh, Sheriff Truluck, where you reckon she done gone? C'ain't no one figure it out. She must've met her lover at this dirtbag motel, and then they toddled off together. Near as we can tell'."

Simmering. "I don't have a lover."

"'Well, Sheriff, I heard her and her college-boy husband wasn't getting along that well. Heard they'd had problems. Heard she had a penchant for spreading her legs for every dick that swung her way, Sheriff.' That sound like a reasonable story? For a college woman like you?"

"Shut your mouth," she said. "You filthy bastard."

"Shut me up." Sticking out his tongue. "Go on and try."

"Untie me and I will."

"I double-dog dare you."

"Macon, I'm gonna see you rot in jail for this."

"Over what? Tell me what I done. You couldn't put me in jail if you tried."

"What do you call pistol-whipping and threatening to rape me?"

His face twitched. "I'm saying, before all this—you was the one spying on a man raising dogs. Following me around. And finally showing up at my house and threatening my god-durn mother." In a flash his face became pinched, furious. "Pestering my poor old mother, messing around with my dumb brother. You're the one who ought to be put in jail. Who's acting half-crazy. Not me."

"You have a ridiculous definition of insanity, pal."

He lit up a fresh smoke. "Every one of you college fucks come back dumb as rocks."

"Oh—like your sister?"

A serious thunderhead formed, a gray aura enveloping him. "What about my sister, rest her soul?"

"I heard she was a college girl, too."

"Nobody's perfect."

Randi, rasping and thirsty. "Look. It's illegal to fight those dogs, but more than that, it's wrong. I don't care how long you've been sucking that fat sheriff's prick."

Ignoring her profane assertion. "All this over a mess of dogs? And as for laws, I follow God's law. You do, too, whether you'll let your cracker ass admit it."

She gasped, tonguing at tears streaming from the injured eye to assuage her brutal thirst. "But you profit from their suffering. Doesn't that seem sinful—?"

Disgusted. "I bet y'all are vegetarians. You're from California, ain't you."

"Slaughtering animals to eat is one thing, but letting them tear each other apart for money? You're sick, you and your Jesus talk." Randi's ire, stoked by the sinking, unreal feeling she'd never leave the blockhouse alive. What had she left to lose? "They should drum you out of that church of yours."

"My granddaddy built that church, lady. Get real."

A sudden flash of Cullen—she saw his face, laughing and happy; her heart ached. At this rate, he might never find out what happened to her.

No, he'll know—he'll tell the police about her dog-obsession. And they'll come down here to check.

They'd get Esau after all. Only she wouldn't live to see it.

Or would she? Her will to fight, resurgent.

Esau, a seeming state of astonishment. "I never seen anyone more wrong about anything in my whole damn life."

"Wrong to want to prevent suffering and pain?"

Scratching at the scars on his face. "You wouldn't know the first thing about suffering and pain."

"Look—it won't matter if you get rid of me. They'll still come for you. I've got the goods on you spread out all over my goddamn dining room table. Pictures, audio recordings of Julius, even video of this place," laughing at him. "But you know, there's more. The organized crime element in this county won't know what hit it."

"Organized crime?" Explosive laughter, a pitying head shake as he fished in his pocket for another cigarette. Esau looked as though he couldn't figure Randi out. "*For raising dogs?*"

"You'll find out, asshole."

Esau now seemed impatient, wearied. "Them dogs are in my blood—I was born into it, like you was born into being a dumbass college boy's wife." He snorted with derision. "I don't know who you think you are."

Coughing and choking, running out of air: "You are fucked either way, mister. You either go to jail for kidnapping and assault and organized crime, or yeah, maybe also for the murder of your own sister."

He blanched. "Do what, now?"

In an instant she saw the truth of what she'd asserted—decades of deception, guilt, worry flashed across his frightened features. It might not convict him, but Randi, knowing. A satisfying, ephemeral rush.

"I know what you did." She spat at him with what little saliva she could muster. "Your mother told me about Ruthie-Lynn. Told me about you beating her."

Shook his head.

Paced around.

Smoked.

"My sister was a sinner—she rejected the Lord, and rejected our ways."

"I'll bet she did."

"But if I tried to bring her to God through the sacred ritual of baptism —yea, in that green river flowing outside, it was—then I have nothing to answer for. Not to you. Nor Mama. Nor God."

The enormity of it all washed over her like the cold water in which he had murdered his own blood. Randi had no chance.

Finally easing back down on the stool, Esau crossed his skinny legs. "So let me get this straight: you Yankees move in here and decide you're gonna become amateur deputies policing my ridge? And me and my brother raising dogs and selling them—like mo-fos all over the blessed world— seems like high crime to you? I can't get my mind around it. It ain't *legal*, you say?"

"No, and for good reason."

"Wellsir, you could knock me over with a feather—I plead ignorance, judge. Ignorance of the law. Ain't much of an excuse, I know." He pulled a wicked, curved hunting knife from a sheath on his belt. Cleaned from under one thumbnail. "I guess I better cut you loose. So you can call the law on me."

Along with her physical survival, Randi had become intent on getting through to this cretin. "It isn't about the law. These dogs—they're God's children. Just like us."

"Mercy, but you don't know your bible-learning none too good."

"Enough to know that Christ couldn't possibly have advocated your kind of cruelty and suffering."

"Don't come here and start telling me what Jesus Christ wants and thinks—Jesus *talks* to me. I know Him. And I know what is true and right."

"This is insane. You're gambling, you're inflicting all this pain—"

"Gambling? No, ma'am. That's like Pete Rose betting against his own team. That's not the angle I come from. Besides, I got plenty of money."

"And what angle is it?" Randi could have sworn the rope, a bungee cord, had slipped over the knuckle on her right thumb. She fought to keep her face frozen in its angered grimace. Ignoring the pain, she kept twisting her wrists against one another.

"How my Daddy raised me a certain way. How we are closer to the land and to God than somebody like you—an outsider. A *heathen*," he shouted as she supposed he might have back in his preaching days. "Worst of all, a usurper of our values."

A minor revelation; a way out. "You realize Julius will help me, don't you?"

"Julius ain't gonna help nobody."

"You've got him brainwashed. But I broke through it."

Esau, troubled. "Bullcrud."

"He loves these dogs—he told me. Cleo especially."

"Ah, so you've been messing with him after all, that fat-faced liar. When?"

"Doesn't matter."

"The hell it don't—now talk." A shiny, black 9mm pistol appeared from underneath his grungy shirttail. She assumed her temple, throbbing, held the imprint of the butt.

"You keep Julius out here like he's no better than an animal himself."

"No better than an animal himself?" Esau, ruminative. "Now we're getting somewhere."

"Enlighten me."

"Animals were put here by God to serve us—not for us to bow down to, and not to talk foolishness, like them curs out there could also be children of God. As though they got souls."

"How do you know they don't?"

"You can look in a dog's eyes and see many things, Mrs. Graveyard. But I can guarantee you won't see God in there. A piece of God, maybe— like one of his fingernails, or a hair off his ass. But not the essence of Him. Not like in *my* eyes."

"You're so full of shit that—"

"Before you die today—and you're going to, oh, yes—I ask that you repent your sins and drink the blood of Jesus Christ. Do it and none of this mess will matter: you will live forever."

"What was Julius's sin?" She didn't bother to question the Biblical reasoning behind her coming murder, or how Esau's actions fit into his pious and depraved worldview. "Tell me why he deserved this life."

"He ain't sinned. Julius is washed in the savior's blood."

"He said you didn't even take him to church anymore."

Probing. "You act like you and him is best friends."

"He's a human being, one who deserves to live and be comfortable. Like you."

"He don't deserve any more than he's got—in some ways, he ain't no smarter than them dogs. Why the hell you think we keep him out here?"

Randi's gut burned as Esau went on to complain about Julius and Cleo. How they'd had to spend so much money on fixing that "damn dog" for his enfeebled brother. "If it had been left up to me, I would have put it down. It wa'n't no good to anybody anymore. Barely had been in the first place."

"Let's change the subject."

"But no, he had to go and cry to his Mama till she give in. Of course, she ain't never had good sense about Julius. She probably should have put him down too, come to think of it. Him, and that worthless, piece of shit dog."

She fought to keep her face calm—her entire thumb had slipped free. Pushing at the coil of the bungee, she wiggled her hand.

A tipping point.

"Where are they?"

"Outside, in his little world. When he seen what I had laid out in the back of my truck—that's you, sugar—he got all flustered. Started whining. Now I know why."

She tried to shout, but only a harsh whisper came out. "Julius—"

Furious, he kicked her in the side, knocking out her breath. She gasped as he grabbed her by the hair. "You know what? Let me go and get him and his little pooch. Find out what's been going on here behind my back."

"Esau—please."

He threw her back against the pole. What was left of Randi's bond fell free, but she held her hands tight behind her as though still bound.

The dogs in their runs had gone mad with barking. Esau shouted commands until they quieted. A blast of frigid air rushed in before the door slammed shut behind him.

Cold, and thirst, gripped her mind. Randi, frantic, wrenched her body around, yanking so hard on her wrists that her shoulders hurt.

Esau flung the door open and shoved Julius through. She fell back into position, keeping her hands, now free, clutched behind her.

Esau kicked at Cleo's hindquarters. The dog yelped.

Randi, gritting her teeth. *"Don't you dare touch that sweet dog."*

Cleo trotted over. Whining, she licked Randi's icy feet. Nosed her calf.

"Hey, sweetheart. Come to mama."

Esau, snapping at his enormous brother: "What you been doing farting around with this woman?"

Randi could see that Julius trembled all over. He stole a glance, whistled and motioned for Cleo to go lie on a pallet of old blankets shoved in the corner. The dog loped over and flopped down.

"Ain't—ain't done nothing."

Quick as lightning, Esau backhanded his brother with a *smack*. "You wanna keep coming for Friday dinner? Tell the truth, shit-heel."

"She made me do it." Pointing and angry. "She didn't say nothing about messing around with Mama back at the big house, though."

Randi considered anew the possibility she might be finished. "Julius, I thought we were friends."

"You made me do it."

"Right." Esau pointed. "Stand over yonder with that worthless cur of your'n."

Chastened and scared, Julius stood shaking beside Cleo. The other dogs began barking again.

"Quiet them down."

Julius whistled. Like a miracle, the agitated dogs fell silent. Kong, the brute, kept his eyes trained on Randi, who stole glances at Cleo, lying with her head between front paws, tail wagging.

"Do you love Cleo, too?" A mocking singsong. "Of-course-you-do."

Randi saw evil flitting across his face. "I don't love her any more than Julius does. You deformed redneck."

"I think I just had one of them moments of clarity, like drunks get." Esau, with a sagacious nod, patted Cleo on the haunches, three quick smacks that made Julius grunt and shuffle his feet. "So you care about that dog. Like he does."

"Why wouldn't I, you monster?" She needed a distraction. Long enough to make a break for the door. She'd head straight for the river—

would dive in again. Swim for her life. Her confidence bloomed; it had
been done before. "Julius seems to have a heart."

"You and my brother, peas in a pod. Ain't that sweet."

Esau pitched his cigarette onto the floor, crushed it out. Pulled the
pistol from his waistband, this time checking the chamber. Called to his
brother. "Come here, son."

Julius, shuffling over and mumbling a mantra of contrition. "I'm sorry,
I'm sorry."

"I swear, but you're as worthless as them fellas hanging around all day
outside Murtaugh's bait shop."

"I told you—I don't know the red lady."

"It's back to that? You need to get your damn story straight, idiot."

"She made me do it. That's right."

"Made you do what?"

Julius switched back again. "I—don't know no lady from up the ridge
in the house with the big TV and the sandwiches."

Esau, exasperated. "Go stand next to our honored guest. Y'all get reac-
quainted."

Julius went to scratch Cleo on the head—an automatic gesture—and
waddled his bulk over toward Randi.

Cleo, sleepy, yawned and smacked her lips.

"Now here's a lesson for you, lady, and you too, lunkhead. Sometimes
you got to rid yourself of that which is weak. Of that which can do no
good works. Can add nothing to your life and efforts but be a burden. A
useless burden."

Desperate. "Esau—don't. I'll do anything. Please."

Winking at her. "Julius, he's got the touch—that Macon touch—with
these beasts. Otherwise? I'd a done this to him, too, before now."

Her captor took a step toward Cleo, pointing the weapon and
grinning.

"NO."

Julius, startled by Randi's outcry. By rote: "I don't know her. I don't—"

"Stop him, Julius!"

His brother saw Esau aim the gun at Cleo.

Shouting and lunging faster that Randi would have thought possible,
Julius leapt and grabbed Esau into a bear hug.

But the gun exploded anyway, a great boom that slapped back from
the cinderblock walls and caused Randi's eardrums to bulge. The air filled

with smoke and the smell of cordite. The caged dogs all went mad with fear. She shrieked anew, expecting to see the horror of what Esau had done.

Cleo, unhurt, yipped and yelped as Julius and Esau grappled for the gun. Another shot went off, scoring the concrete.

This time Cleo fell silent, dropping to the floor. Julius cried out in agony.

Horrified but moved to act, she leapt to her feet and flung off the bungee cords. But Esau Macon, breathless, still held the pistol, turning it toward Randi.

50

JULIUS KEPT SCREAMING AS CLEO'S BODY LAY TWITCHING AND spasmodic, the dog's tongue lolling onto the filthy concrete floor.

Esau, unsteady but holding the gun on Randi, who stood dizzy from injuries, grief and fear.

"You big dummy," Esau said to Julius with a wheeze. "I told you to stand over—"

Julius, a war cry. Awkward but lightning-quick, he swung his huge arm and knocked Esau headlong against the concrete block wall.

The pistol, tumbling from Esau's hand, bounced across the floor and struck her across the top of her right foot.

White-hot pain. Dogs barking. Esau, moaning.

But the gun.

At her feet.

Julius, looming over Esau, who lay face down. "I'm-a kill you for this."

He laughed, rolling and reaching up at his brother's bulk, an almost playful gesture.

Julius sucked wind and pitched forward onto his knees. Got into his brother's face.

In a mad trance: "I ain't messing around. I'm-a kill you for what you done today."

Her mind reeled. She made herself look over at the dog's slack body.

Blood, dark like wicked wine. Stillness.

Death.

Randi wept.

"Mama said she could be *my* dog." Julius, roaring with ire, choked Esau anew. Picked up his brother, again flung him against the concrete wall like a broken marionette.

Dazed, Esau crumpled to the grungy floor in a fresh heap.

As a Taoist might put it, the only time was now: Every nerve ending on fire, Randi snatched up the gun.

And hurled herself through the door and into the cold outside.

She heard Esau behind her. "Julius, she's a-loose. Don't let her get away, boy—"

Randi didn't tarry to see what would happen next. Snowflakes swirling, the wind cutting through her, she ran best she could in her icy, bare feet across the hard-packed dirt of the yard. Slipping in mud, she came charging out of the compound, righted herself, and headed for the river.

The pistol, the first such weapon she'd ever held in her life, felt heavy in her hand, much more so than she expected.

Wait—she had the gun. She could go back and kill Esau for what he'd done.

She fumbled around, hunting for the safety.

No. Randi, not a killer.

Despite a lack of shoes she hustled her way along the footpath toward the fishing spot, and the river beyond. She ran, branches slapping her, brambles tearing at her face.

Along the river's edge, her feet stabbed over and over by the knotty roots sticking out of the damp ground, she heard Esau calling out, his voice echoing across the water. "You can't get away—*my granddaddy's people made these god-durn woods.*"

At Esau's call, Randi's blood roared. He continued shouting, his voice trailing behind on her traverse through the forest on the ridge. She ran.

51

DASHING DOWN THE RIVERFRONT PATH. DETERMINED, ADRENALIZED, also terrified and in pain. A grim summation.

Randi's flight through underbrush and deep, ankle-twisting holes hidden by the dense layer of fallen leaves, turned hellish. Her vision, doubling. The gun in her hand, heavy as an anvil. She heard the dogs barking, but it didn't sound as though they'd been let loose upon her.

In spite of her desperation, she marveled at the beauty of the snow falling upon the rushing river, but no time to enjoy it.

As the pathway petered out at the beginning of the river's sharpest curve, she had no other choice but to start up the ridge. The deadfall would be the worst obstacle—she'd try to stay as close to the water as possible, a route she hadn't taken on her original trek along the branch.

Here in the deeper woods, only a scattered snowflake from the flurry made it through the dense canopy overhead. Still, with the air cold enough for snow, she knew two things—she couldn't stop, and despite her earlier bravado about swimming for it, she couldn't get wet. Her feet were already scratched and numb. She had to get warm.

The woods blurred by in flash-frames; she felt like she'd stumbled into someone else's bad acid trip, an order of magnitude worse than the one dose she'd consumed back in her wild teenage years, and with it an ordeal of psychic terror and lower GI distress from the strychnine-cut psychedelic drug.

But this, no bad trip: she'd stumbled into a true waking nightmare, with the stakes being greater than her mere sanity.

Her head throbbed where she'd been struck; her back hurt, she supposed, from being tossed around, unconscious, in the truck bed. But whatever her physical ailments, at the sight of Cleo killed for no reason than bloodlust her soul had sputtered and turned dark, a filament flaming out. She would see Esau go to prison, not only for the dogs, and her kidnapping and assault, but she didn't doubt, now, he'd also killed his own sister. For whatever insane reason.

And who knew how many more?

Others who had come snooping around?

The foliage became too thick to negotiate—a cluster of thorny vines, old and undisturbed, thick as saplings. Randi headed up the ridge, angling toward the branch meandering along the hillside toward her property.

She clambered over the deadfall, at this southernmost end only about head-high. Tumbled down into the damp leaf-cover; the gun, slipping from her hand.

Randi, quick to her feet, now covered in black peat. Desperate, she searched until finding the weapon buried in leaves, but only after her toe collided with the sharp-edged metal of its barrel.

She heard howling from back downstream, echoing through the trees —not a dog. Esau, in the depths of madness?

No—the voice had been higher. As though the spectral call had come from Julius.

What a fool—she'd gotten his beloved pet killed. With her own life threatened, however, her empathy for Julius—Cleo aside—had become muted. What if he'd snapped in such a way she'd now find him instead of Esau on her tail? Or waiting at the house?

In his simpleminded state, could Julius believe he had to get rid of Randi? She couldn't imagine his thought process, clouded by grief.

He'd calm down, listen to her. She'd explain that she'd do what she could for him. Tell the authorities he'd been kept against his will, by his brother and his own mother. Tell the police that despite his behavior, Julius loved the dogs. Had a good soul.

Did he, though?

Gentle Julius appeared to be the real dog expert, the trainer, the one and true master. He put the bait animals on the hooks and ran the dogs on the treadmill. He used the bloody poles, tied animals to them. Set the dogs upon one another. Watched as puppies he'd attended from birth tore at one another's flesh. Even Julius had to be smart enough, she now decided, to have known better.

Again—she'd tell the cops as much as she could about the Macon family dynamic. Let the courts and the reporters sort out the nightmare.

———

Reporters.

She pictured Cyn-Anne readying the on-air copy: *Former WKNO Producer Kidnapped by Backwoods Dog Cultists.*

The old routine flashed through her mind—Randi handing out field assignments to the news-gatherers, each challenging the other to come up with the silliest, most irreverent logline for their story.

The sound of their laughter.

The camaraderie.

Getting up in the morning.

Having a purpose.

Remembering how her boss, Spencer Mathison—a man she once respected, sharp and assured—had praised her instincts and her eye.

One day he'd mused over how much Randi's heart truly remained in working broadcast news, however. A bit of an outrage—this, after a few of her attempts at muckraking local journalism had been discouraged, if not outright spiked by him.

Far from insulted by his hypocrisy, she'd shrugged—if it rang true, was he wrong to note how she not longer seemed all that hungry and ambitious? And how, barely ten years on the job, she'd turned cynical, and perceived journalism, like most other institutions, as debased and tainted to high heaven? I'll go and raise my son instead, thank you very much.

For all the good that had done anyone. Denny most of all.

Besides, Cullen was riding high, the Southeastern cinema guy, all but tenured. He claimed that, from his freshman year in college when he'd realized that one could pursue such a life, he'd dreamt of nothing but teaching film—not a failed filmmaker, only an enthusiast. She enjoyed seeing how happy he seemed in his chosen life.

But what had she dreamed of doing?

Network news, like Cyn-Anne?

Hardly. The idea of living in New York or DC or Atlanta had never appealed to her. Not after Denny came along, certainly, but not even before that.

She'd never known what she was "supposed" to be. What was expected of her. Other than being a mom, after that happened.

But it'd all been taken from her.

Her marriage.

Her son.

And now, her life. Even if she got home, got safe, she'd still be at square one.

Still without Denny.

But Cullen—he awaited her. Making a fresh start. Willing. And loving.

Someone to run to.

———

As the trees thinned and the ground grew steeper, the snow fell harder. She found the branch gurgling along, its banks dusted with snow.

Pausing to splash the earthy water into her mouth, gasping and gagging. Retching it back up. Coughing.

But the faraway yelping of the dogs spurred her back into motion. Not far now; almost home.

52

THE SHARP BRICKS OF THE PATIO CUT INTO HER ALREADY PAINFUL heels. Worse, she stumbled and skinned her right knee, the gun falling from her hand and skittering across the deck toward the sliding door.

She rolled over in the dusting of snow to see a rip in her pants and a bloody flap of skin hanging down, another on the growing list of injuries and ailments.

Struggling back to her feet Randi snatched up Esau's pistol, fell against the patio door. She howled again, now in frustration—the door appeared locked. She pushed harder, and it gave. Unlocked after all, only heavy. Relief.

In a fresh burst of adrenaline she tumbled inside and flipped shut the small locking mechanism, which now seemed inadequate to the task. Fearful of seeing Esau lumbering up the ridge like a malfeasant golem, she yanked Cullen's theater-drapes shut.

Threw the heavy gun onto the plush sofa.

Felt her energy settle into the sudden silence of home.

Unreality—all of it a bad dream.

Except not a dream.

Lurching into Cullen's office, she had to get to a phone.

Not on the base.

Searching—her cell, left in the rental car.

Upstairs.

First, however, she staggered into the laundry room, sliding on the tiles and leaving splotches of red. She grabbed her house slippers, a pair of threadbare, woven Pakistani mukluks with hand-stitched leather soles. Wincing, she pulled the colorful, thick wool over the raw soles of her feet. Pain flared bright and exquisite.

Randi froze—a thump from upstairs: footfalls on the floor over her head.

A voice, muffled: "Honeybunny? You down there?"

Cullen.

Randi girded herself to hobble up the metal spiral staircase, the thin moccasin-soles of the mukluks providing only a modest cushion. The discomfort didn't matter, only getting to her husband.

For a second she thought of leaving the gun, but Cullen had to know.

Randi slid into the kitchen, flipped on the fluorescents. The dim kitchen and dining room, flooded with white light. Stood holding the pistol.

Cullen, leaning on the island with mail in hand, hadn't yet looked up. He whistled. "Look at this power bill. And what's that old beater pickup parked outside for—?"

At the sight of a bloodied, bedraggled, and armed wife, his mouth dropped open. "Randi?"

A freak out. "*They tried to kill me—oh, baby. I'm so sorry—*"

Cullen threw down the mail and rushed around the counter toward her.

Before he got to her, however, a bloodcurdling howl startled them both: Esau, hurling himself out of the shadows of the great room.

Bloodied and enraged; brandishing the hunting knife.

"Good god, man, who the hell are—"

Slashing at Randi's husband. He raised his arm, but too late—Esau thrust the knife, clean and neat, in and out of Cullen's side.

He collapsed, gasping and gurgling.

Time stopped; Randi's voice roared out from a deep place of anguish. She raised the gun, pulled at the trigger, but the safety seemed on.

Esau lunged and knocked the gun out of her hand, which fell cracking one of the kitchen tiles. Randi lost her balance and began to topple over.

Looming over her, Esau's face, swollen on one side. Blood trickled out of an ear. Leaves and twigs stuck in his wiry hair. Julius had done a number on his brother. "What took you so long to get up that ridge?"

Randi, frantic, tried to crawl over toward Cullen, who lay moaning and bleeding.

"Now we're gonna finish this my way."

When Esau went to reach over her for the gun, Randi kicked upward and kneed him in the gut.

Back on her feet, she threw herself across the island for the knife set, the big slicer.

Esau attacked, grasping for Randi's shoulder and slashing with the hunting knife. She fell backwards onto the stove, hard. Rather than grabbing hold of the butcher knife as she'd intended, all the blades had gone spinning across the island and onto the tile floor with a clatter.

Coming around the island, Esau's head collided with several of the copper pots. They too fell in a clangorous, metallic cacophony.

"You ain't gonna beat me, woman, so might as well just—"

Randi now offered her own cry, primal and urgent, thrusting her fist into Esau's good eye; she rocked his head back. Throwing elbows. Slapping at his face. A feral, shrieking dervish.

He thrust the hunting knife, a flash of silver, and she felt the sharp pressure of the blade going into her abdomen: no pain at first, but then heat, searing, like she'd been burned.

Her breath thinning, she slung an arm around his head. The knife popped out, hurting worse than when it'd gone in.

With her other hand she grabbed for the heavy knife-block, ripping a fingernail she caught in one of the empty slots, a minor injury in the grand scheme. With a savage cry of affirmation, she brought the heavy block around.

It connected with Esau's nose. A spray of red.

He dropped the bloody hunting knife. Fell against the stove, his legs buckling, groping for purchase and managing to twist the control knobs.

Two of the gas burners, their electric pilot lights sparking, flared into life. Esau shut his eyes and reached up to his face with both hands.

"God *damn* you," thick and nasal like Cullen in the midst of an allergy attack. "My nose—"

Randi grabbed him by the hair, kicked at the side of his knee. Shoved him down, brutal, with all her weight.

Face-first into the lit burners.

His cries, high and desperate. The smell of scorching hair, acrid and sour.

But a face full of ignited natural gas gave Esau newfound strength. He convulsed as though hit with an electric charge. Threw her off, back against the island. Randi slipped on fallen knives, the tip of one jabbing into the tender meat of an ankle.

Esau, slapping at his head, hollered for her blood. A bright pink ring had formed around his face; his hair, smoldering. He blinked his searching eyes as though blind. "You done half killed me."

"It's going around."

Randi, thinking only of the gun, hustled around the island. She glimpsed her fallen husband in her path, screamed anew.

She had to get help.

Bolting out of the kitchen, racing headlong for the front door, an object caught her eye—the house phone, sitting on the dining room table. She grabbed up the black rectangle and burst through the front doors, reeling, out into the delicate, dancing snowfall.

Randi staggered down the stone walkway toward Esau's truck, sitting at the end of the driveway with its lights on and driver-door hanging open.

She stabbed at the buttons on her phone, calling not 9-1-1, but someone closer: Ebby Nixon, whom she'd programmed into the memory.

He answered right about the time she made her way around the truck, looking inside to see that Esau had taken the keys. As she got farther from the house, the wireless landline began to crackle and buzz.

"*Hel*-lo, Miss Brandi," Ebby sang in a mellifluous twang. "What up?"

Her feet in agony and the knife-wound in her side leaking warm blood, she started running down the rough macadam of the road toward the Nixon house down at the bottom of the hill. "Esau Macon stabbed my husband—*he's trying to kill us both.*"

"Ma'am, what on earth—?"

"Up the hill," she yelled. "Ebby, call someone—"

From behind came Esau, wailing and cursing her eternal soul. She heard the truck engine thrum into life.

She heard the sharp crack of gunfire. A hot, angry bee buzzed past her head.

Randi damned the agony in her feet and ran faster, curving down away from her house. The cordless phone, out of its range and useless, slipped from her hand and shattered on the hard roadway.

Her stomach in a knot.

Every joint aching.

White hot fire from the stab wound.

But running.

Randi rounded the first curve. She saw a figure approaching from way down the hill—Ebby on his bike, pumping with fury. A deer rifle, slung across his back. Hollering into a mobile phone.

She angled toward him, waving her arms.

Behind her the truck engine roared. She heard the gears grind.

Esau, the tires squealing and sliding in the snow, rounded the bend. He fired again, but wild.

Ebby stopped, straddling his bike, blinking with disbelief. He snapped out of it. Fumbling with the phone, he tried to unsling the rifle, all but tumbled off the bicycle.

Esau roared around the bend, tires on the shoulder.

Randi, trying to fake him out like an adept running back. She stopped on a dime and cut back across the road.

Esau jerked the wheel and the truck veered, first into the muddy ditch and back onto the pavement, its bumper clipping Randi on the hip and sending her flying across toward the opposite ditch. She landed with a sick thud, possessing enough presence of mind to cushion her head with her forearm.

As she rolled over she saw Esau fishtailing down the road, fighting to regain control of the vehicle.

Ebby raised the rifle and fired, far too late.

Esau's truck plowed into the skinny old man, knocking him into the air. Ebby's spindly arms and legs flopped doll-like. He landed in the opposite ditch, his head lying snapped back.

Esau's truck slid around in a one-eighty, came to a stop.

Randi's toll had increased by another.

She gave herself over to being the next.

53

RANDI, IN AGONY BOTH PHYSICALLY AND OTHERWISE, LAY STILL. SHE'D cost not only her husband's life, but now that of innocent Ebby Nixon as well.

All the warnings, rushing back to her.

Everyone had been so right—why hadn't she listened?

The truck rumbled up beside her.

"Now we got ourselves a dead Ebby Nixon, and a dead busybody city woman, and another dead mo-fo on top of that?" Esau, tearful and desperate, talking to himself. "What we gonna do? Drag them back up yonder, I reckon? Oh, lord—guide my hand. I beseech thee."

He now whimpered more like Julius than the tough-talking redneck dogfighter. He got out his phone, tried to punch in a number with fingers singed and trembling.

In that moment Randi realized she might have one more opportunity for survival. She let her face go slack—God knew she must already look the part of a dead person. If she could get the drop on Esau one last time, maybe she had a chance.

Head lolling back as far as she could stand it, she willed herself to remain limp as Esau's rough hands grabbed her by the wrists. Pulled her up onto the truck bed, rough and hard.

She bonked her already sore temple.

The pain in her stomach flared beyond reason.

Teetering on the edge of consciousness, Randi smelled smoke—*oh no*.

The stove burners, still aflame.

She'd caught the scent of her house up the hill on fire.

Cullen—she couldn't let him burn that way. Like Denny, in the plane wreckage.

Yeah. The passengers, they'd all burned to death.

She'd asked, of course. Had looked into what happened in the crash. Everyone told her not to, but Randi, inquisitive investigative journalist, couldn't let it rest.

Some of the victims might still have been alive once the plane came to a stop amidst broken pine trees. But then the fuel, igniting.

He'd burned, her sweet little boy. Beyond recognition. That's the part she couldn't get behind her—how much he must have known the horror and unfolding moment of his own death.

Alone.

Her precious boy.

Give up, a voice whispered.

No—if what she had in mind worked, her own death would be a side benefit.

After Esau had dragged Ebby's broken body into the truck bed, she took a measured, subtle breath and peered up out of one eye as Esau, hunched and grunting, cranked the old pickup. Above her, an opening in the back windshield: Cullen had explained how in a place like Edgewater County, they called it the beer window. In Esau's case, no cooler of PBR or Bud tallboys chilling in a cooler, only one battered, pissed-off, but quite alive human being.

Snowflakes fluttered onto her skin like moths. Cold ate at her. Pain, burning from a dozen points on her body. Warm blood trickling down her side—too much blood. And a dead man lying next to her.

She heard Esau groan with his own discomfort—the effort of shifting gears.

Once he had the vehicle moving, Randi knew the moment had arrived.

As Esau got up a little speed, she rolled onto her knees, counted to three, and pushed herself up, thrusting her arm through the sliding window.

Shrieking in his ear.

Grabbing at his face and throat.

Randi, arisen.

Esau, gasping and startled, punched the gas. "Oh, great God *almighty*—"

She clawed at his eyes and choked him with one arm, grabbing for the steering wheel with the other. She buried her face in a clump of Esau's burned hair like a lover nuzzling her betrothed. Jerking the wheel toward the trees.

Releasing him, she rolled back into a protective ball and braced herself: The truck slammed into a large pine tree, violent, an explosion of shattering glass. Randi screamed and felt herself flung backwards against the tailgate, so hard it burst open.

A blur of trees. Randi, floating in the air. A ghost.

The shock of coming to rest face-down in the muddy water of the ditch. Choking, gagging and weak. Now at the end.

Her neck, sprained; her back, wrenched; her blood, draining. Death— it would be a relief.

And yet: Randi.

Alive.

Still.

Vomiting ditch-water, she dragged herself away from the truck sitting nosed against the tree. Back, hip and ribs on one side on fire with pain, her vision doubling, she crawled toward the cab of the truck. Had to know.

Inside she saw Esau, slumped over the steering wheel and knocked cold. His bloodied face looked serene, she thought, almost like that of a contented child asleep in its mother's arms.

If she lived now, she wondered how on earth she'd begin to explain it all—to Cullen's folks. The police. Poor Ebby's family.

The worst, however would be Randi's own judgmental mother.

Fury and grief blazed anew as Esau, injured but alive, moaned from behind her.

She tried to stand. To get away.

But shaking and weak, Randi fell over. Began to gray out. Fought for consciousness. In the air, woodsmoke, acrid and biting.

Shuffling footsteps. A figure, looming.

Julius.

"Help me," a wet croak.

"When I'm-a done with him?" Pointing to Esau, Julius, his face covered in both mud and blood, spoke in a frightening, dissociative monotone. "I'm-a come back for you. Yes, I am."

He lumbered over to the truck. Pushed aside his brother's body, climbed inside. It cranked. The belts slipping, the brakes shrieking, the motor sounding as though it had thrown a rod, Julius backed out of the ditch and drove up the hill.

Past Cullen, who stood blinking and bleeding, white as a Romero zombie. He clasped his bloody side with one hand, reaching for her with the other.

Randi, no longer alone on the road.

Yelping in pain, she tried one last time to climb to her feet.

"Honeybunny—" Cullen, bursting into tears, collapsed onto his knees.

She dragged herself over to him. "I'm sorry. I'm so sorry."

"Randi—is this some kind of bad dream?"

Her only answer? Tears of relief; and of grief.

The sound of approaching sirens came. The snow had stopped. The hilltop felt peaceful. Who knew so much violence had been transacted.

Randi, at peace. She lay her head back onto the hard macadam and went to sleep for perhaps the last time.

It would be fine—Denny awaited. She anticipated his embrace. What outcome could be better than reuniting with her boy?

54

THE LONG TOLLING OF A BELL, THE SOUND INCREASING IN FREQUENCY until its true nature revealed:

An electronic beeping.

The smell of disinfectant.

A hospital room.

No Denny.

Randi grasped and clawed through gray, psychological cotton candy until achieving a state resembling consciousness. Back from the abyss, somehow, after traversing a tortured, fading dreamscape now transmuted by gradations into diffused almost-wakefulness.

Awake, and alive.

Randi could see out of both eyes, but reached up to find a mass of bandages, thick and immobile, covering the side of her face. Similar bandaging on her forearm and leg; a tightness in her side; tubes, running this way and that.

Her mother, hair a wreck and eyes dancing with disbelief, sat perched on the edge of a lounger. From the sheets and pillow and stack of books on the window ledge, it appeared Aylene been camping out for some time.

"My sweet girl—are you really awake this time?"

Randi, parched and sticky of tongue. "Water?"

Hands trembling, her mother poured a cup from the Styrofoam hospital pitcher on the bedside table. "Bendy-straw?"

"I guess I'd better. Feel weak."

Tearful, she kissed Randi on the forehead, careful of the lump where the butt of Esau's pistol had landed.

"You lost a lot of blood," came a voice from the doorway. Garen Oakley, out of uniform in tight jeans and a Carolina Panthers sweatshirt, stood slumped against the doorframe. "You're lucky to still be here."

"How'd you know she was awake?"

The deputy, winking. "Just a coincidence."

Randi struggled to separate reality from the dreamtime. She choked on the water, asking: "Cullen?"

Aylene, exchanging a look with Oakley.

"They stitched you both up just fine, honey. He's in his own room."

Oakley, his hands prayerful. "Sheriff Truluck's eager to talk. As are reporters."

"Lots of idiots want to." Her mother, annoyed. "Believe me."

Tears ran from Randi's eyes as the image of Ebby Nixon's broken body came back to her. "Mr. Nixon—he tried to tell me to leave well enough alone."

"As did I." The police officer, grim. "Appears as though he died trying to save you, if we've pieced the story together with accuracy."

Aylene cut her eyes at Oakley. "She's in no shape to make a statement yet."

"Understood."

Her mother, sitting on the bed. "Cyn's calling every hour on the hour, as does this Spencer Mathison character you used to work for. I suspect your old colleagues have been titillated by such an unlikely and lurid story." Randi's parents had always decried broadcast news as equal parts pap and propaganda, adding to her father's displeasure with his daughter's choice of career. "Deputy, your men will keep all petitioners at bay, I presume?"

Oakley nodded to Randi. "You do realize they're calling you a hero."

What little blood she still had pulsed in her veins. "*What?*"

Oakley waved her off. "Mrs. Macon told us everything that happened, at least up to your kidnapping. She said Esau had been behaving oddly for a long time. That something about you 'visiting' her there, as she put it, caused her son to go crazy. To kidnap you; to go on a rampage."

"Pretty much the way it happened."

"Last she saw, you were sprawled under a tarp in Esau's truck. Thought he'd killed you already. Now, both her boys are dead."

"Wait—Julius?"

"Afraid so."

Randi, demanding the details. Oakley described a scene of horror: Julius had strung up his brother in the Macon compound, the deputy speculated, where he planned to let the dogs loose on him.

"Unfortunately, by the time we made it down the ridge Esau Macon had passed away, but Julius—he had a rifle. Shot at the officers. They returned fire."

Nothing more needed saying.

A chasm of grief. Perhaps a story as sad as Julius Macon's had been fated to end in tragedy. "He had nothing left. And from a life that had offered him so little in the first place."

A pall, settling in the room.

Randi suffered a wave of complexity: relief mixed with revulsion, even empathy for Mrs. Macon. If Randi knew anything, how much it hurt to lose a child ranked near the top of human travails. This woman, at the end of her own life, had now outlived all three of her adult children—how must that feel?

"Did Mrs. Macon say anything about why I was bothering them?"

"All she could figure was how you must love dogs as much as they all did."

Fresh tears.

Oakley, making to leave. "Just a warning about that media: They'll hound you to death over this, if you let them."

Randi, her tears turning to painful laughter at Oakley's inadvertent pun. "Sir, I *was* the media. I can handle them."

Her mother, fussing around in Oakley's wake. "Marandi, you simply must calm down. Lie back."

Catching her breath. "I want to see my husband."

"Soon." Aylene, reassuring and warm. "I promise."

Randi, asking what was left of her house. Her mother, suggesting disaster remediation followed by a course of interior design and remodeling.

"What a nightmare I wrought."

"Dear, certain hoary old aphorisms, like how good intentions pave roads all the way to Hades and back, possess not only the spice of longevity, but the sharp bite of truth."

Randi had heard this wisdom many times, but in her father's voice; one of his own sayings. "Dad was right. Wasn't he?"

"His was the sharpest intellect I ever encountered." A wistful look flitted across her mother's face, the lines deepening, lips pursed and holding back the tide of time. "But he wasn't always right."

An assortment of nurses came and went, administering meds and making notations. Fresh injections. A doctor breezed through and checked her over. Questions, light in her pupils. Flipping through the chart. Small talk. A thumb's up on her prognosis.

A wheelchair visit to Cullen's room arranged, finally. She found him sleeping under sedation after surgery to repair the damage from the knife wound, but on the way to a full recovery.

Leaning down to his ear. Whispering how sorry she was for all the trouble. Kissing his hand. Randi, swearing that he smiled in his sleep.

55

Once alone again in her own hospital room, Randi dozed until hearing a knock: Sheriff Truluck, his bulk threatening to spill over the edges of the door frame, had arrived.

Came in, removed his hat. "Mrs. Margrave?"

She struggled to sit up. "Sheriff—I'm so sorry about all this. But—"

"You little stinker." He ambled over to the bed, sat down heavy. "What the hank did you get yourself mixed up in?"

Randi, burning with ire. "Why'd you let it go on, sir?"

"As President Reagan once said, 'facts are stubborn things.'"

"Meaning what?"

"Meaning, now I got all the facts at hand. Facts I didn't have before."

Dry. "So at last you're looking into the dogfighting? Well, glory be."

Ignoring her sarcasm. "The Macon boys is both dead from what looks like trying to kill each other, and over them damn dogs. None of which don't surprise nobody. Hell, twenty years ago I'd-a put a dime to a dollar it would've happened long before now. Barring some surprise revelation in your statement? Case closed on the dogfighting."

"The Macons didn't run the ring. They only bred and trained the dogs. Rembert, he's the one. He's—"

"Ma'am? Don't take this the wrong way. But you don't know what all them boys was into, nor do you know anything about Mr. Rembert, who is not only a fellow Mason but a longtime supporter of my department. But as for old Esau—?" The wattle beneath his chin jiggled. "Crazier than shit, all them Macons. Told you not to mess with them."

She ignored his admonition. "Not Julius. He wasn't like Esau."

Sheriff Truluck snorted and slapped a meaty thigh. "Ma'am, I think it's time I left you alone again. I'm gonna go talk to your doctor, see when he'll clear you for a proper interview, one where you're gonna confirm for my department and SLED your side of what happened with all these dead bodies."

"The short version? I caused all this."

His narrow eyes, judging her. "All quite unnecessary, if you ask me."

Randi, mulling words certain to sound blunt. "I'm still not sure what's true and what's not here in Edgewater County. To be honest."

Pausing at the door, he hitched up well-filled trousers. "You and me neither. But I'll tell you this much: I'm not sure how missed Esau Macon is gonna be. He was a hard old barnacle on this world. Probably done more harm than good in the end."

Randi again felt dreamy, out of herself. "You can thank me later."

The need to make one further inquiry startled her back into full consciousness: "Sheriff, wait—the dogs."

"Now, don't worry about none of that."

"*What about the dogs?*"

Truluck, running a wide, old man's thumb across dry lips. "We had to put them down. A real shame, too. Them was some fine animals."

Fighting not to cry. "You people are savages."

"Now look here—Edgewater County ain't much different than anywhere else. Them dogs was a danger. Trained killers."

"Which is news to you. Right? About the Macons and their dogs?"

"Stubborn, them old facts. Ain't they?"

He went to go out, but before the door closed fully behind him, another man appeared.

A familiar face—Spencer Mathison.

Randi watched as the men exchanged hushed words. Shook hands.

Spencer slapped Truluck on the shoulder. "Thanks for taking care of her, Sheriff."

"It's what we do."

Her old boss came in the room. "3M—you're a wreck."

"What the fuck is going on out there between you two?"

Spencer pulled in his lips, a familiar old gesture: that she needn't trouble her imagination about how the sausage got made behind the closed doors of the elite class. "Your story's going to be told far and wide. It's a good thing."

"I'd like to be in control of exactly what that story tells."

Winking and heading back out. "Take it easy. Get some rest. You're exhausted. We'll talk."

Spencer was right: exhaustion came over her, so much so she had no tears left for the feeling settling into her gut: nothing in the world would ever change, the scales of justice forever tipped in the favor of powerful, secretive men—even in a place like Edgewater County.

Her eyes drifted up. Images flickered on the shimmering screen mounted high in a corner, a cable network run-down of the top stories of the year: A schoolyard massacre with two dozen dead, the biggest ever, had edged out both the President's acquittal on charges of high crimes against the state as well as Y2K prep to avoid the coming apocalypse portended by computers unable to recognize the year 2000: the end of commerce, the end of all culture and civilization. Duck and cover for the new millennium. Households and businesses preparing for the failure of the electric grid. If we weren't careful the world would find itself reset to zero, a looming threat that human beings might again be reduced to an animalistic state of affairs.

Randi laughed, bitter—as though the animals were the real monsters in the world.

She fumbled around for a remote, but finding none simply averted her eyes from the screen. Randi wasn't ready for the outside world again.

Not yet.

Alone but for the humming of technology monitoring and maintaining her life force, Randi had but one last question: whether the survivor's guilt she'd suffered over Denny would now also linger for the dogs of Parsons Hollow.

EPILOGUE

The terraced, hillside Berkeley Rose Garden, quiet but for birdsong and the wind.

Another hillside; a different coast.

The inland morning mist had long burned off, but in the distance Randi could see how the fog, resolute, still whispered across the white-capped, green-black of the bay below the expansive bridge: The Golden Gate, a shrouded linkage between promontories looming rocky and steep, symbols of tragedies haunting her:

Denny; and now the dogs.

And all that might have been.

But no might-have-been would ever suffice, and she had learned to let the past dwell in the past, Faulkner's famous aphorism be damned. Only right now existed, and what she would make of it.

Randi sat at the top of the rose garden tapping at the keyboard of her laptop, plugging away on the long-planned memoir intended as tribute to her late son. A beautiful Bay Area Sunday, the roses in full bloom, fragrant, healing, alive—a place she'd gone many times with her father, who liked reading and thinking there in the park. He'd declared how the beauty of the roses transcended any and all meaning his work as an anthropologist studying the cultures of mankind could ever hold; he said such perfection left him humbled. Put him in his place.

Here in the land of her birth Randi sought a similar renewal, another in a series as she and Cullen, on sabbatical from Southeastern University, rented a little house in Marin County and pursued their own creative projects—Randi, getting back in touch with her roots, while he toiled on the German New Wave tome for which he'd gotten a contract from an academic press.

She got to a good stopping point and closed the chapter she'd been working on, the one describing the drive through the backwoods of Edgewater County to what would become her new home.

Now she opened another file: She read through her résumé one last time, as well as the cover letter now ready to drop off at the Best Buddy Ranch, an animal sanctuary. This facility featured a certain specialized program involving the retraining of dogs suffering abuse before their blessed rescue; dogs deserving of another chance.

Randi, unsure if such work represented her true purpose, but felt that her experience qualified her. Gave her special insight. And motivation.

She felt a presence behind her. Ever since the events in Edgewater County, she'd developed an almost preternatural intuition: senses heightened to the environment, sharp hearing, an attuned sense of smell. Her newfound condition came as a result, she supposed, of the ordeal, her own animal instinct forever ramped up into survival mode.

But which choice—fight, or flight?

Obey?

But whom?

"Hey," a small voice coming from over her shoulder. "S'cuse me."

A boy of nine or ten. Tousled, shaggy hair. Freckles. Another Denny.

"Well, hey there, Yogi Bear."

The boy glanced back at his presumptive father, who'd engaged one of the park custodians in conversation over a robust and beautiful championship rosebush. "Who's Yogi Bear?"

"No one. An old cartoon."

Pointing at her laptop. "You playing a game?"

Randi wrinkled her nose. "No, sweetheart—no games."

"I play games on my dad's computer."

"I'm sure you do."

"He says too much."

Within the boy's eyes Randi perceived clarity and curiosity. "I'm sure he does."

He came around and sat beside her. "I've seen you before. I know who you are."

"You and your dad must love the roses—I know mine did. I come here all the time so that I can remember him."

"No, we never came here before."

Randi waited, her gut clenching.

"You're that dog lady, aren't you." A statement. "On TV."

Recognition.

The immediate weeks after the *Dateline* story first ran is when she had been recognized the most, her taste of minor fame. Yes, she'd sold her story, over and over until it no longer had financial worth; the film version would appear on *Lifetime* the second weekend of September, 2001, a production called *The Dogs of Cottonwood County* on which she served as an advisor. It was the least she could do to spread the word. Animal abuse— and dogfighting—happens not only in South Carolina, but anywhere cruelty is allowed to flourish unchecked.

Randi, proud now at becoming a kind of patron saint to any number of animal advocacy organizations. At first she held no interest in promoting the lurid aspects of her story, but after getting over herself became convinced of the good it might do. Cyn-Anne's agent had brokered the deals. Had found Randi's ambition not only noble, but lucrative.

But Randi, closing her laptop, didn't have it in her today to acknowledge this notoriety. "I've never been on TV."

Intense, childlike skepticism. "*Are you sure?*"

"I have to go now." But she made no move to leave.

The boy ambled away, a last glance. "You're not supposed to tell fibs."

"Sorry, kid. Sometimes the truth is too painful."

But he didn't hear her.

Another voice from behind her:

"You ready, honeybunny?" Cullen, in T-shirt and jeans, strolling up with a notebook under his arm. "It's about time for your appointment."

"We should go, then."

"Yeah."

She had rehearsed what she would say at the animal rescue ranch:

My name is Randi Margrave. And I'm here because I want to work with the dogs.

As they headed out of the rose garden arm-in-arm, she turned her face to the sun: True daybreak, assured in its inevitability, fell with grace across the obeisant and grateful California hillside, as she knew it must also upon the Carolina ridge far on the other side of the country. This clear and brilliant light glittered with an ostensible benevolence, one Randi hoped illuminated equally all of God's earthbound charges, whether soulless, or otherwise.

ACKNOWLEDGMENTS

A decade after the first draft of *Dogs* was written, and five years after an earlier version got me signed by an agent who then shopped it to imprints at the Big Six (at the time) publishing houses, here it is at last in print.

I first conceived the book as a supernatural thriller like out of early Stephen King, but in the planning and writing the novel's concerns became more literary and character based. Still, with an eye toward commercial viability amidst other difficult to categorize manuscripts of mine, all versions of the story always ended with a long action sequence of Randi against Esau, hurling themselves against one another like two disciplined, determined fighting dogs in a battle to the death. Here's hoping the climax is still as exciting as many early readers seemed to find it.

No finished version of the manuscript, however, can be attributed solely to its author: More than any other of my books, this piece went through several extensive stages of beta-reading and editorial polish by my agent and others to attain its current "finished" status. For helping me whittle down longer and cruder versions of this fourth published novel, my most heartfelt gratitude goes out to Katherine Michaelis, Laura K. Smith, Samantha Goodal, Lewis Lundy, Nancy Brock, Robert Lamb, Faye Whitt, Erika Lynden, Will Thrift, Cindi Boiter, Bob Jolley, Michelle L. Johnson of Inklings Literary, Marisa Corvisario of Corvisario Literary Agency, Jonathan Haupt of Story River Books at the University of South Carolina Press, my local creative collaborators Catherine Shuler and Marc Card-well, my late mother Andria McCallister, and as always, my closest confidant, first reader, and cherished life partner, Jenn McCallister.

Cruel bloodsports like dogfighting still go on all over the world. Whether you're in South Carolina or elsewhere, somewhere nearby you right now, living, breathing animals are suffering, creatures deserving of a fair and peaceful chance at life. When it comes to animal abuse, if you see something, say something... to the appropriate authorities.

James D. McCallister
    July 2017

RETURN TO "EDGEWATER COUNTY, SC"

in

King's Highway
Fellow Traveler
Let the Glory Pass Away
The Year They Canceled Christmas

and

RECONSTRUCTION OF THE FABLES (2018)
DIXIANA (2019)
DOWN IN DIXIANA (2019)
DIXIANA DARLING (2020)
MANSION OF HIGH GHOSTS (2021)
WANDO (2022)

MHP
Mind Harvest Press
COLUMBIA, SC

www.jamesdmccallister.com

COMING IN FALL 2018

A Special FREE E-book Preview
of the upcoming epic nine-part
Edgewater County novel series

BOOK ONE

Dirt Surfer